PRAISE FOR EMILY R. KING'S

THE HUNDREDTH QUEEN

Winner of the 2017 Whitney and UTOPiA Awards

for Best Novel by a Debut Author

"King's debut is built on a solid premise that draws on Sumerian mythology for inspiration . . . The tale maintains a consistent thread as King embarks on a deep examination of sisterhood, first between Kali and her best friend Jaya, and later when she must fight the rajah's other wives to keep her place within the palace."

—*Publishers Weekly*

"King writes multiple strong female characters, led by Kalinda, who has the loyalty and bravery of spirit to defend her friends even if that means facing death. Strong characterization, deep worldbuilding, page-turning action scenes and intrigue, as well as social commentary, make this book stand out. This outing opens a trilogy; readers will be eager to get their hands on the next installment."

—*Kirkus Reviews*

"This lush and lovely first novel brings a beautiful and brutal culture to life. The ending is left open for sequels, and readers will eagerly follow Kalinda and Deven on their future adventures."

—*Booklist*

"Filled with many action-packed sequences, forbidden romance, and unexpected surprises, this debut fantasy will appeal to teens who enjoy epic dramas with strong female characters."

—*School Library Journal*

"A gripping plot with twists and turns, a unique setting, and strong female characters—a solid foray into the fantasy romance genre."

—*VOYA*

"This book is definitely a page-turner . . ."

—Teenreads

EVERAFTER
SONG

ALSO BY EMILY R. KING

The Evermore Chronicles

The Hundredth Queen Series

EVERAFTER SONG

THE EVERMORE CHRONICLES
BOOK THREE

EMILY R. KING

SKYSCAPE

⅊⑃⑃⑃ SKYSCAPE

Published by Skyscape, New York

www.apub.com

Amazon, the Amazon logo, and Skyscape are trademarks of Amazon.com, Inc., or its affiliates.

ISBN-13: 9781542093392 (hardcover)
ISBN-10: 1542093392 (hardcover)
ISBN-13: 9781542043977 (paperback)
ISBN-10: 1542043972 (paperback)

Cover design by Kirk DouPonce, DogEared Design

Printed in the United States of America

First Edition

For my talented father.
I loved your music before anyone else's.

Prologue

The forest will burn.

Long ago, before the worlds were born of the Creator, Mother Madrona foresaw the end of the Everwoods—the immense fire crackling through her boughs, her bark scorching, leaves and acorns incinerating to dust. The mighty forest was felled, razed from treetop to root, and ash rained down from the stars.

Amid the elderwood trees going up in flames, the last image Madrona saw before the inferno devoured her and her sisters was the wicked smile of a prince.

This is one ending.

There is another.

Madrona dreamed of a knight wearing a talisman of time who wielded an immortal sword. Sacrifices were made to set the knight against the prince, but whether the knight would follow the path laid before her was yet to be seen. Some things that never are will be, and some things that will be never are. Even the Mother of All cannot say which ending is yet to come. Only that they both bring death.

Chapter One

The empty clock shop is eerily quiet. The only beating timepiece is the clock heart ticking in my chest, and it's deafening in its loneliness. Every dusty shelf in the storefront has been cleared off and every item sold. My ticker is all that's left of my uncle's magnificent creations.

Uncle Holden's ghost lingers in the sawdust between the floorboards, in the scent of axle grease on the curtains, in his handwritten "Closed" sign in the window, in the clerk's desk where I would sit while he constructed his timepieces behind me, hammering and chiseling in his workshop. My uncle inherited the shop from my grandfather, and he meant to pass it on to me. This place will never be the same without him, without the warm soda bread he would bring home from the bakery, without his hot whisky tea, his nightly prayers to Mother Madrona, and his humming while he worked. While he was alive, I never thought of myself as orphaned. Now, I don't know what I am.

A carriage stops in the street outside, its outline visible through the rain-strewn window. I duck between the display shelves and estimate how long it will take for me to run from the storefront into the workshop. I'm too late. A key turns in the lock, and the bell on the door jangles.

Footfalls fill the quiet. As I hide between the shelves, I press a palm over my clock heart to muffle the quickening ticktocks, my other hand on my sword. The dim light turns the entrant—a man in an ankle-length wool coat, collar up, cap low—into a silhouette. I doubt he's a thief. He had a key, and nothing is left in here to steal.

He may be searching for me.

My wanted poster is hung all over Wyeth. I passed several of them while riding south to the city. Each one stated the same decree:

WANTED DEAD OR ALIVE
EVERLEY DONOVAN, SORCERESS WITH A CLOCK HEART
REWARD: FIFTY GOLD PIECES

A month ago, Queen Aislinn falsely accused me of killing my uncle and labeled me a sorceress. She couldn't otherwise explain my ticker for a heart. In addition to me, she's searching for Prince Killian Markham. Disguised as a human through a glamour charm, the prince from the Land of Promise—the world of the elves—could be anywhere. Whoever catches him will be rewarded with three hundred gold pieces. Markham must love that he's worth more than me.

The man pauses at the clerk's desk and removes his tricorn hat. "You can come out, Evie. I'm alone."

I step out into Jamison's view. "How did you know I was here?"

"I'd recognize the beat of your ticker anywhere." He smiles briefly, his lips tense. "You didn't tell me you were riding to Dorestand."

I didn't expect to see him either. He had a meeting with his naval superiors here in Dorestand this afternoon. "I didn't want to worry you."

Coming into the city was risky, but I needed to visit the shop one last time before the new owners moved in. I've been here for an hour, wandering from empty room to empty room.

"You didn't need to come, Evie. I had planned to bring the last of your uncle's things to Elderwood Manor. Unless you would rather leave them here?"

"For the new owners?" I ask.

Jamison dangles the key to the shop. "No, for you."

My jaw falls open.

"I would have told you sooner, but I wanted to wait until the deed was signed." Jamison offers me the key. "I just came from the housing office. The deed is in my name, but the shop, loft, and workshop are yours."

I stare at the brass key, speechless. It takes me a moment to form a reply. "You bought my uncle's shop?"

"Unfortunately, I was unable to recover his tools before the taxation officer auctioned them away, but I managed to persuade the auctioneer to leave behind the last bottle of whisky from the cellar. I know you shared a whisky tea every evening with your uncle, so I thought to bring it home."

Home. For the last month, Elderwood Manor, Jamison's estate in the northern highlands of Wyeth, has been my place of hiding. As a marquess with no known association to me, Jamison may come and go as he pleases, whereas our friends and I must remain in the shadows.

"You should keep the shop, Jamison. Add it to your list of properties. I cannot return to Dorestand to live, not now and maybe not ever."

The corners of his mouth draw downward. "You mustn't decide what to do right away. Take the key and hold on to it. The shop can wait."

Wait for what? Jamison's conviction that someday I will be accepted for my clock heart and pardoned by our queen is an endearing fantasy, but I cannot delude myself into thinking that's a possibility. Still, he holds out the key.

"Evie, your uncle wanted you to have this."

I stretch out my hand and slowly close my fingers around the key. "Thank you."

"No thanks are necessary. I'm only sorry I was unable to recover his clocks before they were sold."

"Uncle Holden would have wanted his clocks in homes, surrounded by families."

Jamison runs his hands up and down my arms. "You remember the day we met here?"

"I could never forget." It was the day Markham sauntered back into my life nearly a decade after killing my family.

"I heard a song in my head when I saw you. A melody filled my mind."

"You did not."

"No, I didn't," Jamison admits, smiling. "But I did sense everything shift. One look at you, and there was no turning away."

I lift my chin, an invitation for a kiss. He leans forward and hesitates. He's been reluctant to touch me ever since we decided to dissolve our marriage to protect each other and our friends. His pause lasts just a moment, long enough to remind me he's no longer my husband, then he presses his lips to mine. The distance between us closes, but I sense his thoughts have turned inward and away from me.

A bell chimes as the front door opens. In one motion, I spin around and draw my sword.

Osric steps into the shop, his scowl deep. "Has she been here all along? Creator almighty, Everley. You could have told us where you were going."

"Do you think it's wise to come into the city, with so many *humans* around?" I ask, sheathing my sword.

The elf points at his head. "I'm wearing a hat."

Covering his pointed ears doesn't negate Osric's other elvish features—his sharp nose and chin. His peculiar but dashing good looks don't belong to the Land of the Living. Our human world is too plain for a creature of his ageless beauty. His deep-brown skin is flawless, not a wrinkle in sight.

"The Fox and the Cat told me to meet them here." Osric removes a flask from his jacket. He boiled down his dwindling supply of charm apples, which are grown only in the Land of Promise, into a cider.

The potent mixture is poisonous to humans but slows an elf's aging process. Elves live for hundreds of years. By eating charm apples, they can remain younger looking longer. Osric drinks, then licks his lips. "Laverick and Claret saw you ride off. The stable hand told us you were headed for the city."

"You shouldn't have come," I say. "As you can see, I'm fine."

"I couldn't persuade Foxy and Frisky not to follow you."

His nicknames for Laverick and Claret are meant affectionately. The three of them must have leaped at the chance to leave Elderwood Manor. Hiding from the queen has exhausted all our patience.

Shadows approach the front door. Jamison and I crouch behind the desk, and Osric ducks down with us. A pair of constables peers through the windows. I flatten my back to the wall and draw my sword.

"Wait," Jamison says. "They might leave."

"What if they come in?" I question. "Madrona knows how they'll react to an elf."

Osric points at his head again. "Hat."

The corpsmen in their scarlet jackets continue to look in the windows. Crawling low to the floor, Jamison leads the way from the storefront, through the workshop, and into the kitchen at the back of the house.

The bell on the main door rings.

We freeze and listen to the footfalls in the storefront. The back door is locked, and opening the latch will create a loud noise.

The bell rings as the door opens again. The footsteps grow quieter.

We hold still for a few seconds, then Osric turns the door latch. The grating snap echoes through the silence. A constable appears in the workshop doorway and raises his pistol.

"Halt!" he says.

We scramble to our feet and dash outside. Afternoon rain drizzles down, the summer air wet and warm in my lungs. As we barrel down the alley, Osric's hat blows off his head and lands in a puddle. He pauses to retrieve it and catches up.

"Halt or I'll fire!" the constable shouts.

The three of us stop, our backs to him. I curse myself for not carrying a pistol.

"Jamison?" I ask.

His head is down, collar up and hat low over his eyes. "I don't have a firearm on me either. Osric?"

"Oh, right, ask the elf if he has thought to bring a human gun."

"Turn around and put your sword on the ground!" says the constable.

A gun goes off. I reel around at the blast. The ball struck the ground and broke apart a cobblestone. Behind the constable, at the other end of the alley, Claret and Laverick aim their pistols at him. Both wear wool capes over dresses and white petticoats, along with striped stockings and shiny black boots.

"Let them go," says Claret, her firearm billowing smoke.

Laverick winks at me, her pistol leveled at the constable.

"Put down your weapon," he says.

"You first," Laverick replies.

Jamison and Osric start to back away. The constable returns his aim to us, namely me.

"Stay there or I'll fire," he orders. "I know you're the sorceress with the clock heart!"

I lift my chin and glare down my nose at him. "Let us go or I'll put a curse on you and your family."

He blanches but doesn't lower his gun. Either he's foolishly brave or he's calling my bluff.

"Go, Evie," Laverick says, her stance self-assured.

"No." I'm tired of running and hiding. I'm not a sorceress, but I do have a clock heart, and there's nothing wrong with who I am.

Jamison shakes his head. "Everley . . ."

"It's me they want." I start toward the constable. "You can have me. Let the others go."

"Don't come any closer!" His grip tightens on the trigger. Perhaps he is indeed afraid that I'll hex him. "Put down your sword!"

"You'll have to take me in, sword and all."

"Evie, I have you covered," Laverick calls out.

The constable's arm quivers. "I said put down your weapon!"

He stands a handful of paces away, nearly within lunging distance of my blade. My clock heart beats so loudly I hear it ticktocking over the patter of rain. The whites of the constable's eyes are starkly clear. He's young, not much older than me.

"I'll lay down my sword," I say, "but you mustn't fire."

His dry lips part, the skin cracked on the bottom. Raindrops collect in his sandy hair and drip down his pasty face. I take another step forward.

Two guns fire, one immediately after the other.

The constable sinks to his knees and tips over onto his side. His shot at me went wide. Laverick lowers her pistol, her eyes broadening.

Another constable runs out from the kitchen and fires at her. She and Claret bend down to evade his shot. He ducks back inside to reload.

The young constable on the ground does not move. Blood streams from his chest and gathers in a puddle, tingeing the water red. Claret tugs at Laverick to hurry along, and the two of them step around the fallen constable. Laverick slows down for a better look at him, then Claret drags her forward.

The five of us run around the corner of the building to the main road. Jamison whistles for his carriage driver waiting down the way. Laverick leans against a lamppost, breathing fast.

"Are you all right?" I ask.

She stares straight ahead blankly. The carriage stops alongside us. Osric vaults in. Jamison holds open the door.

"Lavey, we have to go," Claret says, helping her inside.

In the distance, a warbling siren goes off. Jamison extends his hand to help me into the carriage. As I reach for him, something white and yellow draws my attention to the ground—a daisy.

The little flower sits in a puddle, so out of place I almost look for another. I know who left the daisy, and I will not be swayed to respond to the message. I crush my heel down on the bloom and climb into the carriage. Jamison gets in beside me, and our driver takes off.

The siren sounds again behind us. Claret presses her lips to Laverick's temple and whispers something. The Fox hardly blinks, her gaze on the floor. Osric throws his soggy hat onto the bench beside him and drinks from his flask. The air inside of the carriage grows muggy with the curtains closed. Jamison loosens his necktie and unbuttons his collar.

After we have left the city and the sirens fade away, I open the curtains, letting in more light and air. I notice a white daisy petal stuck to the side of my boot. I haven't spoken to Father Time since before my uncle's passing. The daisy in the street was the first time he has tried to contact me in over a month. I have nothing to say to him. Never again will he use me like a cog in a machine.

I pluck the petal off my boot and flick it out the window into the rain.

Chapter Two

This day will never end.

After we arrived at Elderwood Manor from the city at a late hour, I ate a quick meal of bread and butter and turned in for the night. Lying in bed, I stare at the plaster molding along the top of the wall. The roses resemble bunches of knots more than they do flowers. My thoughts don't stay on them for long. I keep seeing the constable lying in a puddle of blood in the alley.

He chased us down because of the lies Queen Aislinn spread about me. The queen's Progressive Ministry permits worship of Eiocha the Creator but not of Mother Madrona, who is known by believers as the Mother of All. Those who revere Madrona are accused of sorcery. The queen might as well permit her people to believe in the sun but not the stars and moon. The Creator, Mother Madrona, and Father Time work as one.

I throw back my bedcover to let in the night air. Elderwood Manor is a grand home, but my inability to leave without risk of discovery has transformed these plastered walls into a cell. Someone deserves to be locked away, and it's not me.

All I wanted was to see Markham pay for killing my family. Even now, he continues to take away those I love. He killed my uncle to gain hold of the infinity sandglass, the most powerful timepiece in existence. Then my friends Alick, Vevina, and Quinn left to live at

Jamison's seaside cottage. Not knowing when Markham will return—*when*, not if—made them nervous. To stay in hiding, Alick has quit practicing medicine, and Vevina is separated from her cherished comrades Laverick and Claret. Quinn is becoming more of a young woman each day, and I'm missing it. I'm missing *life*.

I slam my fist against the mattress. None of this is fair. Not the ridiculous allegations that I'm a sorceress, not the constable who was shot, not the anemic life that my friends now live. Fair would be Jamison and me in the same bedchamber as husband and wife, regardless of whether the record of our wedding nuptials was lost at sea. But it's better that our marriage dissolve so our queen has no reason to suspect I'm here. I couldn't ask Jamison to honor a marriage that doesn't exist, especially not one to a wanted criminal.

My finger twists around the open end of the silken pillowcase, over and over, knotting the fabric to resemble the poorly shaped flower plasters on the wall molding.

I get out of bed. The hour is early, after the crickets have quieted but before the cock crows. I pull on my silk robe and slide into my slippers. My sword goes everywhere with me. I grab the blade and my uncle's last bottle of whisky and step into the corridor. A violin melody swells up the stairwell from the main floor. Just as I thought, I'm not the only one who's restless.

Three doors down, lamplight draws me inside a chamber. Laverick is asleep in bed, and Claret is reading in a chair, her stockings and shoes strewn across the floor.

"Can't sleep again?" I ask from the doorway. During our first week in the manor, we had a late-night run-in in the kitchen. Claret had had a bad dream about her time enslaved by the merrows. I'd had a nightmare about my childhood home burning to the ground.

She sets her book in her lap, and her tapered eyes lift to me. "I want to be awake in case Lavey needs anything."

"I brought you this." I hand her the whisky. "I thought you might be up."

"Eiocha bless you. Lavey took the last dose of the sleeping tonic Alick left me." Claret uncorks the bottle and drinks, her naturally tan skin golden in the lantern light. "I wish Vevina were here. She always knows what to say when things go wrong. Lavey and I went into the alley today with good intentions."

"I know you did," I whisper.

Claret's gaze wanders to the painting over the bed, a landscape of a dense evergreen forest with meandering pathways of amethyst wildflowers and sinister bowers of shadows. The manor is full of ornate paintings of odd places and mystical creatures, and the old house itself is riddled with secrets. Laverick and I have found closets that lead to dead-end hallways and doors that go nowhere.

This painting is of the Black Forest, or so the plaque on the frame reads. It's followed by an inscription in the tree alphabet, Mother Madrona's language. Each tree—birch, hazel, holly, aspen, honeysuckle, and others—represents a letter. For the Children of Madrona, her believers, those symbols hold protective, sanctified, or enchanted meanings. They etch them into tombs and doorways or stitch them into clothes. I never learned the full tree alphabet.

"The mark of the weeping cherry tree is a warning of danger," Claret remarks of the symbol, her *r*'s rolling strongly.

"You can read runes?"

"A little." She lays her palm over the book in her lap, a storybook about the seven worlds and our elf and giant siblings. Most of these books have been destroyed by the queen, burned just like the people who read and believe in their words. Claret watches Laverick sleeping. "Do you think she'll be all right? The constable . . . we saw the severity of his gunshot wound. She'll never forgive herself if he doesn't survive."

"Laverick will be all right because you have each other," I say.

These past weeks, I've done little but rattle around this big house. The Fox and the Cat have never been far, bringing me tea, taking me on walks, keeping me company while I carve figurines. They have made this time in hiding more bearable for us all.

I pat her arm and start to go. Upon hearing a creaking noise, I look back. Claret has climbed into bed beside Laverick and put an arm around her waist. She nuzzles her nose against Laverick's neck and long auburn hair. Their friendship turned romance is still fresh between them but stronger than ever. I slip out and close the door.

The violin music is still playing. I follow the soulful strain down to the main floor and into the library. Jamison stands near the fireplace, playing his violin. Radella, our pixie friend, dozes on a pillow in front of the fire, her little wings tucked around her azure body like a gossamer veil. A low fire crackles in the hearth. The mantelpiece is lined with my latest carvings—a horse and carriage, a sleeping cat, and the one I'm most proud of, a replica of the *Lady Regina*, the navy ship Jamison and I were wed on.

I perch on the edge of a sofa to watch him play. His nightclothes— a tunic over loose trousers—are wrinkled from sleep. A large pile of untouched paperwork waits for him on his desk. He travels to the city twice a week to handle clerical matters regarding his inheritance. Every time he returns, he plays music in the middle of the night.

He finishes one piece and switches to another, his bow stroking the strings with practiced finesse. The first measures of the new song send shivers up my arms. This composition has a broad sense of rapture. The call of life, the beauty of creation power, is so strong that my clock heart slows, ticking to match the cadence.

Jamison enters the second refrain and pauses. He replays the same stanza four times in succession before exhaling loudly. "I can't remember the rest."

"What you've played is lovely. And from memory too? You've a talent."

He lowers the violin. "I like your robe."

"I'm still getting used to my new wardrobe." I tug at the sash. These silks and satins and laces are lovely, but I don't belong to them nor they to me. "I've never heard that song before. What's it called?"

"I don't remember. My mother used to play it for my father on the pianoforte. She taught me the piece during my first years of violin lessons. I used to know the melody by heart. It's been some time since I've played." Jamison sets his violin on its stand. "I gave my resignation to my superiors today."

"You did? Why?"

"I joined the navy before I learned how to run my family's estates. My father had his flaws, but he ran our properties like, well, clockwork." Jamison turns around so I can see his quirked lips. "Secretary Winters is expediting the papers."

Winters was with the queen when she sentenced me to burn at the stake. He's also the one who confiscated my sword, which is reason enough to dislike him, but more so, I question his integrity. Queen Aislinn lost favor with her council after my escape, and Secretary Winters spoke out against her to keep the council's favor. My personal feelings for Winters aside, I'm concerned for Jamison. "Won't you miss sailing?"

He ambles over to me, his strides languid and heavy. "I have too much to do here to think of the seas. Every day, I fall further behind. I have countless ledgers to review, and I haven't even taken care of my father's final wishes. We have a place on our property, a gazebo overlooking a pond with swans and lily pads and flowering rush. Our family would have picnics there to celebrate the summer growing season. My father's final wish was to have the gazebo restored. I haven't even found the time to ride out there."

"I'll go with you," I offer. His gaze sharpens on me, then his focus drifts away. "I meant I'll go with you when you're ready."

Jamison rubs at his tired eyes. "I'm sorry, Evie. I'm distracted. I should be focused on taking over my father's duties, but Killian is still out there. When will he act? When will his kind intervene?"

"Osric expects a reply from his queen any day," I say.

"He's been saying that for weeks. What's she waiting for?"

In truth, I hope Markham stays away longer. I have seen a glimpse of what Jamison and my life could be like away from the prince's destructive aspirations. Our circumstances are far from ideal, but this forced exile has fueled my longing for normalcy. I could never forget Markham—the very tick of my clock heart denies me that pleasure—but when I look at the scars he has given me, I don't want to think of how much they hurt. I want to rejoice in how well they have healed.

I take Jamison's hands in mine. "This will come to an end," I promise.

"Then what?"

"We live our lives how we wish." I touch my lips to his, and he stills, letting me take the lead. I kiss him again, my fingers threading through his hair and pulling him against me. His hands slide up my throat to my jaw as he kisses me back.

Something shivers under us.

"Did you feel that?" he breathes.

Another stronger vibration shakes the walls and floor. Radella wakes, shooting into the air and chirping in alarm.

I don't speak pixie, but I can guess her meaning. "I think the shaking is coming from outside."

Jamison and I go to the window. The pixie perches on my shoulder, and the three of us peer out at the misty dawn.

"I don't see anything," I say.

"There." Jamison points at a man approaching on foot whose black cape is billowing in the dusky morning light.

Radella growls and my gut turns to ice.

Prince Killian.

Chapter Three

Jamison marches across the room and grabs a musket from the gun cabinet. He checks that it's loaded and braces the barrel against his shoulder, the stock in his hand.

"Radella," he says, "warn the others."

The pixie salutes him and zips out of the library.

I take up my sword, and we enter the receiving hall just as the prince knocks. Jamison levels the barrel of his musket at the entry. I pull open the door.

Markham grins, his wolfish eyes luminous in the lamplight. In his burgundy trousers, waistcoat, and overcoat, he looks as though he has come for a dinner party. "Good morning, Evie. Did I wake you?" He takes in my rumpled nightclothes and Jamison's mussed hair, and his lips slide upward. "Or did I interrupt something else?"

"Go sod yourself," I say.

He chuckles darkly. "Lord Callahan, *you* were raised with manners. Won't you invite me in?"

"You'll find my conduct less impressive than hers," Jamison answers, aiming his musket at the prince's face.

Undaunted, Markham enters the hall, a bag slung over his shoulder, and notices Osric at the top of the stairs. "Osric, my old friend. I didn't think I would find you holed up with humans. Have you completely lost your dignity?"

Osric walks stiffly down the stairs. "I've more dignity than you, *old friend.*"

The two of them have not been friends for centuries, and even then, they were more like partners, smugglers of the charm apples Osric depends on.

"I'm here to speak with Everley," Markham replies.

Jamison's grip tightens on his trigger. "You'll speak to all of us or show yourself out."

"Very well. Good day to you all." Markham tips his head in farewell and turns to leave.

"Wait," I say. "Five minutes."

"Twenty," Markham counters.

"Fifteen, and that's all you'll get."

"Everley," Jamison warns. "Need I remind you—"

"I know what he is." A disrupter of peace. A mercenary of life. A bad omen. But this cat-and-mouse game must end. "I want this in the past."

Jamison works his jaw from side to side and directs the prince to the study. Markham strides in ahead of us and peruses the room. I stay at the threshold and repress the urge to gut him just so I can watch him writhe on the floor. His momentary pain would be a waste of my strength. The prince's evergreen youth and unnatural healing ability provide him an impossible advantage, for he can feel pain but he cannot bleed or die.

Osric rolls up his sleeves as if preparing for a brawl. "Be careful, Everley. Killian has trod more paths in his six hundred years alive than you could possibly fathom. He only heads down a path if he knows where it ends."

Jamison's gaze sears into mine. "Fifteen minutes."

I nod and step inside. They shut the door behind me.

The prince pours himself whisky from the decanter. The grandfather clock in the corner reads the hour, a quarter to seven o'clock.

Markham swallows the spirits and lifts his glass. "Care for a drink?"

"Don't pretend you came to socialize."

He makes a wounded expression. "Your quick temper will get you into trouble." His attention slides to the grandfather clock. "How is Father Time?"

"I don't know."

"You two aren't on speaking terms?" Markham wags his finger at me. "I told you not to trust him."

I rub the back of my neck, achy from my sleeplessness. "What do you want, Killian?"

"The same thing you do—I wish to return home."

"I *am* home."

He tips his head back to evaluate me. "Humans will never accept you, sorceress with a clock heart. You'll never belong to their nobility, no matter how much silk you wear."

"Is that what you came to tell me?"

Markham runs his fingertip across the back of the sofa while he considers the gold-framed portrait of Jamison's family over the hearth. "You know the purpose for my visit. Muriel showed you what's to come."

The sea hag would have required a payment, years off my life in exchange for a vision of my future. I had no years to spare to pay her, nor would I do such a thing. Time is too precious.

"The sea hag didn't read my fortune," I say.

"No?" Markham picks up one of my carved figurines from off the console table. I once struggled over whittling the half-fish, half-human body, but after spending time with the merrows, my depiction of them is almost as good as my uncle's. "The last time I met with Muriel, she said she had a contract to offer you."

"You heard her wrong. I didn't sign a contract with the sea hag."

"And now she's dead. She must have left it up to me to show you."

Markham slides out of his cloak, drapes it over the back of a chair, and removes the infinity sandglass from his bag. Time moves untouched within the vessel, the iridescent sand filtering from top to bottom in a steady, silent stream. I restrain myself from snatching away the most powerful timepiece in the worlds from him. My uncle Holden devoted his life to serving as Father Time's helmsman. Before Markham stole it, my uncle's task was to turn the sandglass twice daily for decades to keep time flowing throughout Avelyn.

"Evie," says Markham, "kindly set down your sword and come with me. I have a story to share with you."

"Why would I go anywhere with you?"

"Because you wish to see what awaits humankind."

I wish for him to go and leave me alone, and if going with him will accomplish that . . . "You have twelve minutes left. My sword comes with me."

"As you wish."

Markham offers me his arm, and I grasp his elbow. He turns a small dial on the top of the infinity sandglass. This small movement releases a brilliant rainbow that intensifies into a blinding light.

Our spirits lift from our bodies, slipping out like snakes shedding their skins. We jump up, straight through the roof and into the sky, ghosts of ourselves. The whole process takes seconds, an abrupt but exhilarating separation of body and soul. The radiance whisks us away from our bodies and shoots us far away.

We land a moment later in a forest. My sword, the immortal blade of Avelyn, still hangs at my side. As the relic of a broken star repurposed by the Creator, it exists both in the heavens and the material worlds. I'm grateful it's with me. Spirit jumping is an ability I have been practicing in secret, moving from place to place while my body stays behind. It's difficult to master, a rare skill.

"How did you . . . ?"

"I've been exploring the limits of the infinity sandglass," Markham says. "This extraordinary tool marks time across Avelyn, but that's only the beginning. I'm learning that time itself bridges the worlds and can be crossed almost anywhere."

"Have we left our world?"

"There's no need. What we seek is in the Realm of Wyeth."

He lifts his attention to the canopies. Trees encircle us, their thick trunks and tangled boughs black and their needles green gray. I imagine the scents of moss and pine weight the morning air, but I smell nothing. My senses are unable to reach our surroundings. While in spirit form, I can act upon the world around me if I concentrate hard enough, but the world cannot act upon me.

My clock heart spins and spins, unloosed from the strictness of time. We're visitors, silent and unseen, leaving no trace.

"This is the Black Forest," he says. "Your human legends tell of a cursed woodland. Do you know of the warnings?"

"Of course. Some say the Black Forest is the color of death because the trees took root over a scourged army. Is this what you brought me here to tell me?"

"I brought you here to tell you about the triad war."

"You shouldn't have wasted our time. I know of the war. The giants attacked humankind to obliterate us and take our world. The Creator intervened and put them to sleep." I give Markham an impatient stare. "You brought me all the way out here for no reason."

He appraises me, his expression droll. "You're not very teachable, are you?"

"Only when my teacher is someone I respect."

Markham clucks his tongue, scolding me, and ambles off, setting our trail through the underbrush. Normally, we would trample through the ferns and scare off the nesting groundbirds, but our spirits whisper past them.

"Long ago," he says, "before the Black Forest grew up to become this great woodland, this was a field. Man, giant, and elf gathered here to fight for dominion over the Land of the Living, the Creator's first and most cherished world. The giants believed this world was their rightful inheritance as the firstborns." Markham kneels and places his palm to the ground. He must be concentrating, because his hand makes an imprint in the fallen pine needles. "Below us slumbers the army of giants, enchanted into an abiding sleep by the goddess of all creation through a song played on her violin. Here they lie to this day, yet over time, the shortsighted humans have forgotten their foes—and their redemption—and how close they came to annihilation."

"Your kind fought with us against the giants. You took our side, yet you speak of us so?"

The prince drops his chin to his chest. "That is another story."

"Tell it to me. You brought me here, and you don't seem to be in a hurry to go!"

He rises quickly and shoves his face toward mine. "Lower your voice. Show respect for the elven soldiers who died here so that your kind might live."

I hold firm against his glare. "Tell me your story."

"It is the story of the creation." He steps away and his voice gentles. "Long ago, at the dawn of time, when all creation came to be, my elven ancestors dwelled in the Everwoods with Mother Madrona. It was there, in that sacred grove of elderwood trees, that each group of the triad was born for a task. Giants—Eiocha's firstborns—were given the role of crafting and beautifying the Creator's lands. Elves—born second—were tasked with tending to and leading creaturekind."

"What were humans tasked to do?"

Markham rises and glides out of the forest into a field. He pauses, expecting me to follow along. I move over to him. "In the elven version of the *Creation Story*, humans were created centuries after the rest of the triad. The elves and giants were struggling to fulfill their tasks, so

Eiocha plucked an acorn from Madrona's bough and cleaved it in two. From the split acorn grew a woman and a man. Eiocha tasked them to serve as helpmates to their elder brothers and sisters. We elves obey our purpose to watch over all creaturekind. Thus, when the giants attacked the humans, our servants, my father intervened."

"Your *father* was in the war? But the triad war must have been—"

"Nine hundred years ago, during the beginning of his reign over the Land of Promise. My sister and I were not yet born. Our father led his troops into battle."

Speaking to someone who knew a soldier who'd fought in the triad war sobers me. The legendary event feels truer, more tangible.

A bed of daisies sprouts around me. I scan the tree line for Father Time, and the field and woodland transform into a ravaged battlefield. The Black Forest has been felled, as if the goddess pulled every tree from the ground and tossed them aside like weeds. In the wreckage, giants laden with armor swing mighty weapons at an army of elves and humans.

Father Time must be showing me the triad war. But then why are the trees felled? Markham said they grew after the giants were put to sleep.

I spot a woman on the battlefield, and my stomach plunges to my ankles. She's me—another Everley—riding astride an ivory mare with a gray diamond on its face, leading the charge against the giants. Jamison and our friends are fighting alongside her.

This isn't a scene of the past. This is like the nightmares I've had, though those never felt this real, and never were the trees felled.

Markham goes on, seemingly oblivious to the ghostly war paralyzing me. "For centuries, elves brought humans to the Land of Promise to tend to our orchards and vineyards. After Eiocha enchanted the army of giants to fall sleep, so few humans had survived their slaughter she forbade us from taking in more."

A giant leaps on a soldier beside us. I flinch as he tears the human to pieces with his hands. Across the way, a gunshot strikes down Laverick. Claret bends over her, and a giant impales her in the back with a spear. As Jamison runs to the aid of the Fox and the Cat, he's struck down by a giant's mace. He falls on his side, staining the meadow with blood. The Everley on the white mare still fights across the field, far removed from her fallen comrades.

Go after him. Help him.

The Everley in battle turns away from Jamison and runs farther away, deeper into the fray. Jamison does not get up.

I shut my eyes, nauseated. *This isn't real. This isn't happening.*

The battle cries die off, and I reopen my eyes. The ghostly battlefield has vanished; the trees are righted again, the field no longer bathed in blood. Markham doesn't seem to have noticed my stillness. His attention turns inward to his own thoughts.

"Humans were created to serve their elder brothers and sisters," he says, conviction in every word. "Eiocha's command to leave your kind alone is no longer relevant. Your people have recovered and repopulated. There's no need to leave humans in ignorance of their purpose." Markham comes forward and taps a single finger against my spinning clock heart. "But you aren't like other humans. You, like me, make your own purpose."

I step back and glare. "You and I are nothing alike. You destroyed a world. The Land of Youth is gone because of you."

"You still don't understand," he says tiredly.

He clutches my arm and turns the small dial on the sandglass. A rainbow avalanche sends us into the morning sky. We shoot across an immeasurable expanse and land on an overhang by the sea.

I stumble sideways, catching my bearings. Waves crash against the sandy base of the drop-off, huge breakers slamming against the beach and spraying into the air. A bank of gray clouds churns off the coast, building into a stormy coil. Briny winds sweep in gusts across the pitch of wilting wildflowers.

Higher up the hillside, the charred remains of a manor overlook the sea. Grass and weeds strangle the crumbled foundation. My childhood home. This is all that's left after the prince burned it to the ground.

"Why are we here?" I demand. My spinning heart has begun to slow from spending this amount of time outside my body. "Did you bring me here to apologize?"

He makes no remark, not a change of expression or a dry chuckle or a wry smirk. He gives me nothing, not an inkling of remorse.

I raise my sword to his throat. "Have you nothing to say?"

Markham grabs the hilt and slowly pushes, lowering it. "You think too finitely, Evie. The Evermore timeline isn't fixed. We change the future every day through our choices. Father Time insists he decides when we are born and when we die, but, in fact, *we* do. We decide our paths." He lifts the infinity sandglass. "This timepiece can navigate the stars and take me anywhere in Avelyn, except where I need."

"You said you want to go home."

"Time has changed my home," he says, both sullen and belligerent. "Look at your own home. It's proof that nothing stays the same forever."

So, if not home to the Land of Promise, where does he wish to go? He said the infinity sandglass can take him anywhere, except . . .

The Silver-Clouded Plain—the giants' world.

He must want to go there. Their portals are closed to those seeking to enter. The giants are locked in their world, and for those who leave, there is no return. Expulsion from Avelyn was their punishment for trying to wipe out humankind. Markham stole magical seeds—"skyseeds," Osric called them. Supposedly they can bypass the curse on the Silver-Clouded Plain. But if the seeds can get him there, why is he here with me? What is he waiting for?

Markham's attention drifts to the charred foundation of my family's home. "What would you do if you could change the past?"

25

At one time, I longed to bring back my family. Then I hoped to have a real heart instead of my ticker. Now I wish Markham had never been born.

His stricken gaze falls to mine. "I've tried to let go of the past," he says, "but no amount of time will change my heart. Therefore, I must change time."

Nothing exists that has the power to undo the past, not even the infinity sandglass. Whatever he's searching for must be more powerful than anything humans have heard of. Osric once proposed that Markham was after an artifact, an object like my sword and the sandglass, that has been hidden away, perhaps in the Silver-Clouded Plain.

"You cannot change what's been done," I say, "no matter how hard you try. This is your life, Killian. You are a monster."

"Perhaps I am," he muses. "But you needn't worry, Evie. I won't kill you or destroy the sandglass. Not yet."

He turns the knob on the sandglass and leaps into the air. I jump at him, but my hand misses the rainbow light shooting him away.

"Markham! You cannot leave me here!" I spin in a circle, searching the sky. Off to the east, the sun blazes a piercing trail into the blue. "Damn blaggard prince!"

I stab my sword into the field and slump against the hilt, turning my back to the ruins of my childhood home. My uncle often offered to bring me here to say goodbye to my family. I never came. My family wasn't—isn't—here. Their souls have returned to the Mother of All and found rest in her embrace. At least that's what my parents believed would happen after we died.

A sea wind flings itself at me, swishing the grass around my floating feet. My clothes and hair are untouched by the gusts. My clock heart spins even slower.

"I have to return to my body. Which is the quickest way?" I ponder aloud.

My sword vibrates and warms in my hand. Not since I searched for the gate to the Everwoods has it responded to me. I yank the blade from the ground and hold it out.

"Can you help me return to the manor?" I feel foolish waiting for a response, especially when nothing happens. Just as I begin to lower my sword, the blade warms and vibrates. I aim it inland. "Will you show me the way?"

My sword quivers, then yanks me forward, dragging my spirit into the distance. I soar across Wyeth, a land of saturated greens and gray skies, and slow over a massive manor. I shoot down through the roof and into my body.

I gasp awake in the study. Staggering up onto my wobbly legs, I drag my sword up with me, my ticker beating steadily, once again compelled by time.

Markham pours himself the last of the whisky. "Well done, Evie. You were only a minute or two behind me." He toasts me with his glass. "Do you see now? You needn't depend on Father Time. The Evermore timeline is yours to explore."

"My sword showed me the way back; otherwise, I would still be stuck out there."

"The sword of Avelyn is mighty, but time is the real power." Markham peers inside the sandglass. "We are slaves to time. To break free, we must bend time to our will."

I raise my sword, my arm quaking from exhaustion. "Give me the sandglass, Markham. No more games."

"You think I'm playing games?" His expression darkens and cools, his mask ripping away to reveal the monster who stood over me as a child and plunged his sword through my chest. "Do not confuse my mercy with complacency. I've only so much tolerance for your small mortal mind."

"Then leave me be. Go away and never come back."

A tremor shakes the ground, a roar from the land that can be felt in my joints.

"What did you do now?" I ask.

"My childhood home is surrounded by acres of orchards. Did you know an apple tree produces fruit six to ten years *after* the seedling grows into a tree?" Markham's eyes shine; he's fascinated by this random fact. "The number-one ingredient a planted seed needs isn't sunshine or water—it's time."

The grandfather clock chimes the hour. Seven o'clock. Osric swings the door open, and he and Jamison hurry in.

"Your fifteen minutes are over," Jamison says, his musket at the ready.

Markham swallows the last of his whisky and sets down his glass. "Thank you for the drink, Lord Callahan. I'll take my leave now."

"You aren't going anywhere," I say.

The prince grasps the timepiece with both hands. "You know how much I enjoy these spats of ours, Evie, but I don't have time for your empty threats at the moment."

Another tremor rattles the manor, swinging the chandelier and knocking a vase off a table. Jamison, Osric, and I brace ourselves against the heavy pieces of furniture. Markham calmly puts on his cloak, twists the top of the infinity sandglass, and vanishes.

Chapter Four

I run to the place where Markham stood seconds ago and turn in a circle. Where did he go? He cannot have spirit jumped or his body would still be here.

"How did he leave?" I ask.

"It—it can't be possible," Osric stammers. "I don't understand how, but I think he used the infinity sandglass as a portal."

Jamison isn't convinced. He searches the room, looking behind curtains and furniture. "So he left, just like that?"

"Harnessing time to portal jump isn't unheard of," Osric answers. "Some say the infinity sandglass itself is a portal. The same has been said of the sword of Avelyn, but I thought those were myths."

The blade in my hand has been in my possession for years, and I have never carved a portal through time.

"But where did he go?" Jamison asks.

Osric drinks deeply from his flask of cider before answering. "To his place of hiding, I suppose. The vermin coward."

My reflection in the glass front of the grandfather clock frowns back at me. Regardless of how he vanished, Markham can move from place to place without locating an existing portal. The infinity sandglass can take him anywhere in Avelyn except for two places—the Silver-Clouded Plain and the Everwoods. He didn't want me to know he could escape easily; otherwise, he would have had us travel in such a manner to the Black Forest and coastline instead of spirit jumping.

The ground shakes anew, vibrating so hard the empty whisky decanter falls and shatters. The portrait of Jamison's family over the mantel slides sideways and drops off the wall. Both of us lunge to catch it, but the frame hits the ground and tips backward into the fire. He yanks the painting from the flames and stomps them out. He saved the portrait, but the top outer edge of the canvas is blistered.

"What in the name of Eiocha is causing those quakes?" Osric asks.

I throw up my hands in exasperation. "I asked Markham if he was responsible, and he prattled on about apple trees."

Jamison crouches over the portrait, his expression crestfallen. The damage can be repaired, but it will require skill and time. "The day this was painted, my mother fed my sister and me pieces of honeycomb to bribe us to sit still for the painter. Father was exasperated by our sticky fingers and faces, but he didn't raise his voice." He rehangs the frame over the hearth. His father didn't start his violent outbursts until *after* Jamison's mother passed away.

Claret appears in the doorway, her face heated. "You need to come see this."

"Where's Laverick?" I ask.

"Still asleep. Come on."

Radella zips into the room and tugs at my hair to hurry. We hasten after Claret out the front door. The servants have woken, roused by the quakes, and gathered on the front steps.

Claret hands me a spyglass and points. "Look there."

I peer at some sort of tower in the distance. "Is that . . . ?"

"A skystalk," Osric finishes grimly. "He did it. The bastard planted the skyseeds."

Jamison looks through the spyglass next. "Remind me what they do again."

"Skyseeds have been enchanted with creation power by the Creator herself," Osric explains. "The seeds sprout up faster than any other plant. Even tiny elderwood-tree seeds take longer to grow, or so I've been told. Mother Madrona's roots fan out from the Everwoods to the Otherworlds, linking all of Avelyn together. For skyseeds to grow into skystalks, they tap into that ubiquitous power."

My mother had a picture of Madrona over her favorite chair. The image depicted a mighty elderwood with a massive root system connecting the seven worlds. Markham hasn't created a new way into the Silver-Clouded Plain. He's found a pathway that already existed.

Jamison points to the skystalk. "That thing will help Killian bypass the curse on the giants' world?"

"Think of it as a causeway," Osric says. "Giants were builders and inventors tasked with developing and beautifying the worlds. Long ago, they would use skystalks to travel from world to world to complete their work. They planted skyseeds in specific sites so they wouldn't have to depend on portals."

The household staff makes no remark. They are loyal to the Callahans; some of their families have been working here for decades. The butler and maids have become accustomed to the pixie, elf, and even my clock heart, yet they shift uncomfortably. We all do.

"Prince Killian means to climb that stalk to the giants' world?" Claret asks, her brows creased in confusion.

Osric grunts, a disparaging sound. "Only a supreme idiot would try. Most giants are flesh-eaters. They feast on elves, gnomes, humans . . . More to the point, Killian won't know his way around. No one has been there in centuries, and the infrastructure is bound to have changed. Any surviving maps of the Silver-Clouded Plain will be inaccurate."

The ground shakes again, gravel bouncing along the carriageway. Radella buries herself in my hair while Claret peers through the spyglass. She curses under her breath and passes it to me.

"The skystalk has grown taller," she says.

I look through the spyglass. The top of the skystalk extends higher, disappearing into the clouds. "This seems extreme, even for Markham. He has to know this will draw attention."

Jamison's gaze turns flinty. "He doesn't care. Once Killian climbs that monstrosity, he'll leave the stalk behind for us to deal with."

Radella flies out of my hair and motions widely down the carriageway at the arrival of a horse and carriage escorted by several single riders.

"Secretary Winters's carriage," Jamison says, urging all of us toward the door. "I wasn't expecting him to pay a visit. Hurry inside. I'll send him away as fast as I can."

The servants scatter throughout the lower level of the manor, and the rest of us go upstairs. Laverick stands in her doorway, awake, rumpled, and puzzled. I leave Claret and Osric to explain what Laverick has missed, and go to my chamber. Radella and I watch Jamison greet Secretary Winters from the second-story window. The two men disappear inside, followed by the secretary's escort. Radella sits on the windowsill and stares at the skystalk stretching taller into the sky.

"I have a terrible feeling about this," I say.

Not only did Markham plant the skystalk in Wyeth, he did so near this estate, knowing it would draw authorities. He means to flush us out of hiding. He's baiting me with the infinity sandglass. The prince must assume I'll try to get it back—or that's what he intends for me to do.

I dress quickly in trousers, a white button-up shirt, a cloak, a hat, and my mother's red wool gloves. Jamison has been downstairs with the secretary for several minutes. With each added second, my anxiety winds tighter.

"Has the secretary left yet?" I ask.

Radella shakes her head.

"Would eavesdropping be wrong?"

The pixie gives me a look that says, *As if that will stop you.*

I lie down on my back on my bed. She flies to me, hovering in place, her little wings fluttering quickly. "You're coming with me, Radella."

She puffs out her chest and salutes me. Radella has been present during all my spirit jumping trials. She hails from the Everwoods, a spiritual bridge between the worlds, so she's the only one in the household who can see me while I'm in spirit form.

The first time I spirit jumped without Father Time's assistance was by accident. I was falling asleep, and the next thing I knew, my spirit was above my body. I was so startled I dropped back down into myself. The next evening, as I drifted to sleep, I did it again. Radella saw me, and after a long discussion through hand gestures and some failed attempts, we concluded that sleepiness is not necessary, only that I am relaxed. I close my eyes and focus on my quiet ticker.

Tick . . .

Tock.

My spirit rises off my body with a gentle pull. I stare down at myself. To anyone else, I appear to be sleeping.

Radella motions for us to go. My spirit can pass through solid objects, such as walls and ceilings, but Radella pushes open the door out of habit, and we go downstairs.

A maid carries a tea tray into the library and leaves the door ajar. The secretary's guards are just inside. I fly across the corridor and slip in. Radella darts in after me and ducks behind a side table. Jamison and the secretary are seated across from each other in slim armchairs while the maid serves them tea.

"We have been investigating the destruction of the *Lady Regina*, the prisoner ship you sailed to the penal colony," says the secretary. My gaze flickers to the replica on the mantel that I carved of the ship. "A sailor who survived the wreckage reported that you and Everley Donovan, the sorceress with the clock heart, were wed at sea."

Jamison's grip tightens on his teacup. "Miss Donovan was our prisoner. I became acquainted with several of the female convicts under my care. The sailor must have misinterpreted what he saw."

"The ship's logbook has been found in the wreckage and is being returned to Wyeth. Soon record of what happened on the *Lady Regina* will be public knowledge. Captain Dabney was a meticulous man. Will his logbook confirm or deny the sailor's report?"

"I've no idea what the captain's logbook will say, sir. I only know what I did and did not do aboard that ship."

The secretary sips his hot tea. "Tell me about Miss Donovan."

"I hardly remember her, sir. But from what I recall, she was quiet and kept to herself. She didn't seem to like people much."

None of his accounting of who I was at the time is inaccurate. I wasn't the friendliest person when I was keeping my clock heart a secret.

"Hmm," says the secretary. "You purchased Miss Donovan's uncle's clock shop at auction. Yesterday, a constable was found shot dead in the alleyway behind it."

I drop closer to the floor. Laverick will be devastated.

"That's . . . unfortunate," Jamison replies with a suitable amount of regret.

"Where did you go after the meeting with your superiors yesterday, Callahan?"

"I briefly visited the clock shop to survey my investment and returned here. I presumably just missed the incident."

Winters billows out his cheeks with a quick puff of air. "The constable corps are searching for the shooter. She's been identified as the convict Laverick Driscoll. Driscoll was accompanied by her companion, Claret Rees. Their street names are the Fox and the Cat, respectively. We believe both are aiding Everley Donovan." I drop even farther to the floor. "Driscoll and Rees were also convicts aboard the *Lady Regina*. Another constable identified Driscoll as the shooter in the alley. Two men were spotted with the women. Do you remember them?"

"The women?" Jamison puts on a show of searching his memory. "I must have met Driscoll and Rees aboard the prison ship, if you say they were there, but I had over two hundred convicts to look after. I can hardly be expected to remember them all."

The secretary licks his lips and sits forward, his voice low. "Everley Donovan is a dangerous sorceress. She blew up the roof of the courthouse and damaged several buildings in the city square to escape execution. Queen Aislinn believes Donovan works with Killian Markham. They are a peril to the realms."

"I'm telling you, Winters," Jamison replies, maintaining strong eye contact with the secretary, "you're wasting your time looking here."

Winters grips his teacup closer, his big hands swallowing the delicate porcelain. "I'm relieved to hear so. Harboring criminals would be grounds for stripping you of your nobility."

Jamison cocks his head to the side. "Clearly."

The secretary sets down his teacup and crosses his arms over his chest. "The queen suggested that you might be under the sorceress's enchantment."

Queen Aislinn's paranoia of me is almost flattering.

Jamison rubs at his top lip with heavy movements. "The only enchantment I'm under is my own desire for privacy during this time."

Winters's features soften. "You must be lonely out here all by yourself. Come to Dorestand. Once you're through your grieving period, my wife can introduce you to the eligible young ladies of the court. Our neighbor has a daughter, Brida. She's comely and quiet and well mannered." He sounds as though he's describing an old mare. "Brida is part of my niece's needlepoint group. Her father, a baron, has five daughters, the poor man. You could choose Brida or one of the others. The baron would be glad to introduce you to them."

Jamison's attention wanders to the fire in the hearth. "I'll think on it, sir."

"I hope you do. You're the son of my oldest friend, Jamison. I'm here for whatever you need." Winters grips the arms of his chair and rises. "Before I go, my men will have a look around your property."

Jamison looks to him coolly. "Does this search come by order of the queen or from you?"

"From the council. Surely you understand. Precautions."

Jamison arches a brow, simultaneously haughty and withering. "I was just leaving for my morning ride around my property. A peculiar structure has appeared in the distance and alarmed my staff. I'm eager to investigate it."

"I saw the structure as well and sent a messenger to alert the council. You best stay away from it until the army investigates." The secretary pats him on the shoulder. "I'll tell them I delayed the search of your property in favor of returning to the city to address what I saw. But I'm only one member of the council, Jamison. Your acquisition of the clock shop raised some questions. Your cooperation would go a long way toward tamping down suspicions."

"My fascination with the clock shop was inspired by my father's memory. He was an admirer of Holden O'Shea's work." Jamison clears his throat, expelling his thickening emotions, and rises to his feet. "It was a pleasure to see you again, sir."

"And you, Lord Callahan. I'll leave you to your day."

Winters bows, and he and his men file out.

Jamison sinks into his chair and buries his face in his hands. I float over to his side. Both of us agreed it was better that we not stay married, but in all honesty, I only let go of our vows to protect him. Now that the ship's logbook has been found, I don't know what else I can do to turn suspicion away from his household. He has now lied to a member of the queen's council about our nuptials. Not even coming forward to turn myself in could help him if our wedding is recorded in the logbook.

Radella darts out of the room. I slowly follow her upstairs and slide back into my body. I come awake, my heart beating soundly in my chest and my mind echoing with Jamison and Winters's conversation. Radella trills, a question I have come to recognize as, *Are you all right?* Which is not to be mistaken for, *Get up, lazy toad.*

I roll over onto my stomach and press my face into the pillow. Jamison has shown a brave front, but some part of him must regret taking us in. Had he chosen the type of woman the secretary suggested—quiet and polite, a lady—he wouldn't need to lie to an old family friend or dodge searches of his property.

Radella tugs on my hair. I roll over, and she lands on my clock heart, her feet on the glass face. She points at my ticker.

"No, I told you I'm not speaking to him. How could I in good conscience after Father Time let my uncle perish? Nor did he help in stopping my execution."

Radella rests her fists on her hips and glowers.

"You needn't stay to appease me. You can return home whenever you'd like."

Her wings wilt. As an ambassador of the Everwoods, her loyalty should be to Father Time, yet she has stayed with me instead of going back to him. I know she's sorry he let me down. Sometimes I wonder if she's staying to compensate for his lack of support. Father Time *says* I'm his Time Bearer, a knight of the Evermore, but I don't care to be.

I peer into her sad eyes and sigh. "I'm sorry you're in the middle of this, Radella. I hope you aren't in trouble."

The pixie shrugs, though her expression is torn, then she perks up and darts to the window. I get out of bed, and we watch the secretary's group ride off.

"I'm going downstairs," I say.

Halfway down the corridor, Jamison comes upstairs. His attention lifts from the parchment he's reading to me.

"Osric just stopped me on his way to the stables," he says, tucking the paper away. "He's waiting for us. I assume you're coming?"

"To the skystalk? Yes." I fiddle with the pommel of my sword. "How was your conversation with the secretary?"

Jamison breaks eye contact and shrugs. "He had a few questions about why I purchased the clock shop. I knew that might draw attention for a little while. It will pass."

"What if it doesn't? Maybe Laverick, Claret, and I should hide somewhere else."

"Evie," he says firmly. "I've no regrets about buying your uncle's shop or housing your friends. None at all."

But will he have regrets if he's caught harboring us?

He yawns and rubs at the crease between his eyebrows.

"Why don't Osric and I investigate the skystalk?" I say. "You stay here and rest."

"I already told him I'm going, though I do need to speak with Laverick at some point." Jamison releases the rest of what he's about to say all in one breath. "Winters told me about the constable who was shot in the alley. He didn't recover."

"Let me talk to her," I mumble. "I owe her that much."

"What happened wasn't your fault, Evie. No one intended for the constable to get hurt."

But he did, and now I'm nervous about what else could be waiting around the corner for us. I have to intercept Markham before he climbs the skystalk to the Silver-Clouded Plain. Capturing the prince and turning him over to Queen Aislinn could convince the council I'm not Markham's ally and shift suspicion away from Jamison.

The queen should be willing to bargain. Markham's crimes have concealed the real reason she's hunting him. I know she had her father, the king, murdered with Markham's help so she could assume the throne. To bury her secret, she may be willing to pardon me and my friends in exchange for him. What she and the council do with the prince once he's in custody is up to them.

I once longed to see Markham stand trial. Now I would settle for never seeing him again.

Chapter Five

A fogbank drifts over the grassy highland. Jamison leads the way over the hills while daylight burns through the morning clouds. Osric rides his horse beside mine, as stiff as a statue, his tricorn hat low over his scowling eyes. Jamison and I pass a smile back and forth. The elf seldom appears less than dignified. Until recently, he was a pirate in the Land Under the Wave and spent all his time at sea. He's out of practice at riding.

I grip the key to the clock shop around my neck. I haven't been on a horse for some time either. In the city, I walked or drove my uncle's wagon. The last time I rode on horseback, I was accompanying my father into Dorestand to visit my uncle.

We approach a vast wheat field, the site where Markham planted the skyseeds, and halt at the perimeter. The skystalk has grown taller than any structure I have seen, stretching to the heavens so high it hurts my neck to look up.

I start across the field, and Jamison and Osric follow, our horses trampling through the low, tawny wheat. The monstrosity's trunk is wider than two longhouses set in a row lengthwise. Only creation power—sorcery, as Queen Aislinn would say—could create this behemoth.

She's going to throw a fit when she hears of it.

A half dozen farmers have gathered at the base. I draw my hood, casting my face into shadows. Jamison opts to go to the other side of the skystalk to avoid the farmers. We stop a good distance away from them, next to the skystalk.

A great rumble rises from the ground. The stalk shoots up several more feet, higher and higher, winding into the clouds like a corkscrew. The farmers shout in alarm, and our horses spook. Jamison and I stay on ours, but Osric is bucked off. I hop down to collect his fallen hat. He jams it back on his head while Jamison chases down his horse and returns it to Osric.

"Rotten animal," Osric mutters, getting back on his horse.

The farmers haven't seemed to notice the elf from a distance. Osric falling off his mount was the lesser spectacle.

The three of us ride closer to the skystalk. Swordlike thistles protrude from the dingy olive trunk, some longer than my legs. Gnarled and sinister, the skystalk bears no leaves or berries or acorns. Had I not witnessed it growing, I would think it was dying or dead.

"How long until the soldiers arrive?" I ask.

"From Dorestand?" Jamison replies. "Before the end of the day."

Shouts from the farmers sound down the way. Several men are pointing upward. We step away from the skystalk to look up. Someone is high above, scaling the skystalk's thistles.

Jamison exhales sharply. "Killian."

"I had an inkling the prince hadn't gone far," Osric drawls.

A howl erupts behind us.

Osric's and Jamison's faces drain of color. We last heard this chilling sound in the Land Under the Wave when the elven guard was dispatched by their queen in search of the prince. Their barghest—a bloodhound trained to track its target—led the hunt. Markham escaped, but his companion, Harlow, was taken captive. We haven't seen her since.

The barghest howls again. Down the way, the farmers glance around for its source.

"My queen received my letter," Osric says in a daze.

Jamison dismounts and climbs up the stalk, his feet level with our heads. "There." He gestures east. "They're coming this way."

"They better hurry," I snap. "Markham is getting away."

Jamison hops back down. "Let that be their problem. This is what we wanted, Evie, for the elves to take responsibility for their unruly prince."

But how else can we start over if we don't hand Markham over to our own queen? If the elves take him, he will be gone, and so will our chance to sever ourselves from his actions.

A rumble shakes the ground, and the skystalk grows taller. I pacify my horse, then dismount and step onto the lowest thistle.

"What are you doing, Evie?" Osric asks.

"Going after Markham."

"Wait," Jamison says. "The skystalk is unstable while it's growing."

"Either I go now, or Markham gets away."

He glances at the elven guard running toward us. "Go. We'll fend them off."

"*We will?*" Osric asks.

I start up the stalk. Markham is so high above me I grow dizzy looking up at him. My ticker booms in my chest, solid and strong. I set a swift climbing pace.

Another howl from the barghest comes from below. I'm still close enough to hear Osric bickering with Jamison about how his queen might be unhappy with us for interfering. The elf queen will have to accept our involvement. She and her kind waited to come to our aid, and now they expect us to stand aside? Not bloody likely.

The stalk begins to shake. I hold on as it shoots up several lengths higher.

I cling to the trunk, my head reeling. I catch my breath. The ground suddenly feels much farther away, then closer, then farther again.

Another piercing howl carries up from below. The farmers flee the wheat field as a rangy canine the size of a black bear dashes for the stalk. Charging after the barghest is the elven guard.

Jamison and Osric hold their ground against the approaching party.

I set out more quickly. Clouds slowly pour in around the skystalk, masking my view of how far I have to go to reach the top. Markham has climbed higher than any treetop in sight, but his heavy pack is slowing him down. I go faster, my heart booming. The next time I look up, he's closer. I'm gaining on him.

Finding a burst of strength, I ascend even faster, pushing into the rising winds.

Flying arrows arch toward me. One of them embeds in the stalk near my foot. Another strikes Markham through the arm, pinning him to the skystalk. The elven guard is firing at us from a distance with accuracy I have never seen.

I clamber upward again, my chest heaving. The gusts of wind rip at me. Markham is directly above, near the low-hanging clouds. I swipe at his ankle. He kicks free and jerks the arrow out of his arm. More arrowheads sink into the stalk around us. I grab upward and grasp his leg.

He extends the infinity sandglass out, dangling it in the air, many stories above the ground. "Don't make me do it, Everley."

"You wouldn't."

His hair falls forward into his steely gaze. "You know better than to doubt me."

"You won't drop it," I repeat, my grip firm on his leg. "You need time as much as the rest of us."

"Time only serves itself."

He holds the sandglass out farther, and his sleeve rides up to his elbow. His forearm is bandaged, covering what I suppose is an injury. I cut him there with the sword of Avelyn a month ago when we spirit jumped to a moon. He's already healing from the arrow wound he received moments ago, as he always does. Why would he need a bandage for an old injury?

Markham glares down at me. "Catch."

He lets the sandglass go.

I lunge, but the vessel skims past my fingers. I snag one corner of the wooden base and hang off the stalk, suspended over the ground. My weight is too heavy to pull myself back again.

My grip on the sandglass starts to slip. The thistle anchoring me cuts my palm as I slide farther away from the skystalk. I hold on tighter, hissing against the pain. My grasp on the thistle is failing. I cannot hold on. I try to readjust my grip, and the sandglass slides out of my other hand, plummeting and pinwheeling end over end.

I brace myself, hoping a merciful power will intervene. The priceless timepiece smashes into the ground and explodes into pieces.

Chapter Six

My ticker stops. Everything stills as I wait for the world to crumble apart, the moon crashing into the land, the sun melting from the heavens. The noise of Markham still climbing yanks me out of my horror. My clock heart stamps out a healthy beat, and the world doesn't fall to ruin.

Time goes on.

Markham pauses just before entering the low-hanging clouds and lifts a sandglass overhead—the true infinity sandglass. The bastard made a duplicate. He laughs and ascends into the mist, the distance left to the top impossible to tell.

I hug the skystalk, my ragged breaths booming in my ears. My head whirls, my muscles shaky, my hair whipping me in the face from the wind. My cut hand stings and bleeds down my wrist. I climbed higher than I realized. The expansive view of the countryside extends all the way to the western coastline. I cannot force myself to go higher.

I descend the stalk little by little. The elven guard comes into focus, their arrows aimed at me. Sitting on the ground, held at sword point, are Jamison and Osric. They look disgruntled but otherwise unharmed. I scramble down, jumping the last few feet. An elf disarms me, and the barghest rushes over to sniff my feet. I try backing away, but the massive canine growls.

The guard, clad in black garments under light chain-mail vests, surrounds me. They are all male, except for a female snapping orders in a language I don't understand. She has thick red hair and sooty lashes, her teeth pearly and eyes a stirring green. Her figure has just enough curves for her tall height, her shape neither round nor reedy. A rapier hangs at her waist, and her boots extend above her knees. Her fitted trousers and military jacket would be considered indecent on a human woman, yet the tailored lines are elegant.

She drags her toe through the broken duplicate of the sandglass and whistles. The barghest pads over to her. She leashes the canine with a metal chain and collar.

"Come," she says.

I assume she's speaking to the beast, but her guards heft Jamison and Osric to their feet and gather our horses. Another elf prods me to fall into line with the others.

"Who is she?" I whisper.

"Commander Asmer." Osric's tone verges on admiration. "She's Queen Imelda's top guard. Asmer was the soldier who caught Prince Killian with my sister, Brea, and reported their romance to the queen."

"I remember things differently," replies Commander Asmer from the front of the group. She glances over her shoulder. "You've been gone from home too long, Osric."

His gaze and voice flat, he answers, "I'm not welcome in our world any longer."

"Perhaps you no longer feel welcome because it's no longer your home."

The commander's comment throws Osric into a sulk. He was ordered by his parents to find his wayward sister after she ran away with the prince, but Brea passed away tragically, and centuries later, Osric has not returned home. His self-imposed banishment isn't a topic he speaks of often.

Commander Asmer faces forward and makes no other remark.

Jamison wraps my cut hand with his kerchief. I would tell him about the bandage I saw on Markham, but the elven guard may overhear me. The bandage makes no sense. Yes, Father Time once implied that the sword of Avelyn could harm Markham, but I've stabbed him multiple times, and he has always recovered. Was the bandage a ruse, just like the duplicate sandglass?

After about half an hour, Jamison begins to favor his bad knee. He could ride one of the horses, but the elves don't offer. Just as I open my mouth to complain, I spot Elderwood Manor. More elves are stationed at every door of the huge house and patrol the gardens. The guard posted at the main door blinks at Osric as we approach.

Osric slows in front of him. "Dalyor?" he asks. "You haven't aged a day."

The guard flushes. "It's been a while, Osric. How have you—"

"You two can catch up later," Asmer says. She ushers us inside and strides into the study. Pianoforte music comes from within.

As we follow her, I whisper to Osric, "Who's the guard out front?"

"Dalyor is an old friend."

"None of *my* friends blush when they see me."

A flush creeps across his cheeks. "Yes, well . . ."

The guards shove us into the study. Laverick and Claret are nowhere to be seen, but an iron birdcage has been set on the floor. Radella is locked inside. She peers out at us, her usual azure color tinged bruise purple.

A statuesque, willowy elf plays the pianoforte. Her fine ash-blond hair is tucked into a slim gold crown studded with diamonds that match her earrings. Her long, lean fingers fly across the ivory keys. The music is not of our world, all at once gentle and discordant and impetuous, like a sparrow taking flight for the first time. Her attention stays fixed on her instrument, her rosebud lips pursed in concentration. She's adorned in a floor-length ice-blue velvet dress that complements her eyes, the bodice tight and the sleeves billowing. On the seat beside her is a short-handled stave.

Her song ends with a flurry of notes followed by a rambunctious crescendo of bold chords. As the sound dissipates, she maintains her pose, fingers arched and waiting. The guards applaud. Osric joins in, and I shoot him a frown.

The crowned elf—their queen, I presume—twists toward us. "I haven't visited the Land of the Living in many decades," she says. "For centuries, humans dwelled in dens. Your living conditions have much improved, and you have such fine things. How much for your pianoforte, human lord? I'll pay in diamonds."

"It's not for sale," Jamison answers.

"Disappointing." She tings the highest treble key. "This would suit my music library."

Commander Asmer edges forward to the front of the group. "Queen Imelda, this is Jamison Callahan and Everley Donovan. And you remember Osric Llewellyn."

Osric lowers to one knee and bows his head. "Your Majesty, thank you for coming."

Queen Imelda picks up her stave and glides past Osric to me. She smells strongly of lemon and verbena, a light, enamoring scent. She looks a few years older than us, but as Markham's elder sister, she must be at least six hundred years of age.

"Everley," she says, her voice suspiciously sweet, "you're the human who has been pursuing my brother across the worlds."

I sense that she expects me to kneel, but I cannot bring myself to bend the knee to an intruder in our home, let alone Markham's sister.

Commander Asmer passes her my sword. "Everley is the bearer of this."

"The sword of Avelyn?" The queen's statement carries a hint of puzzlement. She lifts the weapon to the light as though the answer is engraved in the blade. "The Creator's hallowed sword should belong to someone who can control its might."

"I can," I answer. "And before me, the sword belonged to my father."

"Ah, yes, Brogan Donovan, the great human explorer." Her praise verges on sardonic. "Father Time has a bleeding heart for your family. First your father and then your uncle. I was sorry to hear of Holden's passing. A rare man."

"How did you know him?"

"I've known of every helmsman and Time Bearer in my lifetime. One dies, and Father Time chooses another, replacing them like clockwork." Her gaze examines me, dicing me apart. "You *are* a surprise."

"As are you," Jamison says. "I don't recall Osric's letter inviting you into my home."

Queen Imelda hardly spares him a glance. "I've come to the Land of the Living to fetch my wayward brother."

"You're too late," I say. "He escaped up the skystalk. He'll be in the Silver-Clouded Plain by now. We shouldn't be wasting our time. We need to go after him."

"Killian is my responsibility." Queen Imelda arches her chin, her grip tightening on her stave. "No one knows my brother better than I do. I will retrieve him."

Now she's taking ownership of the prince? Where was she when he destroyed an entire world? My family?

"We need to work together," I reply. "Markham is a danger to us all."

The queen catches her breath. "I haven't heard that name in a long time." She rubs at her throat, adding softly, "Markham was our father's name."

I'm too impatient to let her sentimentality derail this conversation. "Your brother stole the infinity sandglass. I owe it to my uncle to get it back."

"That's admirable, Everley," she says, and I believe she means the compliment, or at least wants me to think she does. "But you needn't worry. I'll return the sandglass to Father Time after I retrieve Killian." The queen waves for Osric to rise from the floor. "You should have educated the humans about our duties so they wouldn't question my capabilities, Llewellyn."

His nostrils flare as he takes a slow, controlled breath. "Respectfully, Your Majesty, nothing we say will wipe away our former actions. We neglected to protect their kind from our prince."

"You're still angry about your sister," she replies coldly. He opens his mouth to object, but she raises a finger, silencing him. "No, you are."

"You never cared for Brea." Osric's answer is simple, but there is nothing simple about his resentment.

"I never wished her harm, and I was as blindsided by their elopement as you were." The queen sounds truly perplexed, even now. "Never in a thousand years did I think my brother would give up his people, heritage, and future for someone well beneath his station."

Osric clasps his hands so tightly his knuckles turn white. I speak up before the queen disparages his sister again.

"Markham worked hard to find a way into the Silver-Clouded Plain. You say you know him better than anyone, so what's he's after?"

"I don't know, but whatever it is, he means to make a fool out of me." Queen Imelda fidgets with her earring, her tone distraught. "He is jealous that I inherited our father's throne and seizes every opportunity to disgrace me."

Markham's actions reflect poorly upon his sister and their people, but this is more than a sibling rivalry. "He wants to go back to when elves kept humans as servants."

"Killian has always felt an elf's place is to lead, a sentiment passed down by our father, but I disagreed with their definition of leadership. I've no interest in utilizing humans as servants. The Creator set forth a mandate after the triad war for elves not to interfere with the humans. I won't defy the goddess, nor will I let my brother vilify me or my people. Commander Asmer will take a small party of soldiers to find Killian and bring him home."

"Your Majesty," Osric says, "please let us help—"

"You and your human associates had your chance to seize him and failed. We will do this without your interference, or I'll be forced to detain you alongside Killian's human pet."

Jamison's eyebrows jump up. "Do you mean Harlow Glaspey?"

"She's been uncooperative and quite surly to our guards," Queen Imelda replies. "Now, I must return and report to the elven council. Members of my guard will stay behind to ensure you're not tempted to follow Commander Asmer."

"Your Majesty, your people's visit won't go unnoticed," Jamison states. "Our ruler, Queen Aislinn, is already sending soldiers to investigate the skystalk. The farmers will tell them they saw your guard."

"Your queen won't permit her subjects to claim they saw elves. Such utterances would support every belief she's fought against." The elven queen reads our expressions of astonishment. "We know about the happenings in your world. As elected stewards over the Land of the Living, it's our duty to stay appraised. When your queen denounced Mother Madrona and the Otherworlds, it caused quite a stir among our council. The foolish woman doesn't even believe in pixies."

Queen Imelda signals for a guard to pick up the iron birdcage. "Take this one to the nearest portal and see that she returns home."

Radella flutters her wings and wrenches against the bars.

"Why are you taking her away?" I ask. "She wants to stay with us."

"She's been ignoring Father Time's summons to return to the Everwoods." The queen peers into the cage at the angry pixie. "He asked that I send her back."

The guard starts to carry Radella away. She bangs against the bars and trills furiously. I rush forward.

"You'll be all right, Radella."

Her wings droop, her color a miserable dusky purple. I stick my pointer finger through the bars, and she grips the tip.

"We'll see each other again," I whisper. "I promise."

The guard carries her out of the study, and her trills fade away.

Queen Imelda points at me with her wooden stave. "As for you, Miss Donovan, I'll let you keep the sword of Avelyn, but only because you're the Time Bearer, and only because I trust that, as Time Bearer, you won't test the might of the Land of Promise. Once word that Commander Asmer has seized my brother reaches me, I will notify my guards, and you and your friends will be permitted to move freely."

Jamison draws up taller, his shoulders straight. "You're holding us captive?"

"You and the members of your household will be unharmed, as long as you stay out of our way."

A pair of elven guards prod Jamison and me into the corridor. Imelda snaps at Osric in their foreign tongue. He bows his head and stays behind in the study. We are led down the hall to the library, shoved through the door, and locked inside.

Chapter Seven

Claret and Laverick rise from the sofa in surprise. A wave of relief courses through me at finding them in the library.

"Are you two all right?" I ask.

"Except for the pushy elf queen who put us in here and told us not to leave, we're fine," Claret replies.

Jamison marches to the window to look out at the front courtyard. "Guards are stationed outside our door and windows. Commander Asmer is riding off with her troops."

I quickly explain our encounter with the elf queen to our friends.

Laverick pushes at her temples. "Maybe Queen Imelda is right. Maybe we should let her commander track down the prince. Every time we try, something bad happens."

"I don't trust her." Jamison paces in front of the window. "I think she knows what artifact Killian is looking for. If not, why did she answer Osric's letter right after the prince found a way into the Silver-Clouded Plain?"

His question sends us all into dour reflection. Does Imelda have an urgent need to capture Killian? Or does she know what he seeks in the giants' world and want it for herself?

"I need a drink," Laverick says.

"I'll get it." Claret goes to the serving cart. "All the bottles are empty."

Jamison crosses the room to her. "Let me look. I could stand for a drink as well."

They search for spirits while Laverick fiddles with a small bundle of fuses in her hand, playing with the frayed ends. I should tell her about the constable, but now seems like an extraordinarily bad time.

"You know what I hope happens?" Laverick asks, her voice tired. "I don't care about the prince. Not really. I want to open a firearm-and-ammunition shop with Claret, like I told you about when we were in the Land Under the Wave."

"You should," I say. I think of my own dream to one day sell my wood carvings in my uncle's clock shop and be with Jamison. Such a wish feels so far away. I don't know how to get us from here to there without removing Markham first.

"I've been deluding myself." Laverick laughs softly, a lackluster sound. "The things I did while living on the streets, the folks I pinched coin from . . . I thought pickpocketing didn't hurt anyone. I was wrong. I *did* wrong. What happened with the constable is my comeuppance."

"He had a gun too," I reply. "He shot too."

She goes on as though I didn't speak. "I was so arrogant. I held him at gunpoint, and I never thought . . ." Her voice chokes with tears. "When I saw him start to fire at you, I didn't think. What sort of person doesn't hesitate to shoot?"

"You're a good person, Laverick. You were trying to protect me."

Her wet gaze rises to me. "The Creator may not see me that way. She probably views me the same as she does any other murderer."

Claret lets out an exclamation of victory. "I found a bottle of port!"

"I'll pour," says Jamison, collecting the glasses.

A moment later, Claret brings over full tumblers. I take mine and join Jamison at the window.

"The queen left," he says flatly. "Is what you told her true? Does Prince Killian plan to enslave our kind?"

"He wants to try, but I think he ultimately wants to change something from his past." I shake my head, indicating I have no idea what.

Jamison shifts his weight off his bad knee and rubs at his upper thigh. "We all have things we wish we could undo."

"But none of us has the arrogance to try," Claret says from where she's listening from across the room.

Laverick sits forward, setting her elbows on her knees. "I know what I would undo."

"Me too," Jamison mumbles.

I also know which moment I would return to and alter.

"Enough." Claret sets down her glass with a clink. "We aren't going to waste our time wishing for impossible things. So, our lives are in shambles at the moment? I had no one when I was a little girl, just the streets and uncertainty. I'd never wish those years away, because they brought me to all of you."

Her statement pulls me up. Markham took away my family once, and I couldn't do anything about it. But I can stop him from taking my family now. I swallow my drink in one gulp. "I'm going after Markham."

"*We* are going after him." Jamison strides to the library shelves and begins moving books about and looking behind them. "The queen left with two guards. By my count, eight more remain at the manor. Everley and I will get the horses. Claret and Laverick can—"

"I can't," Laverick rasps. "I'm sorry, Evie and Jamison. I'd like to help, but I can't go with you."

Claret grips her hand. "Lavey and I will stay behind and watch over the manor."

Jamison gives a grunt of agreement and continues to shuffle the books on the shelves.

"What are you doing?" I ask.

"I may know of a way out of here that doesn't involve you stabbing a guard. My grandfather liked puzzles. As you may recall, he built hidden chambers in select rooms that led to concealed passageways. I remember seeing an opening in here somewhere. Or maybe it was in the study? In any case, there may be a book with a tree on it, a holly tree."

While Jamison shuffles books, I whisper to the Fox and the Cat. "Should you get the chance, there's something I would like you to do for me while we're gone." I quickly summarize my request so Jamison won't overhear. Right as they agree, he calls out.

"Aha!" He tips down a book and unlocks a lever in the wall, releasing a narrow pop-out door. The three of us go to see what he's found.

"Holy elderwood," breathes Claret.

"Holly, actually." Jamison points out the symbol on the leather book that acted as the lever to open the secret door. "This marked the opening."

Claret traces the tree symbol. "In the tree alphabet, holly means 'freedom.'"

"I knew I remembered seeing a secret door in this room," Jamison says, beaming. "My grandfather was an eccentric man with a tendency toward paranoia or, as my mother would say, fanciful indulgences." He picks up a lantern and ducks through the opening.

I pull Laverick in for a hug. "You're one of the best people in all the worlds," I say. "Whatever happened before or happens next, you're my friend, and I love you for always."

She squeezes me back. "Be safe. Teach that prince a lesson."

"I will."

Claret pulls me in close next. "Evie, don't worry. Lavey will be back to her usual antics in no time, blowing things up with her black-powder inventions and lighting things on fire."

"And you?"

"I've never had a real home, not one I could be proud of. The chance that I could have one with Lavey is worth fighting for."

Claret's inference that, in time, everything will be all right worries me. She can hardly sleep at night because she's still haunted by the merrows, and Laverick won't soon forget how she wounded the constable. How often do we place all our hopes and dreams on time? We trust that in time, justice will prevail, scars will heal, or wrongs will be forgotten. I haven't the heart to tell her that time isn't all-powerful. Some wrongs are never righted, some wounds never heal. We simply learn to live with them.

Jamison waits for me to enter the hidden room, then shuts us inside. The narrow chamber is filled with crates of mismatched pottery and dusty furniture. A mirror glass with daisies etched into the frame leans against one wall. A silver-handled comb has fallen to the floor beside baby clothes and a bassinet. Trunks overfilled with women's clothes are set about. A doll lies on its side near an old playhouse.

"What is this place?" I ask.

Jamison lifts the lid off a small wooden jewelry box and takes out a silver shell brooch inset with diamonds and pearls. "My grandfather built this manor as a wedding gift for my grandmother. The hidden doorways and passageways were his idea, though they were never used much. My father seems to have converted them into storage. Most of these things belonged to my mother, though some were my sister's. I thought my father had discarded them."

I pick up a small painted portrait of a girl. "Is this your mother?"

"My grandmother. She worshiped Mother Madrona. Back then, Children of Madrona were teachers of the old ways. Grandmother named this home Elderwood Manor after her esteem for its namesake."

I set down the portrait and crouch over a milk crate packed with books. They are titles similar to the one Claret was reading last night, books forbidden by the queen for depicting Madrona in a reverential manner.

"Those were once in the library," Jamison explains. "My mother, like my grandmother, studied the old tales. When she was too sick to leave her bed, Mother would read stories aloud to me about pixies and gnomes coexisting in the Everwoods, playing among the elderwood trees' mighty branches."

I wipe the dust off a book's cover and read the title: *The Mother of All*. "Perhaps it's time to bring these things out of storage."

Jamison turns the shell brooch over in his fingers. "My father kept my mother's and sister's rooms intact for a long while before clearing them out. It would be odd to put their things back where they were."

"I mean that you shouldn't hide them away. I would give anything to have more pieces of my home or family. All I have left are my mother's gloves." I lift my hands, showing him the faded and mended wool. "If you've ever wondered if it's possible to love something to death . . ."

Jamison offers me the brooch. "I would like for you to have this. You're right. My mother's things shouldn't be stowed away. They should be enjoyed." He pins the brooch on the breast of my cloak and stands back, his lips sliding upward. "There. Now you have another thing to love."

I manage a quiet thank-you. The brooch is something meaningful that I can appreciate and wear to feel pretty, but in truth, what he has given me to love isn't a thing I can wear on my cloak. It's him.

Jamison raises the lamp, extending its glow down the passageway. The tunnel gradually narrows, and the ceiling lowers. I stay close to him and hunch to avoid hitting my head, ignoring the cobwebs and creeping things skittering from the light.

"Any guesses where this leads?" I ask, the musty air itching my nose.

"None whatsoever."

"Grand."

We follow the passageway for so long, I lose track of how far we have gone. Elderwood Manor is a massive estate, but we must have trod the whole length of it by now. We finally come upon a brick wall with no markings.

Jamison searches for a way out. "This can't be right."

I study the walls to our right and left, running my fingers over them, and locate a marking of a holly tree near our feet. Under the engraving is a notch in the brick. My breath snags at the sight of a big beetle running away, but I slide my finger into the notch and pull.

Clicking noises go off like a spattering of gunfire, and dust rains from a crack appearing in the wall. Jamison pries the door open, and we step into a dim room. The large quarters are skimpily furnished with a bunk, a dressing cabinet, and a stool. A narrow rectangular window is high over the bed, too far to see out of.

"We're in the groundkeeper's quarters." Jamison passes me the lamp and kneels to rummage around under the bunk. I listen at the exterior door, my ticker thunderous in the charged quiet. He pulls out a spade. "Here it is! This is what I was looking for."

"A shovel?"

"Our former groundskeeper fended off thieves with a shovel this size."

We slowly open the exterior door and sneak out. The day has gifted us with sunshine and a parade of fluffy white clouds. Jamison leads us around a corner of the manor toward the stables and drags me back again.

An elf guard is posted outside the stables.

"Blaggard pricks," Jamison says.

"Wait, look."

Someone creeps up behind the guard and knocks him over the head with a shovel. I suppose gardening tools are good for more than digging. The elf goes down, and his attacker disappears inside the stables. We dash across the clearing and in through the same door.

A shovel swings at my head. Jamison raises the spade between us, and the tools connect.

"Good sin, Osric," he says, "you nearly took Evie's head off."

"I thought you were guards." Osric lowers the shovel. This encounter could have gone worse. He also carries a short sword. "I stopped by the library. Claret said you'd left, so I came here. I was afraid you'd gone without me."

"How did you get out?" I ask.

"I told Dalyor I was going for a walk." Osric tosses Jamison a pistol and passes me a pouch of Radella's pixie dust that we'd been saving in case we found ourselves in a pinch. "Saddle up."

Jamison prepares a horse for the two of us while Osric and I saddle his. "If we hurry," says Jamison, "we can be up the skystalk in less than an hour."

"We cannot be brash or we *will* wind up dead," says Osric. "The elven guard will have the skystalk surrounded. We will never get past them, and even if we could, we would be mad to go to the giants' world without someone guiding us."

"Who do you have in mind?" I ask.

Voices sound outside.

Jamison launches into his saddle. I sheathe my sword and vault onto the horse behind him. Osric mounts up as well, and we ride out of the back of the stables just as three elven guards rush in. Arrows stream past us, lodging in the doorways. I lean forward into Jamison, hugging his waist, and hang on. Our horse gallops us away from the manor, away from the skystalk, away from the peace that the prince of elves has again stolen.

Chapter Eight

Jamison and I lead the way on our horse down the riding trail. Osric bounces in his saddle behind us, his hat low over his surly eyes. We have been riding for two hours, and the elf looks no less vexed to be on a horse.

We travel the edge of the cliff through the late-summer colors of yellowing green and dull gold framing the coastline. A stony beach spreads out below, fringing the base of the limestone cliffs and blending into the sparkling blue-gray sea. We pause at a lookout to peer over the ledge.

Between the beach and the top of the cliff, suspended in midair, is a patch of kaleidoscopic sky as big as our horses. The radiance is almost imperceptible, but when the sunlight catches it at the right angle, the brilliancy shimmers every color of the rainbow, simultaneously dazzling and otherworldly. To the plain eye, the prism of light could be a trick of the imagination. But this isn't the first portal I have encountered, and it won't be the last one I will depend on for travel between the worlds.

I dismount first, then Jamison gets down. We sidestep up to the drop-off, pushing into the sea winds, and peer over at the subtle patch of iridescence.

"Why are the portals always in inconvenient places?" I bemoan.

"Creatures would wander through them without a thought otherwise." Osric slides awkwardly off his horse, his grip tight on the saddle, and rubs at his sore legs.

Jamison touches my elbow. "You don't have to come along."

"I've survived the Land Under the Wave once," I say. "I can do it again."

Osric holds down his hat before a gust of wind sweeps it away.

"No one is here," I say. "You've no need for a hat right now."

"I surely do. I found a gray hair on my head this morning—and a wrinkle!" He yanks off his hat to show me.

I examine his flawless, youthful face. "Where?"

Osric points to the tiniest wrinkle along his hairline. "I'm rationing my dosages of cider until I restock my supply. The effects of the charm apples have begun to dwindle." He drops his voice to a sheepish whisper. "I'm *aging*."

He's nearly six hundred years old. All things considered, he's outlasted time rather well. "Maybe this is a good time to stop depending on the charm apples for your youth?"

"And let time ravage me? Never. I've no time to grow old." Osric shoves his hat back on his head and scans the cliffside. "We must go and come back quickly. Time moves slower in the Land Under the Wave."

"Then let's get to it." I back away from the stone ledge. Every portal to an Otherworld is a leap of faith. Fortunately, for this journey, we've no need to seek out a whale to swallow us.

Jamison and Osric back up beside me. The three of us stand in a line facing the cliff, the portal out of sight below.

No one budges.

The sword of Avelyn warms and vibrates in my hand, urging me to go. I cannot move my joints. I worked hard to return home from the Land Under the Wave. Never did I imagine I would willingly go back to that inhospitable world.

"Fine." Osric sighs. "Let your elder show you how it's done."

He takes off running and leaps over the cliff, one hand on his head to hold down his hat, and drops out of sight.

Before I can think too deeply about what I'm doing, I sprint after him. "Bloody bones!" I curse and jump.

A brisk wind whooshes up at me, wailing past my ears. Osric has disappeared without a trace. The rainbow of light stretches beneath me, translucent, gossamer, flimsy. I can see the ground through the band of multicolored radiance. My boots meet the opening of the portal, and the scent of the sea grows stronger. Feet, legs, hips, chest. I hold my breath and plummet out of this world.

The next thing I see is Osric's outstretched arms. He catches me as he would help someone step off a chair. We landed on a raised platform built on a barren hilltop. The structure was erected beneath the portal for ease of travelers coming and going.

The mild evening sky hosts a backdrop of stars pinned with an enormous bone moon. I'm uncertain of the local hour, except that it's nighttime.

Jamison lands beside us and folds forward, grasping his stomach. Portal travel has left him woozy. "We're back?"

"We're back," I confirm.

A swelling breeze snaps at my cloak. The winds of this world constantly punish those of us who don't dwell under the waves. My hair tangles in the shell brooch still pinned to my cloak. I take off the shiny treasure and stow it in my pocket.

"Are you certain Captain Redmond is the best guide?" Jamison asks, still bent in half from nausea. "Mundy's been locked out of the giants' world for decades. He may not be a reliable resource any longer."

"Do *you* know any other giants we can ask for help?" Osric counters.

Neither of us offers another solution. Captain Redmond is one of the only giants we've met who was banished from the Silver-Clouded Plain and made a home in another world. He isn't a man-eater, but that doesn't mean he's fond of humans.

"I thought not," Osric says. "Collect yourself, Jamison. We must be swift. You and Everley don't want to come back to the Land of the Living and find you've been away several months like you did last time."

No, we certainly do not.

The three of us thump down the stairs of the platform to the rocky ground. I half expect to encounter the boggart, the sinister-looking guardian of this portal, but the ghoulish hooded figure doesn't show himself.

We waste no time trudging down the arid hill to the lantern-lit village of Eventide. With less than a third of the houses occupied, the place feels sparsely cared for and abandoned. Eventide is a haven for castaways—pirates, traders, and those, like Redmond, who were banished from the Otherworlds. Four ships are moored off Merrow Lagoon. Included among them is the *Undertow*, the captain's vessel.

"How do we find the captain?" Jamison asks.

"After the disturbance Mundy caused in the village, trying to prevent us from leaving, there's only one place he could be," Osric answers. Osric is Captain Redmond's former first mate, so I trust his judgment.

The trail weaves down the hillside to the upper levels of the village that ring the lagoon in half-circle tiers. Strings of azure lights lit by effervescent plankton mark the underwater trails and highways that lead down into the deep, far below the surface of the water, to the merrow king's castle at the bottom of the sea.

Osric's arm shoots out, blocking our path and motioning for us to halt. Ahead, stalking in the shadows, a strange figure comes our way. The creature's bony legs are emaciated, all tendons and kneecaps, and its upper body, from navel to crown, resembles a fish. Big, round black eyes bulge from either side of the finperson's head, and serrated teeth protrude from its puffy lips.

We duck behind a shed and hunker down. Osric draws his short sword, and Jamison readies his pistol. The finperson marches past, a musket held between its bony fins for hands. Since when did finfolk start wielding firearms? The last time we were here, they carried tridents and were contending against their sworn enemies, the merrows, for underwater territory.

I start to get up. Jamison tugs me back down again. Two more finfolk, also armed with muskets, patrol the road up the way.

"The transition of power has begun," Osric whispers. "The finfolk occupy their new territory."

Good sin. It's really happening.

In one of his more asinine moves, Markham promised the merrow king residency in the Land of the Living and exclusive rights to our seas. As elves are appointed stewards over our world, Markham felt that the decision was within his authority. The finfolk—his allies—will benefit by taking possession of the Land Under the Wave, which, apparently, they have already begun to do.

"How long until the merrows leave for our world?" Jamison asks.

I search my memory of the prince's conversation with King Dorian—the ruler of the merrows. "Markham said they could claim their new territory after the next full moon."

We gaze up at the swollen moon above.

Osric swears under his breath. "Looks like the full moon is tomorrow."

A day in the Land Under the Wave equals a month in the Land of the Living. We have approximately thirty days before the merrows infiltrate our seas and target us with their nightly song of enchantment, luring victims into the water to drown or enslave.

My anxiety is wound so tight I startle when Osric gives the signal that our path is clear to go. The finfolk patrol everywhere, muskets leaned against their shoulders, their ugly, toothy sneers and bulbous eyes nightmarish. Osric waits for openings, then we dash from shadow to shadow. Eventide was already quiet when we were here last. Now, with the world occupied by the finfolk, this drought of activity in a prominent seaside port is downright eerie.

Finally, Osric hunches behind a large single-story building and tells us to wait here while he creeps around to the front. He comes back a moment later and waves us forward. We sneak to the front of the building and take turns peeking inside the closest window.

Captain Redmond sits behind bars with his crewmate and fellow older giant, Neely. The pirate giants are locked up with members of their elven crew from the *Undertow*. Some of the elves wear headscarves marked with their ship's symbol, a sandglass over a skull and crossbones. In terms of dress, none is as polished as Mundy. He sticks out in a black velvet jacket with a scarlet satin lining, his long hair combed and tied back from his scruffy face. Neely looks just the same as before, with his simple cotton clothes and wiry gray hair.

Four finfolk guard the cell from inside the prison. Their leader, who colluded with Markham—I never caught his name—sits in a chair by the door. He's the only one armed with a trident and a pistol. His underlings carry muskets.

We return to the back of the building.

"What do we do now?" Jamison asks.

"We use the dust," Osric whispers. "Captain Redmond and Neely are sitting on a bench on the other side of this wall. Everley, will you do the honors?"

"Happily." I remove the pouch of pixie dust from my pocket and sprinkle a pinch on the clay bricks at about eye level. An opening as large as an egg appears, as if a hole were drilled through the wall.

Osric whispers through the opening. "Captain Redmond?"

A big eye appears.

"First Mate Osric?" asks Neely. "Is that poppet with you?"

"Yes, it's me." Though I can only see his eye, I can tell by Neely's bright tone he's glad to see me. "Get the captain, would you, please?"

Neely disappears, and Redmond looks out the hole.

"What are you riffraff doing here? Haven't you caused me enough trouble?"

"We need to speak with you," Osric replies. "Turn around and lean against the wall, or you'll draw attention from the guards." Redmond grumbles but does as he's told. "Mundy, we need your help."

"My help? How about you help *us*? Queen Imelda found out about the prince's bargain with King Dorian and threatened to align with the finfolk if one merrow enters the Land of the Living, which, of course, King Dorian didn't appreciate. He attacked the finfolk's border, and they retaliated by seizing Eventide with firearms from smugglers."

Their internal strife could mean safety for the Land of the Living. The merrows may abandon their designs to invade. I doubt they can triumph against the finfolk *and* the elves.

"As for you lot," the captain snaps, "since I was betrayed by my former first mate"—I glance at Osric—"my life has been nothing but strife. My pet crocodile passed away, my clock collection was destroyed, and my ship was commandeered. The finfolk slaughtered most of our crew and took the last of us hostage."

"Blame Prince Killian," Jamison says. "This civil war is his doing, and now he's found a way into the Silver-Clouded Plain. The elven guard is searching for him. Queen Imelda said she wants to bring him to justice, but we aren't convinced."

Osric tenses at the mention of his queen and our first impression of her.

The sound of a door shutting draws me to the corner of the building. I look out at finfolk walking away from the prison. I creep back to Jamison and Osric.

"A pair of finfolk have left," I report. "They're going toward the lagoon. Just two remain inside. Their leader and one underling."

Captain Redmond doesn't want to hear from me. We have a tumultuous history. He put me in his clock collection and tried to sell me and my friends to traders. In return, I injured his crocodile. But Redmond is the guide we need. He has the self-assurance of a leader and the gumption of a pirate.

"Captain," I say, "you told me once that you didn't think you could find a way back to your world. This is your chance. You and Neely can go home."

My ticker counts out the seconds of silence. Each beat feels as though it lasts a whole minute. Why is he taking so long? He's wasting our time.

I shift my lips over the opening. "If you won't help us, then Neely will. We'll leave you here to rot."

"All right," the captain growls. "We have a bargain."

Osric tugs me away from the wall. "Back away and be ready to run, Captain. You and Neely both."

I grab a fistful of pixie dust and toss it at the wall. The glitter rains down and dissolves the bricks in patches. As the openings spread, I see the prisoners gaping at me through the disappearing wall. One of the finfolk raises his musket. Neely reaches through the slots between the cell bars, grabs him by the neck, and slams him against the irons. The guard collapses and drops the weapon.

Redmond wedges himself in the gap in the brick wall, his shoulders as wide as the hole. The ceiling cracks as he wriggles out.

I draw my sword as the other prisoners swarm the escape route. A guard fires a gun into the crowd of them, triggering a panic. They all shove and push to get outside first.

Neely tries to leave at the same time as three elves, the whole lot of them becoming lodged in the opening. More prisoners shove at them from behind. Dust and rubble rain from the ceiling, the cracks there spreading out and down the walls. Neely wrenches himself out of the gap. Another gunshot goes off. Prisoners pour outside as the nearest section of the ceiling crumbles and collapses.

A torrent of debris sends a cloud of dust pouring over us. I cough, my eyes streaming tears to clear my vision. Osric lies on the ground, his leg bleeding. I drop beside him and press down on the wound. He's been shot.

Three finfolk patrolling nearby run at us and lift their weapons. Captain Redmond bashes one on the head and takes his musket. He bludgeons a second in the temple with the firearm stock. Jamison grapples with the third finperson and smashes the creature over the back of the head with a brick.

"Carry him," Captain Redmond says to Neely, who then slings Osric over his shoulder.

The elf groans. Redmond leads the charge up the hill. Our assailants are first to meet him, and the giant throws a formidable punch. For all their firepower, the finfolk aren't well trained in firearms. Their shots go wide and high. Perhaps their striking Osric was luck.

Jamison, Redmond, Neely, Osric, and I steadily make ground uphill to the portal. As we reach the steps to the platform, Osric becomes limp and unconscious, and his flask falls from his pocket. I stop to grab it, and a trident pierces the ground near my hand.

The leader of the finfolk stands behind us. Captain Redmond reels around as the finperson raises his pistol at me. A wind billows toward us, plastering me with the creature's scent: rotten fish.

"You reek of fear, human," he snarls.

"You don't smell much better."

The boggart suddenly manifests beside the finperson. His jawbone juts out from under the lowered hood of his shapeless black robes. He hovers above the ground, the heavy cloth hanging past his hidden feet.

He extends his skeletal hand from under his robes and unfurls a sharpened nail at the finperson. "Let them go," he hisses.

The finperson bares his teeth. "Begone, boggart. These are my captives."

"You may not have them."

The boggart's chilling voice sends Neely up the stairway with Osric. Jamison hesitates, staying close to me. Redmond stands by, ready with his fists.

"My kind has taken possession of this land," the finperson snaps. "I command you to go."

The boggart sweeps his gaunt hand down the finperson's arm. Scales and flesh peel away to reveal his skeleton. His skin and muscle gone.

The finperson flaps his fin to shake free of the illusion. "What have you done? Turn it back!"

"Beware of time," hisses the boggart. "For the tides cower to the days, and the moon and sun revolve around the hours. Trod carefully lest your eleventh hour should speedily come."

He sweeps his hand over the finperson's arm again, and the grisly image goes away. The finperson stumbles back, clutching his scaly limb, and the boggart floats toward us.

"Go," he rasps.

Jamison and I take off up the stairs, Redmond's heavy steps sounding after us. Glancing back, I see the boggart vanish. The finperson, still shaken by the illusion, doesn't pursue us. Our feet pound up the stairs.

"Does the boggart serve Father Time?" I ask.

"You could say that," Captain Redmond answers. "The boggart guards the portal, and portals are instantaneous conduits through time."

We arrive at the platform where Neely waits. Osric hangs loosely in his arms, his leg a bloody mess. The boggart reappears, blocking the entry to the portal that floats above the ground at the end of the platform. He extends his wasted hand toward me. I flinch at the daisy in his skeletal fingers.

"What's that for?" I ask.

"You know."

A chill fires up the back of my neck. "I don't want it."

Redmond huffs at me. He must think I'm being difficult for declining a flower and slowing our exodus, but this daisy represents an apology, and I'm not ready to forgive Father Time.

The boggart steps forward even closer. He has no breath to flow over my face, as he doesn't appear to be breathing. Under his hood, I glimpse his white skull, stained teeth, a hole where his nose would be, and empty eye sockets. In those orbs of nothingness, a scene plays out like a vision. I see myself running through a shadowed woodland, darting between trees and lunging over ferns. I sprint hard, away from what or toward whom I cannot tell. I only know that I am afraid and alone. The image comes to me in an instant, between the tick and tock of my heart, but the fear from the vision lingers longer.

Fate has shared a secret. A warning.

The boggart pulls his hand back under his draping sleeve. "The eleventh hour is nigh, Time Bearer."

Before I can ask what that means, he vanishes and clears our way to the portal.

"What was that about?" Jamison asks.

"I don't know," I mutter. "Let's go home."

My grip firm on my sword, I step up to the colorful prism and leap into the light.

Chapter Nine

I land on a bluff. Upon first glance, I see that the portal dropped me back at the seashore, a rocky beach fringing a sunset-lit sky and sea. My companions arrive seconds later. The second they are through the portal, it vanishes. The giants remain on their feet, but Jamison drops to his knees and stays down, his head hanging.

"Are you all right?" I ask.

"I heard the song."

"The song?"

"My mother's song. The one I can't completely remember. I heard it in the portal." He leaves his head down and whistles the song I last heard him play on his violin.

Gooseflesh rises up my arms. The music has a profound, stirring undertone, like a lullaby. My beating ticker slows to match the rhythm. My muscles turn soft and loose, and my mind becomes fuzzy. I fight off a yawn.

Jamison stops and lifts his head. A haunted look dims his gaze. "We landed before I heard the ending. Did you hear the music?"

"I heard nothing."

A voice calls out from close by.

"Everley! Jamison!"

Quinn runs toward us from up the shore. Alick and Vevina stand behind the lass outside a two-story seaside manor that overlooks the sea. It's the only structure in sight. This isn't the same shoreline we left to go to the Land Under the Wave. Peculiarly, the portal returned us here, farther up the coastline, where our friends have been hiding at Jamison's seaside manor.

Jamison catches the lass in his arms. "This is a surprise. What's the day?"

Quinn rattles off the date, just one day after we left our world, and narrows her eyes at the giants. "Are these the pirates you warned us about? The ones who killed the sea hag?"

"They are," Jamison replies. "This is Captain Redmond and his comrade Neely. For the time being, they are, um, our associates."

Quinn pauses to examine the giants from head to toe skeptically, then she grabs my hand, turning me away from the water, and points inland. A lofty pillar shadows the eastern horizon. The skystalk is impossible to miss, even from afar.

"Have you seen this, Evie?" she asks. "It showed up yesterday. Alick said it must be the work of a sorcerer."

"Not a sorcerer," I correct. "We'll explain later. Right now, Osric needs Dr. Huxley."

Quinn runs ahead of us to the house. Our party follows, the giants' mighty steps quavering the land in unmistakable thuds. Each one pounds into my belly. The last time such a noise was heard in our world, the giants had come to slaughter our kind.

The seaside manor is a shrunken version of Elderwood Manor, with fewer windows and floors but a similar boxy structure. Alick and Vevina are dressed in work aprons, tools and woodpiles set out around them. One segment of the house's siding has been repaired. Broken and warped patches cover the rest. A charming, low driftwood fence encloses the home, and chest-high daisy bushes flourish by the front door.

Alick rushes forward to meet us and quickly examines Osric's injured leg. "The wound appears shallow, but we must remove the musket ball. Bring him upstairs."

Too tall and broad to squeeze through the door, Neely passes Osric to Jamison, who carries the elf in. Quinn goes inside, as well, to assist Alick, leaving Vevina to welcome me.

She has cut her hair to less than a fingernail's length all over. The style emphasizes her high cheekbones and large brown eyes and shows off her ebony complexion. She looks beautiful—she always does—but I regret the reason behind the change. She and Alick are wanted by the queen for helping me escape execution. Coming here, chopping off her hair, they're all because of me.

Captain Redmond brushes rubble off his velvet jacket while Neely stares at the front door, clearly put out that he's unable to fit inside the house.

Vevina drags her curious gaze away from the pirates to me. "We were wondering when we would see you next. I certainly wasn't expecting this." I have so much to tell her, but I won't delve into details in front of the giants. "Where are Claret and Laverick? Are they coming?"

"They stayed behind at Elderwood Manor, but they miss you. Claret told me so just yesterday."

Vevina puts on a tight smile. "You've no need to explain, darling. The Fox and the Cat and I don't have the sort of friendship where we have to see each other often." She removes her work apron and drapes it over the tools. "Alick and I have been doing little projects to pass the time. He likes to work with his hands, and since he can't practice medicine at the moment, we've been fixing up the house. That man is unbearable when he's bored." Her complaint holds no rancor. Vevina and Alick get on well. Her affection for him rings through every word.

Captain Redmond releases an impatient sigh. The sun has sunk into the watery horizon, and night has begun to close in. "Must we stand out here all evening?"

I shoot him a look of annoyance. "Do you have somewhere they can stay?"

"Come," Vevina says. "We've just the place."

She leads us behind the manor to a barn with sagging eaves, and slides open the tall main doors. Captain Redmond ducks inside and winces at the waft of manure. Hay bales are stacked on one side, and livestock stalls line the other. Swallows coo from the rafters. Quinn's cat—Prince—prowls around.

Vevina lights three lanterns, casting a soft glow across the straw floor. "It's drafty but dry. I'll bring blankets and some drinking water."

"This will do fine," I say. "Thank you."

Captain Redmond grumbles to himself.

Neely wanders to the lamb pen and peers down. He picks up a small black sheep and strokes its fleecy back. "Look, Captain," he says, his eyes wet and shiny, "a wee lamb."

"Didn't have many of those in the Land Under the Wave." Redmond shrugs out of his velvet jacket and hangs it on a tack peg. "House woman, do you have a washbasin? Or have humans no appreciation for cleanliness?"

Vevina arches a brow. "I'll fetch you something to wash with from the house." She tugs me to the door. "I thought giants were supposed to be brutish monsters. One's crying like a lost child, and the other's an entitled dandy. Aren't these the pirates who captured you?"

"We need their help. We wouldn't have brought them if we didn't. It's important, Vevina."

"House woman?" Redmond calls. "When will you bring that water? I'm parched."

Vevina harrumphs. "Is he incapable of doing anything himself?"

"Thank you for tending to them. I promise it won't last long."

"I'm only accommodating him because you said it's important." She sweeps out into the night.

Neely sets the black lamb down in the pen and picks up a white one. He hums to the animal while petting its back and rocking gently.

I stomp over to Redmond. "You could have been less rude to Vevina. You're not a captain of a ship anymore, and you're her guest."

"I've every right to point out laziness when I see it. That house woman is an insolent one, I can tell." He undoes the cuffs of his frilly shirt with short, irritated jerks. "How's your clock heart faring, Ticker?"

"Stop calling me by that name. I'm not a clock in your collection anymore. You're in my world now."

He slides me a slantwise look. "Your human world is unimpressive, and your small moon is lackluster. I expected a magnificent landscape from the highly sought-after Land of the Living. You ungrateful humans have dulled the beauty my ancestors created. When giants first left the Everwoods for the Land of the Living, this was an empty tundra. Under Eiocha's direction, my ancestors built mountains and islands, scooped out valleys, and trenched canyons. My kind still creates new and wondrous things. Your kind doesn't appreciate all that we've done for them." The captain sits on a stack of hay bales and loosens his boot buckles. "I cannot fathom Prince Killian's fascination with humans or this human world. You would be an easy conquest."

My mouth goes dry. "Markham wishes to conquer us?"

"Why are you surprised? Elves have always lorded over the rest of us."

"Queen Imelda showed no interest in dominating my kind."

The giant leans back against the hay bale as he pulls off a boot. "Queen Imelda and Prince Killian disagree on many things. He was highly favored by his parents and well liked by their patrons, but the firstborn of the king inherits the throne, so Imelda is their ruler."

"Did Markham tell you this?"

"Aye."

I sit beside the giant. "What else did he tell you?"

Mundy pulls off his second boot, then peels off his stockings and stretches his big toes. "You ask a lot of questions, Ticker. I'm tired. Thirsty. Where is the house woman?"

"Her name is Vevina, and she's very clever, so I would be nice to her, or she will make you regret it. Tell me what you know about Markham."

"Rub my feet and I'll tell you."

"Never in a million lives will I touch those ugly things. We got you out of prison. Answer my questions."

Mundy stretches his long, hairy toes. "I know much about Killian. Some things he told me, some I observed. The prince has a passion for music. He often asked crewmen to play their instruments for us in private."

I know this already. When Markham was Queen Aislinn's governor over the penal colony, he asked Jamison to perform song after song for him on his violin. "What does that have to do with conquering my people?"

Mundy makes odd faces as he massages the instep of his right foot. "Near the finish of the triad war, our warrior giants were on the cusp of obliterating the humans. The elves came to the humans' aid, but they were too late. Our warriors had very nearly reclaimed their birthright. Only divine intervention could stop them, which, as you recall, is how the war ended. Eiocha played a song on her violin that put the giants to sleep. To this day, the warrior giants still slumber under the Creator's spell, waiting for someone to wake them."

I rub my hands over my knees, suddenly restless. This is the same story Markham brought me to the Black Forest to share, and here I am, hearing it again. "The Creator destroyed her violin so the giants would stay asleep forever."

"Forever is a very long time." He looks up at the cobwebbed rafters and listens to the swallows softly cooing. Across the barn, Neely sings an old sea chantey to the lamb and rocks it like a babe. "With the right materials, the same experienced hands who crafted the first violin could re-create Eiocha's powerful instrument."

My ticker booms a hollow thud that throbs down my spine. "But the luthier who built the Creator's violin must be dead by now."

"The Bard—a luthier who fell in love with Eiocha—crafted her famous violin as a gift of his affection. In return, she gave him eternal life." Mundy aims his finger directly at me. "Your kind best be ready, Ticker. If Prince Killian finds the Bard and wakes my ancestors, they will finish their war and reclaim their rightful inheritance."

My vision of the ghostly battlefield and bloodshed returns to my mind. "That's impossible."

"Music is powerful. The Creator cut the worlds from the cloth of the eternities and stitched them into the heavens with a song on her violin. Eiocha even left a piece of her music in all her glorious creations. The call of life that dwells in every living thing is her voice. We carry her power inside us, just waiting to be woken."

A lamb bleats across the barn. Neely puts down the one in his arms and picks up the noisy sheep. He cradles the animal against his chest and hushes it.

I grip my sword and rise. Even seated, Redmond towers over me. "Do you intend to guide us across your world? Or were you lying so we would free you?" I ask.

"I'll do as I promised, but Killian has a head start, and unlike me, the giants in my world will see you as a gristly nugget of meat." Redmond's gaze skims the barn again, contemplative. "Memorize your home as it is now, Ticker, for every season has an end."

Vevina bustles into the barn, her arms full of blankets, an empty pail, and a pitcher of steaming water. As she sets everything down, she accidentally spills hot water on Mundy's feet.

"You fool!" The giant jumps up and strikes his head against a rafter beam. He grasps his forehead and yowls. "Humans have been alone too long! You've forgotten how to serve your betters."

"When I meet someone better than me, I'll serve them," Vevina replies.

"If you were a member of my crew, I would string you up for your insolence and leave you for the seagulls to perch on!"

She sets her hands on her hips. "If I were a member of your crew, I would string myself up to get away from you."

The giant bends over, pushes his huge face into Vevina's, and snarls. His lips curl and his fists ball at his side, vibrating with anger.

Vevina glares up at him, holding her ground. They stay that way, locked in their pride, until she blinks. Redmond snorts in derision. As he turns away, Vevina kicks over the pitcher of hot water, pouring it all over his boots. He gapes at her.

She gives a flippant smile. "Many pardons, Captain."

Redmond scoops up his boots and shakes them out, splashing water upon me. I cannot abide him any longer. I mumble a farewell and push out of the barn.

My racing heart steers me to the beat of the waves raking across the sea. I stand on the cliff and gulp down big breaths, concentrating on the sea to quiet my ticker. My heart hasn't required recalibration in a long while, and I will not end that streak.

I hear Vevina leave the barn behind me. She's muttering a prayer to Madrona to unleash a plague upon the pirate captain. She must not see me, as she goes straight inside the manor.

Several minutes pass before a bleak calmness falls upon me. The gears of my ticker no longer clink, and I'm in no danger of popping a torsion spring, but I stay where I am, at the edge of land and sea, encircled by the cold night.

Somewhere off to the east, the skystalk looms like a leering shadow. Ever since Markham destroyed the Land of Youth for revenge against his wife, Princess Amadara, I've known he could do the same to my world. The prince has been plotting this uprising against the humans for decades. Father Time must know the future he intends for us. The battlefield he showed me of the giants annihilating my friends was a glimpse of what's to come should the prince succeed. How could he let Markham get this far?

My stillness builds inside me, hot panic expanding against my ribs. I have had two great fears since I woke up from near death with a clock for a heart. First, I wouldn't live long enough to see Markham brought to justice. Second, he would destroy whatever life I made for myself.

He hasn't succeeded, I tell myself. *There's still time.*

I've been wrong before.

I gulp down a swell of salty air and march to the manor. Yanking open the door, I call up the stairs. "Jamison!"

Chapter Ten

I yell down the shadowed hall. "Jamison! Where are you?"

Quinn appears in the doorway of a sitting room, her cat snug in her arms. "I think he's gone to bed. Evie, would you like to play with us? Vevina is teaching me a card game. We're placing wagers with coin. I'm up by twenty gold pieces."

"Beginner's luck," Vevina says, shuffling cards in the sitting room. Her back is to us, coin piles laid out on a table in front of her. "I'll deal you in, darling. Do you have anything to put up for wager? How about the lovely brooch in your pocket?"

I shove my hand in my pocket and touch the brooch. Vevina may have left the city and committed herself to a quieter life, but she's kept up with her sly skills.

"Another time." I scratch the cat on the head. "Quinn, watch her closely. Vevina likes to stash extra cards down the front of her bodice."

"Don't tell lies," Vevina replies, aghast. As I start up the stairs, I hear her purr at Quinn. "Are you certain you don't want to wager more, darling?"

I go door to door looking for Jamison. He comes out of a room at the far end of the hall, holding a piece of paper like the one I saw him with at Elderwood Manor. I hurry to him, my worries rushing out of me. "I thought the vision Father Time showed me was a warning that

Markham was gathering an army. I didn't think he could wake the army from their sleep. The story says the violin was destroyed."

"Everley, slow down." He refolds the paper and puts it in his pocket. "What's this about Killian and an army?"

"My vision in the Black Forest was a glimpse of the future. He's trying to end our kind. Well, not all of us. Some of us he'll keep as slaves, but either outcome is awful."

Alick pokes his head out of the door beside us. "Would you two mind taking this elsewhere? My patient needs to rest."

"Our apologies." Jamison leads me into a bedroom and shuts the door. I cling to him, pressing my cheek into the hollow of his neck. "Evie, what happened?"

Mundy's words would not have pierced me so deeply had I not seen the war, witnessed the violence and carnage, or watched my friends— my family—fall by the sword one after another. "I know what Markham is after."

I summarize what the captain told me. As I do so, Jamison's arms stiffen around me. At the finish, the strain between us is unbearable. I lift my head to meet his gaze.

"Evie, this is too much. We should involve Father Time."

"But he'll do nothing!" I pull away, pacing and prowling. "Father Time has always known Markham planned to wake the giants. That's why he showed me that vision. He predicted all of this would happen. He knew and did *nothing*."

"He gave you a new heart when you needed one. He saved your life."

"My *uncle* saved my life. Uncle Holden gave me his life—his remaining years—so I might live." I lift the key on the string around my neck. "My uncle wasn't finished living. He had more clocks to create and more beauty to put out into the worlds. Our family's shop will always belong to him."

"I meant the shop as a gift," Jamison replies. "That key wasn't supposed to remind you of what was. It was a promise of what could be. If you don't want it, that's all right. Take it off and put it in your pocket beside my mother's brooch."

My feet slow, my anger draining out of me. "I didn't mean to imply—"

"My father's passing was too much, Evie. First my mother, then my sister . . . Father's death knocked me off my axis. I was so overwhelmed and lost." Jamison takes my face in his hands. "Then I remembered the first time we met in your uncle's shop and how sure I was about you. Breathing, living, *being* felt possible again."

"I'm sorry." I lean my cheek into his palm. "I didn't mean to sound ungrateful."

His gaze searches me for something deeper, something greater. "You're consumed by the dead, Evie. You live a world away, torn between agonizing over the past and fretting about the future, when I'm right here. I'm right here in front of you."

"I'm here now." I seal my lips to his.

He kisses me hard, leaving a gentle burn. I return the favor by pulling on his lips with mine until they snap back. He inhales sharply, taking in all the air in the room, and then draws closer. His hands roam to my hips, his mouth on mine, and his body presses down the length of me. A necessity for more rises like a hot wind. I tug his shirt out from the waist of his trousers, but I'm all elbows and knees and jerky fingers.

He unbuttons the top of my shirt down to my chest scar above my thin shift. The cloth falls aside to uncover my clock heart. His thumb brushes my chin. He kisses the scar there and continues down my neck, across my collarbone, and to the scar in the center of my chest. His tenderness sears into me. I clutch the back of his head and bury my fingertips in his hair, my mind growing hazy. He straightens and our noses bump.

"Sorry," we say in chorus.

He laughs nervously.

"I never thought this would happen," I say.

"With me?"

"With anyone."

I hadn't noticed I'd lifted my arms to cover the front of myself. I lower them again, and he tugs the straps of my shift down my shoulders one at a time. I draw his shirt over his head, uncovering acres of smooth bronze skin. He traces a circle around my clock heart.

Tick . . .

Tock.

I place my palm over his own heart.

Boom . . .

Boom.

His body slides closer to mine, and together we beat a rhythm of time and life.

The sound of Jamison's humming wakes me. He stands at the moonlit window, dressed in his trousers, staring out at the sea. I was only asleep a few hours at most. I rise and pad over to him, my shift floating around me, and slide my arms around his waist. I lay my cheek against his back. He rests his hand over mine and continues to hum the beginning of the lullaby that has been eluding him.

I kiss his shoulder. "Come back to sleep."

"My mother loved this manor." He presses his lips to the back of my hand. "We would spend weeks here every summer when the violets and daisies were blooming. My sister and I played along the shore, collecting ivory pebbles. Mother called them 'cloud stones.' She said they were pieces of clouds fallen from the sky. After she passed away, my father, sister, and I spread her ashes here. I hadn't been back since. You should have seen this place then. The gardens were cared for and the paint was fresh." His voice coarsens. "My mother would have wanted us to take better care of the property."

"You will. You've been marquess for only one month. Give yourself time."

"My father should have taken care of it, but losing my mother . . . I thought falling in love and marrying meant I would suffer the same heartache as he did." Jamison pulls me around in front of him and sits me on the windowsill, our eyes level. "No matter what anyone thinks, we *were* married on that ship. I know we agreed to forgo our nuptials for the good of our friends and us, but I swore to honor you until the end of time, Everley Donovan, and I will."

I stroke his blond hair back from his face. "I'm not a quiet or polite woman. I'm stubborn and hasty and opinionated. Clock heart or not, I'm no good as a wife."

"Why do you think I want someone who's quiet and polite?"

"A marchioness should be a lady."

He stares past me, out the window at the seaside, and smiles a little. "My father was never fond of this place. He thought it was damp and drafty and too far from the city and high society, but he came here in the summers at my mother's behest. Mother always knew what was best for our family, even if it could get her into trouble. My parents never should have thrown celebratory picnics thanking Madrona for the growing season. The queen could have thrown them in prison, but Mother refused to stop her worship." Jamison grips my hips and pulls me closer. "A marchioness is strong and determined. She knows what's right and doesn't yield."

I kiss his shoulder again. "In that case, I really do think you should come to bed."

His lips skim over mine. "You win." I lead him back. As I begin to nod off, he whispers, "Do you hear the song? The music is louder by the sea."

"Hmm?" I reply blearily.

I don't hear his answer. My clock heart begins to spin, and my spirit jumps out of my body.

"Wait," I say. "Jamison!"

An unseen force pulls me upward, through the roof, and shoots me to the stars. I try to get back down, but the invisible grip pulls me faster.

Halos of light whirl past me—stars zipping along, racing each other. The stars twirl as they fly, a synchronized dance that dazzles. One of them pulls ahead of the rest, the fastest and most nimble. My spirit was not meant to streak across the heavens like a comet. I fall behind, and the force that holds me drags me downward out of the sky, past treetops, and to the ground.

I land on a pathway of daisy petals within an evening evergreen forest. Moss and dew are fragrant in the mild air. Glowing sprites and pixies dart in and out of flowering vines, and gnomes hide in the heaving roots of a grove of colossal trees—the mighty, sacred elderwoods. Moonlight filters through their branches and dusts a silvery hue over the undergrowth.

My clock heart has paused. Time doesn't move in the Everwoods; it's eternal.

"Radella?" I call.

At the sound of my voice, all the pixies and sprites zip away and the gnomes scurry into their burrows. In the quiet stillness, a line of strange glowing spheres floats in place, nestled just off the petal path in the trees. I've never seen them before. The lights are perfectly round, about the size of my head. I carefully approach the first one. Within the light, a moving picture plays—my mother rocking a newborn in her arms.

"Mama?" I reach for her, but as soon as my fingertips touch the soft glow of the sphere, the image disappears.

Down the way, more floating lights line the path in a long row. I walk to the next one and see another moving picture within. My eldest brother, Tavis, grips a baby's hands as he helps her walk across our childhood nursery.

I go to the next globe, my chest tight. In this scene, I must be six years old. My mother and her children—Tavis, Isleen, Carlin, and I—stand at the river docks in Dorestand.

I remember that day. We were waiting for our father's ship to arrive home from an expedition. The day I first met Markham.

The scene shows my father's ship sail into port and anchor. The gangplank drops, and he comes down to the docks. My throat squeezes. I haven't seen him in so long. His boxy chest, heavy eyebrows, quick grin. He grabs my mother close first and then picks me up and spins me in a circle. I can still recall the sensation, like flying.

Markham disembarks the ship down the gangplank. A navy admiral then, he greets my mother warmly, kissing the back of her hand. He ruffles my brother Carlin's hair and pats Tavis on the shoulder. Isleen blushes and lowers her eyelashes, shy in the handsome officer's presence. I step back, disgusted. Our family believed he was my father's friend. We trusted him.

Farther down the path, the next light plays a familiar scene. The evening of my mother's birthday—her last birthday—is a memory I know well. Slowly, reluctantly, I step forward, my feet floating past the petals beneath me.

Our family has congregated in the drawing room after supper. We're dressed in our finest clothes for the birthday celebration. Carlin performs on his flute, his present to Mother. Isleen knits a shawl by the fire while Tavis stands by the mantel, slightly apart from us. I'm wedged between my parents on the sofa, tapping my foot impatiently, bored by my brother's song. And jealous, honestly. I always wanted his musical talent.

My chest aches at the sight of us together. Our final hours as a family were peaceful. A pleasant evening. Until the bloodshed.

Father Time emerges from the shadows beside me, leaning against a cane for support as he walks. The addition of the cane is new, yet his ageless beauty and matchless youth are unchanged—brooding green eyes, trimmed blue-black hair, and a smooth jawline. He's dressed smartly in a top hat and a tailored black jacket over stiff trousers. A genteel fashion.

He stops beside me. In the globe, the scene shows my father leaving the birthday party to answer a knock at our front door. Markham has come calling.

"I don't need to see this," I say. "I remember this night well enough. Why does everyone keep bringing me back to this moment? Markham took me to the ruins of my home. This is no better."

"This wasn't to torment you, Everley. What you stand on is your section of the Evermore timeline. Each being is given their own line spanning from birth to death. This is the day when your timeline was altered. Your life hereafter veered down a less certain path."

Down the petal pathway, the globes henceforward are dimmer and fewer in number.

Father Time motions at my still ticker. "The Evermore timeline can be shifted. Agency must be taken into account. Thus, the timeline expands and adjusts accordingly. When you sought out Prince Killian to bring him to justice, you changed the worlds."

"For the worse? My friends are in hiding. Jamison must lie to protect us. My uncle is dead. Markham has escaped again. I'm trying"—my voice catches—"I'm trying to find happiness in all of this. I'm trying to believe this can end and we can have a fresh start. Your bringing me here and showing me this . . . Do you want me to be miserable forever?"

He places both hands on his cane and hunches forward. "Precisely the opposite. We can encourage you to make choices for the good of all, but we cannot compel you, nor can we alter what has already been set into motion. The consequences would be dire."

"They *are* dire!" I scrunch my eyes shut and turn away from the scene of my family's final moments together. "I want Markham gone for good."

"Everley." The gravity of Father Time's tone compels me to reopen my eyes. His gaze relays a depth of compassion I've never seen him display. "We are aggrieved about your uncle's passing, but please take heart. His spirit rests with Mother Madrona."

I walk away, too raw to accept his trite condolences.

Only a dozen or so globes remain along the path. I'm tempted to ask if the last one will show me how I die, but I'd rather not know.

Beside the next sphere, I spot a tree stump. Strange. The Everwoods are the heart and soul of Avelyn. This conclave of elderwood trees holds up the heavens with their mighty branches, creating a divide between land and sky. Avelyn needs them. I cannot fathom anyone cutting one down.

I concentrate to solidify my form and then rest my hand on the sheared stump. "What happened?"

"This elderwood gave her life for a crucial cause. Heartwood was needed, so Mother Madrona offered up her first sapling."

"What became of the tree's heartwood?"

Father Time walks to a nearby tree and points out cut marks along its trunk with his cane. "Do you recall the *Legend of Princess Amadara?*"

"You mean Markham's elaborate lie about his epic love story with Princess Amadara? I wish I could forget that hogwash."

"Then you recall Prince Killian stole the sword of Avelyn from Princess Amadara to harvest the heartwood of the elderwoods? This is where his tale deviated from the truth. Killian did not come for heartwood. He came to usurp time." Father Time grimaces, a pained expression, his posture bent. "Killian began cutting into this tree. He meant to fell the whole forest and force us to bend to his will. We should have sent him back to his world—that was what was written into his timeline—but we punished him for betraying Amadara by stranding him on a cursed isle so he might perish. By interfering in his timeline and seeking to end his life, we gave Prince Killian freedom over death."

I whirl around. "Markham is immortal because of *you?*"

"Time helps to keep order and prevent chaos. We sought to take away his life before the fated end of his life. In doing so, he was able to throw off the bonds of mortality, for no deity can meddle with the timeline without grievous cost." Father Time steps to my side, his shoulders drooping as though his body is suddenly too heavy. "We should never have sought to end him prematurely, but Amadara was our friend."

"Your friend? Markham killed my *family*!"

Father Time appears to shrink even more. "He must have known our interference would result in his freedom from mortality. The elves have a more complete doctrine than that of the Otherworlds. Their *Creation Story* includes more truths than yours."

I thrust my chin up sharply. Could Markham's claim that humans were created to serve as helpmates be true? Bloody bones, I cannot abide such a notion.

Father Time wipes a shaky hand across his brow and hunches over his cane. He looks *fallible*. He extends his hand, and a globe appears in front of me, the scene of Uncle Holden carving my clock heart out of a piece of heartwood. "Everley, the Evermore timeline has adjusted to compensate for the disruption of Killian's immortality, but his actions have had lasting penalties that continue to ripple out into the worlds."

"But you gave Markham everlasting life. Can't you take it away?"

"We cannot interfere with the timeline again. The fracture has already weakened us. Fortunately, allocations to repair the timeline were made long ago." Father Time hobbles over to the stump with his cane and sits. "This elderwood gave her life so her heartwood could one day preserve the knight of the Evermore."

My hands fly to my clock heart. I watch the scene in the globe of my uncle crafting my heart. "My ticker."

"Through Holden carving the heartwood into a timepiece, you attained more power than any Time Bearer before you. You, and you alone, can navigate the timeline and reset what has been broken." He hunches forward again, his chest sunken in. "We wish you could have seen your life without Prince Killian. You are worthy of so much more."

"The life I have may not be perfect, but I have love."

"You won't for long. Not unless you find the Bard—"

"Don't." I withdraw a step. "No more assignments or lectures. I'll stand up to Markham for my people, not for you."

Father Time sets his hat beside him on the stump. "Someday you will see that everything we have done is for the good of the worlds."

More triteness. The most alarming truth here is that Father Time acted passionately in defense of Princess Amadara. Then he stood aside while my family died, while Uncle Holden died, while I almost died, and he would do it again.

"You don't care about me. Time is indifferent. You only care for yourself."

A hint of hurt flares in his eyes. "You must decide to do this. We cannot force you. But without our direction, you could lose your way and become fodder for the most sinister parts of the eternities."

"I'll take my chances."

He pins me with his all-seeing gaze, as though he has looked straight through my heart. "Your hatred for Killian controls you."

I flinch away. "Send me home. Send me home *now*."

Father Time sighs and opens his hand. Daisy petals stream out of his palm, spinning around me and lifting my form. As I float up through the treetops, I do not look back, but his voice follows me.

"Be wary, Time Bearer. For whether you are prepared or not, the end speedily comes."

Chapter Eleven

I gasp awake, my chest pumping and ticker thumping. Jamison's half of the bed is empty, and he's not in the room. Sunshine streams in through the saltwater-stained windowpanes. From the height of the sun in the sky, the day must be well into morning. I press Jamison's pillow over my head to shut out the light.

The end speedily comes. What in the name of Madrona does that mean? Was Father Time threatening me or warning me? Was the boggart?

I wish Radella were here. She might tell me I'm wrong—Father Time isn't to blame for unleashing a monster on the worlds—but that's precisely what he admitted to doing.

Hearing voices outside the house draws me to the window. Jamison and Quinn are walking down to the beach. I dress quickly, tie back my hair, and grab my sword.

Down the hall, Osric's door is wide open. The patient is sitting up in bed, his injured leg propped up by pillows.

"Well, if it isn't my favorite human."

"Opposed to the humans you like a little less?"

"Opposed to any of them, really. In fairness, you're the only human I'm fond of."

"I'm happy to win by default," I say. "You're looking better."

He grunts and drinks from his flask. "Don't tell Alick. He doesn't trust the cider is good for me, but he's never tended to an elf before. The drink helps me regenerate. Two more days, and I'll be back on my feet."

I hope Osric has a speedy recovery, but I still don't understand why aging is so repulsive to him. "Aren't you low on your supply?"

"I've enough for now. One of the queen's guards at Elderwood Manor offered to refill my flask next time I see him."

"Was it the guard who blushed at you?"

"Dalyor's blush is a matter of debate."

"But yours isn't," I say, pointing out his rising color. "You still have friends in the Land of Promise. Why don't you go home? You could see your parents."

Osric picks fuzz off his wool blanket. "My parents don't wish to see me."

Images of my mother and father, fresh from my visit to the Everwoods, sit at the forefront of my mind. "Don't you want to see them?"

"Quite honestly, I haven't thought about it." Osric pushes up in the bed, wincing at a tweak in his leg. "How did we get here? Alick said there's no portal nearby. The lot of us dropped from the sky out of nowhere."

"I don't know what happened. We went through the portal at the top of the platform in the Land Under the Wave and landed here."

"Portals connect to each other. Like a tunnel, they have two ends, an entry and an exit. To travel them, you go in one side and out another. How did you get around that?"

"What makes you think this was my doing?"

"Oh, I don't know. Perhaps it's because you're the only one with a clock for a heart who's carrying the sword of Avelyn." Osric stares at me, waiting, but I don't know what he expects me to say. "Fine, I'll tell you what I think happened. We went through the entry portal, and the sword created its own exit portal to get us here. As the legend says, the sword of Avelyn can move instantaneously through time, just like the infinity sandglass."

I adjust my sword at my hip. Even if the hallowed blade did what Osric claims, I cannot fathom how. "Say you're right. Do you know how it's done?"

"Me? I've no idea. I thought portal jumping would be something the Time Bearer would know how to do." Osric sinks farther back into his pillows. "I suppose you're off to the skystalk. I'm not fond of sending you up there with Mundy without me, but I'll follow as soon as I'm able. Everley, be watchful. The captain's a self-serving bastard."

I'm more concerned about the probability of encountering other giants. When I was a lass, my uncle read me bedtime tales about giants snatching children from their beds and cooking them into meat pies. I have a healthy amount of fear for most creatures of legend. My misgivings about giants are, well, *bigger*.

"Evie, what is it? Did Mundy do something?"

"Not exactly." I won't explain what Redmond told me about the prince. In Osric's condition, I don't want to stress him. "After meeting Queen Imelda, I was curious about Markham's family. He told me some things, but not much."

"There isn't much to know. Killian and Imelda were best friends growing up. When their parents became sick, Killian cared for them while Imelda ran the kingdom. The king and queen died suddenly, and Imelda assumed the throne. If you're thinking something occurred in Killian's youth that turned him into a rotter, you're wrong. The prince was beloved by his family and his people. He *chose* to become a monster."

"He doesn't see himself that way."

"Monsters never do."

"I should go." As I adjust the pillow behind Osric's head, I spot the wrinkle on his forehead that he lamented before and kiss it. "Be a good patient."

"I'm always good. Tell Alick I want my hat back. I've asked twice, and no one has brought it to me."

"I'm sure they'll return it soon. Don't pester them."

He puts on an innocent face. "Me? A pest? You're not my favorite human anymore."

"Honestly, that lasted longer than I thought it would." I nudge the foot of his injured leg, and he chuckles.

I step into the hallway as Vevina storms up the stairs.

"Evie, you might want to avoid the barn. Your dandy pirate is on a tirade because I refused to shave his face. I'd strangle him dead, but I can't fit my hands around his meaty neck."

"You won't have to tolerate him much longer."

"Yes, I heard. Jamison told me you're going to the giants' world." Vevina's brows lower over her probing gaze. "Darling, should you be trusting those pirates?"

"I'll be all right. Jamison will be with me."

"He's a handsome one, that marquess." Vevina adjusts the collar of my shirt under my cloak for me. "You've come a long way from the lass who said she wasn't made for love. I suppose we've both changed, haven't we?"

"We have." Vevina has been living a quiet life for months now, watching over Quinn and working alongside Alick. She's been with the surgeon longer than any other man. "Thank you for taking care of Osric."

Vevina pulls Osric's hat out of her apron pocket. "Tending to a patient will be good for Alick. Gives him something to fuss over besides my blisters." She levels a stern gaze at me. "Be careful with those giants."

"I will." I head downstairs, outside, and around the back of the house. Mundy's voice carries out the open barn doors.

"No, you may not bring that repulsive creature with us!"

"But look at him," Neely pleads. "He's fond of me."

I stop in the doorway and see Neely petting a black lamb cradled in his arms. Mundy stands next to him, clean shaven in his velvet jacket. Through the opposite barn doors, I see two covered wagons. Jamison and Quinn are out there rigging up the horse teams.

"It's a *sheep*," the captain says. "A sheep doesn't have feelings."

"Every creation has a heart." Neely nuzzles the lamb. "Isn't that true, Rufus?"

"Rufus?" Redmond throws up his hands. "Everley, tell him he cannot keep the lamb."

I offer an apologetic smile. "I'm sorry, Neely. Rufus will be happier here than he would be crammed in the back of a wagon."

Out the far door, Jamison and Quinn finish readying the horses and start inside.

"I want to go," Quinn says. "Don't say I'm too young. I'm almost thirteen."

"Quinn, this is the land of the giants. It's too dangerous." Jamison pauses at the door and reaches out to console her, but the lass storms a few paces away to stew.

Alick hauls two heavy supply sacks into the barn and drops them at my feet. "Vevina asked me to bring you a few things. Inside, you'll find blankets, food, water casks, candles, and a medical box."

"Thank you, Alick," I say. "And thank you for looking after Osric."

"Vevina and I will set him right again. She's been bored out here in the countryside." He runs a hand down the back of his neck, smoothing down his hair. His unkempt locks are the longest I've seen them. "I've tried to come up with projects to occupy her hands and mind, but that woman is hard to keep up with."

I hold back a smile. Vevina and Alick are both trying their best to look after one another. This makes it easier to leave them.

Jamison comes up behind me so quickly I don't notice. I jump, and his lips slowly rise. "Did you sleep well?"

"Did you?" My throat itches and my face grows hot. We did things last night that are too intimate to dwell on during daylight hours.

He brushes his lips across my ear. "How are you with driving a wagon?"

"A what?" I ask, distracted by his touch. "Oh, a wagon. I'll manage."

Redmond is shining his boots, and Neely is cradling his lamb one last time, uninterested in us. But I catch Alick staring, and my cheeks burn. This is ridiculous. I can be apple cheeked for all eternity or . . .

I grab Jamison by the front of the shirt and kiss him on the mouth. He jerks in surprise and softens.

"There," I say loudly. "Now everyone knows."

Alick displays a wide grin. "It's about time."

I flush again, hotter.

"I think he already guessed," Jamison whispers to me, then announces to everyone, "We're ready to go."

Redmond gestures at the wagons. "You don't really expect us to ride in those like livestock. How demeaning."

Neely climbs into the back of one and lies on his side, his knees curled into his chest. "It's not so bad, Captain. An old giant like me can do it."

Redmond mutters as he crawls into the other wagon.

"He's going to complain all the way there," I say.

"Should we flip a coin to decide who drives him?" Jamison asks. "It's only fair."

"No." I sigh. "You take Neely, I'll take Mundy."

A musket has been stashed at the front of each wagon, and Jamison carries a pistol. Quinn still sulks nearby. I take out the gem-studded shell brooch and give it to her. She's unsure about wearing something so delicate, but when I tell her it belonged to the former marchioness, she accepts it like I've given her the greatest prize in the worlds.

Jamison and I load up the supplies and start eastward. I hold the reins steady, my days of driving my uncle's wagon through the city for deliveries helping me settle in.

Winds push in from the sea, heaving at our backs. The gusts are laced with a melody, the lullaby Jamison has become obsessed with. He swivels around to look back at the sea several times. I think he hears the music too.

We travel farther inland, away from the sea winds. The song quiets, but my uneasiness stays. Can someone be haunted by a song? Because I have a nagging feeling that the music isn't after me.

It's plaguing Jamison.

The roadways are deserted. Our wagons haven't passed another traveler for nearly an hour, which is probably for the best. Redmond will not shut up.

He peers out through a small hole he punctured in the canvas. "How much longer?"

"Less than an hour."

"I've been trapped inside the back of the wagon for three."

"You should use this time to rest. We have a climb ahead of us." The skystalk towers directly beyond in the wheat field. My hands rattle on the reins, my nerves growing with every turn of the wagon wheels. Our journey up the skystalk will take us very high into the sky.

Redmond doesn't reply. He must have taken my advice—

"Giants are outstanding climbers," he says. I suppress a groan. "In the olden days, giants climbed skystalks to the Plain of Delight and the Other Land."

My ears perk up. "You've been to both of those Otherworlds?"

"I haven't personally, but my people used to travel everywhere. Skystalks once connected the Silver-Clouded Plain with the Other Land

and the Plain of Delight. I doubt you've heard of their inhabitants, the trolls and spriggans, human."

"Actually, I have." I elaborate to prove I'm not the stupid human he thinks I am. "Spriggans are treelike creatures who live in burrows in the Plain of Delight and are often employed by the elves to serve as guards and animal caretakers. Trolls are industrious metalworkers and hard laborers who hail from the Other Land. Our legends suggest they're half breeds of humans and giants."

Redmond blows his lips. "Giants would *not* debase themselves by mating with mortals. Trolls are stupid, ugly little creatures only good for grunt work." He shifts his position, rocking the wagon. "I cannot feel my foot. If my jacket is ruined by this filthy wagon, you'll replace it."

"There isn't enough velvet in all the realms for a jacket your size."

Over the next rise, the base of the skystalk appears in the wheat field. The middle and top have widened to the same thickness as the bottom, their thorns like enormous porcupine needles. Silver clouds wreathe its top, obscuring the apex. I thought the skystalk was farther away, but we are only minutes from arriving.

Jamison stops his wagon and calls back to us. "Soldier checkpoint ahead!"

A half dozen or so of Queen Aislinn's soldiers block the road. I pull my hood down and slip my sword under my cloak. Redmond quiets, the sudden silence nerve-racking.

We halt at the checkpoint. The bare landscape offers no cover or escape routes. No trees or hedges or turns in the roadway. Just low-hanging clouds and vast wheat fields. An offering to Mother Madrona in thanks for the growing season has been set on the ground, twigs and summer flowers weaved into a hand-size wreath. A farmer or field-worker must have left it, assuming no one would pass through this quiet area and see their token of faith before the wind blew it away. My uncle told me these tokens were once worn on heads and hung everywhere when he was a boy, before the queen outlawed them.

A soldier steps up to the first wagon. "Name, sir?"

"Marquess of Arundel," Jamison replies. "What's the meaning of this stop? My father passed away, and I need to move the last of his belongings to my estate not far from here."

"This area is closed, my lord. We've been ordered to turn travelers around."

Three more soldiers bearing muskets begin to case Jamison's wagon, walking around and looking underneath. I bow my head, my fingers sliding to my sword, and sense Redmond holding his breath behind me.

"Surely you don't mean to keep me from my home," Jamison says.

"Those are our orders, my lord. Please pull ahead and turn around. We'll escort you away from the blockade. You can find another route home."

A soldier lifts the flap at the rear of Jamison's wagon. Neely's huge foot flies out, knocking the man back into our horse team. Our horses rear and reverse the wagon several paces. Neely rips off the canvas covering and roars.

The soldiers at the back of the wagon raise their muskets. Jamison draws his pistol on the solider he was speaking with, and the two of them hold each other in a standoff.

I stand up and snap the reins. We plow past the armed soldiers, and the last guard is momentarily distracted. Jamison whacks him over the head, knocking him to the ground.

We ride past as Neely gets back into their wagon. Jamison wrenches on the reins, and they take off after us.

The soldiers we plowed past stand up and fire. Shots zip past us, some ripping through the canvas. I urge the horse team faster. Jamison charges behind us, and we direct our wagons into the field, riding out of the soldiers' firing range.

The skystalk is in the distance, a gnarled, massive shoot in a sea of golden wheat. No one else is around. We barrel onward, trampling the field.

Roots shoot up from the ground and startle my horses. I try directing the wagon away from my companions, and two of the back wheels lift off the ground. Redmond falls out and rolls to a stop. I right the wagon before it tips over, the wheels landing with a bone-jarring slam.

More roots shoot up, grabbing the wheels of Jamison's wagon, and it comes to an abrupt stop. Neely hangs on and stays in, but Jamison goes flying forward over the horses and lands hard.

I slow my wagon and jump out. Something slithers among the wheat stalks, shifting at my feet. Redmond rises, his jacket torn and dirty. We both go still, then his eyes bulge.

"Spriggans!" he shouts. "Run!"

Jamison gets up and sprints to his wagon for the supply pack. I run with the giants, and a root trips me, making me fall to the ground. The dirt roils with spindly foliage, like tree roots bubbling from below. Little shoots dart out and snatch at me. I yank away and pick myself up.

Redmond's foot is caught. He lifts his leg and pulls a creature out of the dirt. The willowy thing has branch-like limbs covered with hard, wrinkled gray skin. A narrow, eerily young face looks up at the giant and hisses. Redmond pitches it across the field.

A vise wraps around my ankle and tightens. I tug against the spriggan's squeezing grip.

"Where did they come from?" I ask.

Neely's wrist has been snagged by another. "The elven guard stationed them here to guard the skystalk." He breaks the spriggan's binding and rips my leg free.

We sprint for the skystalk, dodging grasping shoots. Jamison beats us there with the supply pack. Redmond has fallen behind. He roars as he plucks more spriggans from the dirt, like carrots from a garden, and hurls them across the field.

Neely starts climbing for the clouds, and we follow. We're not a second off the ground when a root snatches at Jamison's leg. I hack at the tendril with my sword, setting him loose. Several more spriggans snake their grasp around Jamison from calf to thigh. I slash at them, careful not to hit my love, but they wrap around him tighter.

"Go, Evie," he pants. "Go and don't stop."

I chop at another strand. "Not. Without. You."

He takes off the supply pack and swings it up at me. I pause mid-hack to catch the bag. The spriggans give a collective tug and drag Jamison to the ground. A tangle of gnarled roots arches over him in a dome, weaving itself together like a basket. They cover Redmond in the same hill of roots.

A shoot snatches at my leg. I kick it away and climb higher. Neely waits for me a few stories above the ground, out of the spriggans' range. Jamison and Redmond have disappeared under a cage of roots. The skystalk trembles. Spriggans have wrapped their reedy arms around the base and begun to pull. They're trying to tip it over.

"Hurry, poppet!"

Neely and I set off faster, ascending into rampant winds. The shaking peters away the higher we climb. Big clouds rush in around us, a surge of white muffling the winds to an unnerving quiet. I dare not think how far from the ground we are. I focus on scaling the section right above me, hand over hand, little by little.

Neely hisses loudly.

"Are you all right?" I ask.

"I slipped. Keep going."

We push onward into thinner air, and my heart begins to spin. We're leaving this world.

A flash of silver sends spots across my vision, then the sky around us tilts. I hold on tighter as we're turned upside down. Neely and I hang end over top, our hair and clothes dangling. Suspended there, my vision clears to see the world straighten out again.

We resume our climb, but we aren't going up anymore. We're descending. I cannot comprehend how, but I keep moving, my muscles achy and my lungs heaving.

My feet strike white stone—cloud rock. Thick fog encircles us and constricts our view. Neely's big hand grips mine; he's at my side, yet I can hardly see him. A trapdoor opens above our heads. An invisible force pulls us in, and we fall up.

Chapter Twelve

I land on a bed of grass, staring up at the night. My clock heart hitches, recalibrating, and then resumes a baseline rhythm.

Tick . . .

Tock.

I push to my feet with my sword. Neely lies on his back beside me, winded. We landed beside a pond under leafy trees. Frogs ribbit near the water's edge, and huge dragonflies soar over the still water, their wingspans the size of a sparrow's. Though we left the Land of the Living in the daytime, time in this world is far into the evening. The stars and moon offer scant light, their radiance filtered by the tree branches overhead. Everything—the trees, rocks, insects, and flowers—is bigger than back home. The willows are taller than my head.

Neely rips a thorn out of his hand and another out of his heel, injuries from the skystalk. I wrap his hand with cloth torn from the hem of my cloak. He sits on a log and tends to his foot.

"Where did the skystalk go?" I ask.

He hobbles to the grassy patch we landed on, kneels, and feels around. His long arm slides down a hole up to his shoulder, and he pulls out a fistful of white stones. "The Silver-Clouded Plain exists inside a massive cloud bank. The Creator gathered two thick, fluffy clouds and molded them together. Then she blew a hole into the center of the clouds and placed our world inside."

He drops the white rocks. They hit the ground, poof into bits of cloud, and vanish. I cannot fathom how a world could be nestled in a bed of clouds, or how I just saw rocks turn to air, but the skystalk bypassed the curse the Creator put on this world. At this point, anything seems possible.

I hug myself to fight off a shiver. "Will Jamison be all right?"

"The spriggans won't hurt them, poppet. They were defending the skystalk for the elves."

I wish I had his confidence. "Do you know where we are?"

"Stonecross Hollow." Neely indicates a stone pile in the shape of a cross on a rise above the pond. "We're in the prairie east of our stronghold city, Rackfort."

Loud cranking noises fill the night. We still and listen as the clatter rushes toward us in puffs and groans, clinks and clatters. I grip my sword as the noise approaches, passes us, and travels away.

"What was that?" I whisper.

"I've no idea. We'll stay here until daylight and head west tomorrow. My sisters and father live outside Rackfort, about a day's walk from here." Neely sits on the ground with his back against the log. "My sisters will be glad to see me."

Neely's father is the reason he was banished. He turned in his son for stealing food to feed his sisters and himself. A family reunion between them will be interesting.

I step closer to the pond for a peek at the oversize frogs.

"I wouldn't get that close," Neely says. "Last I heard, a grindylow lives in the pond of Stonecross Hollow. Grindylows can live for centuries. Better to be safe and keep back."

Having been nearly drowned by one of the tentacled water creatures, I edge away from the water and inventory our supplies. We should have everything we need, but I double-check the pack. A folded piece of paper falls out of the front pocket. I open it and shift into the moonlight to read the short passage.

*Jamison Callahan from the Land of the Living requests
a divination of the future. Payment for service requires
one month's time. This document and ensuing bargain
are binding, nonrefundable, and unexchangeable for any
other inquiries about the client's past, present, or future.
The client accepts the terms regardless of the outcome of
the foretelling.*

The bottom is signed by Jamison and marked with a bloody fingerprint—his fingerprint, I presume. Beside his name, scrawled in elegant handwriting, is the sea hag's signature.

"Do you know what this is?" I ask, showing Neely.

He pulls his monocle out of his pocket and squints to read the passage in the dark. "Aye. It's a contract of divination with the sea hag. Every pirate in the Land Under the Wave visited Muriel at one time or another, may she rest in peace."

"You mean Jamison asked the sea hag for a reading?"

"Right there it says, 'divination of the future.' She took one month off his life in exchange for telling him his fate."

I'm speechless. I sensed that he was holding on to something private, but this? Why didn't he tell me? He would have revealed the divination if it were good news—the two of us getting rid of Markham, being pardoned by the queen, and starting over. The possibilities of what the sea hag predicted pile up, stacking on top of each other, a crushing force.

"Poppet?" the giant whispers.

"Yes, Neely?"

"Do you think Rufus misses me?"

I need a moment to recall who Rufus is. Ah, the lamb. "I think so. We often remember when someone is kind to us."

Neely pats me on the head. "You have a good heart, Everley Donovan."

I tip my head against his shoulder and sigh.

Tucking Jamison's contract in my pocket, I search inside myself for a calmness I don't possess. I will never be able to fall asleep. Spirit jumping from one world to the next is ambitious, but I have to know Jamison is safe.

My ticking heart fills my thoughts. The relentless sound once pestered me and plagued my every waking moment, a reminder of loss and pain. Now the sound calls to mind my uncle. His life and luster, talents and accomplishments. His love for me.

My spirit lifts off my body. Hovering above myself, my sword in hand, I address the immortal blade. *Which way to Jamison?*

The sword vibrates and warms, then drags me up into the night. We rise through the clouds that ring the Silver-Clouded Plain and hover above the giants' world. I'm uncertain about which direction to go. Jamison could still be in the Land of the Living, or the spriggans could have taken him to the Land of Promise. My clock heart spins.

Strangely, I'm in the dark. The stars are far away, as though I'm still on the ground gazing up at them.

A prickle scuttles across my back. I turn in a circle and see a shadow slide across my vision. My sword vibrates in warning and sets off in a rush, dragging me back toward the Silver-Clouded Plain. A long, thick shadow with toothy jaws hurls after us.

"Time Bearer," the thing hisses.

My sword pulls me faster. From the corner of my eye, I see the shadow barreling right at me. I try twisting away, but its teeth graze my side. The attack knocks me into a free fall. Down I tumble through a bed of clouds, spinning end over end. At the last second, my sword pulls me forward, adjusting my trajectory so I land in my body.

I sit up with a gasp and clutch my side. My hand comes away bloody. The shadow chasing me left shallow slashes where its teeth grazed me. The wounds sting worse than they bleed. I quiver all over, my hands cold and sweaty, my ticker a hollow thud. What was that thing?

I tuck myself closer to Neely's side. Every shadow around me appears to grow fangs. Far off in the distance, the same clunking and puffing noises from earlier come nearer. I stare out at the pond, images of charging monsters in my head, and refuse to close my eyes and let in the night.

Something tickles my nose. I wake up and look into the eyes of the biggest rabbit I have ever seen. I scramble backward, wide awake in a second. The gray bunny, the size of a dog, stares at me a moment longer and hops away.

Daylight has transformed the pond and greenery into a softly lit haven. Morning dewdrops sparkle on the grass like diamonds in the morning light. Neely is up the rise beside the stone cross, singing.

> *"Sea, land, stars. Great Creator, your home is ours.*
> *Animals, plants, trees. Madrona, we rest upon our*
> *knees.*
> *Gathered beneath thy leaves. Brothers and sisters*
> *three."*

I join him up the hill and pause in awe of the brilliant reds and oranges staining the eastern sky and blending downward to the prairie in layers of pink, purple, and blue.

"I was only in the Land Under the Wave one year, but here it's been over thirty," Neely says, tears simmering in his eyes.

"That's a long time to be gone from home. Was your world always so striking?"

"Aye. Before the Creator cursed us, the sunrises and sunsets were even prettier."

I notice a wooden roadway that runs east to west across the prairie. "What's that?"

"I don't know. It's new since I've been away."

My stomach grumbles with hunger. As the sky lightens to periwinkle, I return to the supply pack to eat breakfast—water and two hard biscuits. Neely plucks berries off a bush, eats a handful, and offers me one. The berry is monstrous, the size of an apricot, so I decline. He tosses the berry into the pond. Tentacles rise from below and snatch the fruit under the surface.

"It's good luck to feed a grindylow," he says. "Throw them food and make a wish."

"No, thank you. A grindylow almost drowned me."

"You must have met it on an unfortunate day. They're mostly harmless." Neely drops a berry into my palm. "Go ahead. Make a wish."

Neely urges me to the water's edge. I think of a wish, the first thing that comes to mind, and toss the berry. A tentacle nabs the sweet treat, and the grindylow's eerie face flashes under the surface. I shuffle away from the pond.

"What did you wish for?" Neely asks.

"Jamison's safety." I stare up at the rising sun. Wherever he may be, he might be watching the same dawn. "Let's head out."

We pack up and set off across the grassland at a conservative pace. The cuts on my side ache, and Neely favors his sore foot. He notices me hugging my side but doesn't ask about it. He probably assumes I hurt myself climbing the skystalk or running from the spriggans. We follow the wooden trail west. The entire crisscrossed roadway is staked into the ground. Neely and I take turns guessing what it could be—a cattle fence, a fairy repellent, or the skeletal remains of a huge contraption. None of those ideas feels right, so eventually we give up.

He hums to himself, his steps jaunty despite his hurt foot. The rolling green prairie and clear skies grow more vibrant as the sun rises overhead.

"Why would the giants want our world?" I ask, thinking of my home where the sky is perpetually gray, the weather rainy, and the ground soggy.

"The gates to the Everwoods are there. As firstborns, we want to be closer to the Creator."

I squint slantwise at him. "Your birth order entitles you to take away our world?"

"Giants crafted the Land of the Living. The father of giants, Hanish, assumed he and his people would inherit the first world, but Eiocha insisted humans should possess it and sent our kind here. Giants constructed these plains into glory as well, but Hanish was never the same. He died from homesickness. His eldest son, Nothor, blamed his death on the humans, and he and his brothers began plotting for retribution."

I cringe, remembering the warrior giants I saw in my vision of the battlefield. "My kind know none of this."

"What *do* you know about us?"

"Most of our stories are about giants who sneak into our cities at night, kidnap us from our homes, and eat us."

Neely nods. "Nothor feasted on men, just as you described. The flesh of a human was said to make male giants virile and give female giants strong and healthy babes."

"How awful!" And disappointing. Something from our storybooks is true, and it's this. "Have you ever . . . ?"

"Consumed a human? Once. I disliked the flavor." His brow furrows. "Stay close to me. Your smell may draw interest."

I sniff at myself. Other than my need for a good wash, I smell rather bland. "Does your family eat humans?"

"Not that I know of, though I do have quite a few cousins." Neely winks at me. "You'll be all right, poppet. You're with me."

A trail of smoke appears straight ahead. Neely and I hurry for a copse of trees and hunker down low. Something big and metal charges toward us down the tracks. The front has a blade for a nose and a chimney that puffs smoke. The machine grunts and clangs uproariously, the same mysterious sounds we heard last night. Several wheeled carts are attached to the smoking front portion. The carts are loaded with iron scraps and lumber, while others are closed in with windows. The contraption emits several piercing whistles as it chugs past us down the wooden roadway. Turning wheels propel the machine over the rails, yet I cannot tell what fuels them.

Neely steps out of the trees to watch the contraption steam off. Neither of us says anything, and we don't linger. We maintain a swift pace well into the middle of the day, our path gradually splitting away from the wooden tracks to a meandering road along a woodland.

He stops at a cairn that marks a fork in the road. High up, a hawk circles. I pause for a drink, thirsty, tired. My forehead is warm to the touch. The hottest part of the day is wearing on me.

Neely wanders to the woods to pick wild berries. I put on the pack and wait for him. A cheery birdsong carries out of the trees. The trilling reminds me of Radella. I still to listen, and a shadow falls over me.

The hawk, four times the size of any I've ever seen, dives at me. I duck low, but the hawk snatches the supply pack in its talons and lifts. My feet rise off the ground.

"Neely!"

The hawk draws me higher. Neely runs out of the woods and puts his hands on his head in dismay. I'm too far away for him to reach.

"Jump, Everley!"

I pull one arm free of the pack and dangle by one strap. My side aches, my hold on the cloth tenuous. We're already high above the ground and getting higher. My clock heart skips a beat, then another.

Neely runs to stand beneath me. I let go of the strap and drop.

The hawk swoops away with my pack. I'm still falling. The ground gets closer and closer. Neely catches me in his arms, and I shut my eyes and breathe. Thankfully, my clock heart hasn't stopped.

Neely sets me down, then winces and shifts his weight off his injured foot. I bend over to collect my breath, my side aching, and pat my pocket. Jamison's contract is still there, but the hawk flew away with our supplies.

"Let's get out of the open," Neely says.

I stay close to the giant. I'm not likely to leave his side again. We go down a dirt footpath into the woods. The ache in my side grows stronger. I touch it, and my fingers come away wet with blood. My cuts reopened during the fall. Neely notices the crimson stain on my fingers and frowns.

"We're over halfway there, poppet. We walk past the cairn that looks like a falcon, follow the river, and cross the walking bridge to my sisters' cottage. Can you make it?"

"Can you?"

He's limping worse with each step. He says he's fine, but no more than ten minutes later, I suggest to him that he sit down, and he does so without argument. The giant favors his outstretched foot.

"Let me have a look." I pull off his boot. The puncture in his sole is swollen and seeping. He shouldn't be walking. "I think part of the thorn may have broken off inside your foot."

I poke at the wound, trying to fish out the piece, and he yanks away.

"I'm sorry, Neely." I've never seen him in this much pain. "Soaking your foot may coax out the broken piece. How far is the river you mentioned?"

A howl fills the air. Neely and I look at each other. He slides his boot back on and starts to get up, but the second he puts weight on his foot, he sucks a quick breath between his teeth and sinks back down.

"Maybe they'll go around us," he suggests half-heartedly.

"I'll go and see how close they are. Wait here."

I draw my sword and creep into the trees. Movements sound ahead, footfalls and rustling leaves. I stop behind a bush and peer out.

Commander Asmer and the elven guard are coming up the trail. The barghest pads down the path at the front of the group, sniffing every bush. Sweat beads along my brow, my forehead hotter. The barghest loiters near the footprints Neely and I left in the dirt minutes before.

Commander Asmer inspects the tracks he located and pats his back. "They're close. Go get 'em."

The canine sets off down the trail faster.

I make my way back to Neely quietly and quickly and tug at his arm. "Get up. The elven guard is coming."

The giant rises and hobbles after me. He's too big for me to support, and his foot is in too bad of a condition to leave the path, so I try to choose even ground for us.

The barghest howls. I can hear it tearing through the underbrush.

Neely pushes himself to go faster and keep up with me. A flash of black fur streaks across the corner of my vision. The barghest's howls sound so close to us that my belly tremors.

"Come on," I say, tugging Neely's arm.

He stops and braces against a tree, his face bright red and his breathing labored. "Poppet, find my family's cottage. Do you remember the way I told you?"

"I—I think so."

"Then go!" The giant shoves me behind him and blocks the trail.

The barghest's next howl is followed by the commander yelling for us to surrender. I stand in the path, unwilling to leave my guide.

Neely looks over his shoulder at me. "Everley, run!"

I grab the hilt of my sword and take off. Twigs crunch under my feet, and the tightness at my side worsens. Perspiration rolls down my face and back.

Neely yells in anger. I glance back and see the elves have netted him.

I sprint faster, leaving the trail and racing through the trees across a rocky, shallow stream to the other side. The barghest howls behind me. I start up a tree. My skin is on fire, but I push myself to the highest branch and huddle in the leafy cover.

The barghest appears across the stream, sniffing the ground. The running water should dull my scent, or at least this would be the case with bloodhounds in my world.

Commander Asmer appears behind her canine. She looks around and calls the barghest back. They slowly disappear down the trail.

I slump against the tree trunk, my back slick with perspiration, my skin burning yet chilled all over. My side is bleeding worse than ever. Why are the elves wasting their time on us? Queen Imelda sent them here to find Markham.

By the time the bleeding stops, daylight is growing short. Still, I don't get down. Neely is gone, and no one knows where I am. How did I ever talk myself into coming here? Markham wanted me to follow him. I should have known better than to give him anything he wanted.

A chill racks my body, my teeth chattering together. I want to go home. I want to find out if Jamison is safe. I could call out. One whistle, and the barghest would be back for me. Though I feel alone, I am not.

I hug my sword close. "How do we travel without a portal? Can you take me home?"

The sword does nothing in response.

"Fine. Don't help me."

A good hour or so later, I wipe my brow and carefully descend the tree. The woods are quiet and dim. I walk down the middle of the stream, soaking my boots and stockings. Neely said I have to find a cairn that looks like a finch. No, a falcon.

I walk and walk, cradling my aching side. My fever hasn't gotten worse in the last little while, but it isn't better. I would spirit jump to hover overhead for a bird's-eye view of my surroundings to make sure I'm headed in the right direction, but I haven't the strength.

About the time I spot a cairn shaped like a bird, the sun begins to set. I swipe at my hot brow and stare up at the falcon's outstretched wings. The road splits. One way leads into the trees, and the other way leads to the prairie.

I sit at the base of the cairn. I could easily lie down and go to sleep, but I'd rather not spend the night this exposed. "Which way did Neely say to go next?"

My sword vibrates.

"So now you're talking to me?"

The hilt warms in my hand. I point the blade down the path to the prairie first and then into the woods. The sword vibrates when aimed at the trees.

"Thank you," I whisper.

I set out, the shadows in the trees deepening to night. My entire body aches, my soreness felt in every step. I hear the river before I spot it through the underbrush. Moonlight reflects off the water, acting as a beacon, the trail along the river coming and going out of sight. My sword helps me remain on course, though lifting it gets harder. I stumble to the side of a tree and rest. I'm not sure I can go another step.

Then I see it—a footbridge over the river.

I pull myself up and drag my tired body to the bridge. Lights greet me from the other side. I trudge across, and a charming cottage comes into view, its water mill turning in the flowing river. The thatch-roofed building is huge, an oversize replica of the homes I'm used to. I almost feel foolish calling it a cottage.

Music plays from inside—the bright, intense sound of a brass instrument.

Almost there. A few more steps.

A sharp ache shoots through my side. I drop to my knees a few strides away from the front door. I try to get up, but the cottage lights float in and out of focus.

The music stops. A door opens, and the big barrel of a gun is shoved in my face. Before I can respond, the pain sweeps me away.

Chapter Thirteen

The scent of cooked cabbage fills my nostrils. I blink myself back to awareness and spot two giantesses out of the corner of my eye. One stands by the hearth, stirring a bubbling pot, and the other holds a lengthy brass instrument near a dining table. The kitchen window is dark. I don't think I was out long. From the food the giantess is cooking, the hour seems to still be in the evening. Although my side pangs fiercely, I pretend I'm asleep on the sofa.

"Are you certain she's a human, Mistral?" asks the giantess by the table.

"She looks just like the women in the pictures in our history books," replies the other giantess. She lowers her voice. "Corentine, should we send for the surgeon? She's wounded and feverish."

"No, no surgeon."

"Surely we should tell someone we found her. At the very least the sheriff."

"Mistral, that dumb goat will empty all our food cupboards. He might even eat *her.*"

A shadow falls over my face. The giantess that was cooking, Mistral, stands over me. "She's a wee lass," she says. "Why would anyone eat a human? Not much there worth cooking."

"They're supposed to be good wrapped in bread and dipped in butter."

"Where did you hear that?"

"Read it in one of Great-Grandmother's cookbooks."

I try very hard not to tremble.

Corentine's voice comes closer. "Do you hear that?" Her sour, hot breaths stream over me. "It sounds like she's ticking. Let's wake her up."

A loud blare goes off close to my ear. I shoot up so fast I fall off the sofa and hit the floor. I moan, the pain in my side sharper.

"Poor thing," says Mistral. "She isn't well."

"She doesn't look very bright. Humans are fribbles, the whole lot of them. She probably doesn't even understand what we're saying. Imagine being afraid of an ophicleide." Corentine sets her brass instrument on its stand. Behind the ophicleide, the wall is lined with carnyxes. The last time I saw the long, narrow battle horns was aboard Captain Redmond's ship.

Mistral waves a little. "Hello, human woman. We're the Esen sisters. I'm Mistral, and that's my older sister, Corentine."

The Esen sisters are tall, nearly twice my height, and sturdy limbed. Broad shoulders and hips balance out their girth. Gray streaks lighten their otherwise muddy-brown hair, and wrinkles surround their small eyes and lips. They have the same droopy noses and ears as Neely but longer eyelashes. They wear serviceable wool frocks and aprons that are extremely well constructed, the lines of stitching perfectly straight.

Corentine pushes her sister out of the way to loom over me. "Who are you? How did you get into our world? Why are you here?"

"You're scaring her, Corentine." Mistral grabs the back of my shirt and picks me up, setting me on my feet. "Can you understand us, wee one?"

"Y-yes."

"See?" says Mistral. "She's not a fribble."

Corentine harrumphs.

"Where's my sword?" I stammer.

"Hidden." Corentine crosses her arms over her chest, her expression locked in a perpetual sneer. "What's your name?"

"Everley Donovan. I'm a friend of Neely's." The giantesses go still except for their widening eyes. "We met in the Land Under the Wave. He told me where to find you."

"Is our brother here with you?" Mistral breathes.

"He was. I don't know where he is now. The elven guard captured him."

Corentine mashes her lips into a line. "There are elves in our world? Why would they take our brother?"

"They came for their wayward prince. He planted a skyseed in my world, the Land of the Living, and climbed the skystalk here. The elven queen sent the guard to bring him home. I'm looking for the prince too. Neely was helping me find him."

The soup pot boils over onto the fire. Hissing noises commence, and smoke streams from the hearth. Mistral bustles over to lift the pot off the heat and sets it on the table. I'm held in place by Corentine's scowl. The giantesses' home is clean and organized, the draperies and rugs faded and worn. The layout is the same as our cottages back home, with the shared living space in the middle. A candle clock hangs on the wall. I've only ever read about them. A candle burns down, supposedly at a steady rate that denotes a reliable passage of time but is, in fact, wildly inaccurate, like water clocks. The candle clock's presence is oddly ancient considering the large, complex pistol on the table and the intriguing contraption on a table in the corner. A bobbin of thread sits on top of the metal machine. A wheel is attached on the closed side, and the top extends over the bottom with a needle set at the lowest point.

"What's that?" I ask.

"A sewing machine," Corentine replies abruptly, as though I'm daft for not knowing. "Why is the elven prince in our world?"

"His name is Killian Markham. A glamour charm makes him appear human. He's been in your world for about three days. Has a man been sighted?"

"No," replies Mistral, sprinkling chopped parsley over the soup. "We're at the textile factory in the city all day. We would've heard if a human had been seen. After nearly nine hundred years, that would be tremendous news."

"The prince is looking for a luthier called the Bard," I say. Both sisters look at me blankly. "Maybe your father has heard of him?"

Mistral wipes her hands off on her apron. "Our father passed away fifteen years ago."

"I'm sorry," I reply quietly.

"After he died," Mistral says, "we sold all his mechanic tools and took in grain to grind in our mill. Barely made enough coin to survive. A couple years ago, the railroad was built out here, so we closed the mill and took jobs at the city factory."

"Railroad?" I ask.

"You have trains in your world, don't you?" Corentine asks.

"I can't say we do." The Realm of Wyeth is the most advanced of the four realms in my world, and I've never heard of them. I gesture at the odd pistol. "I have a friend who's fond of firearms. She'd be curious about that one."

"This is a six-shot revolver." Corentine picks up the pistol, spins the barrel, and locks it into place. "They're the newest firearms on the market. I bought it from the gunsmith factory. They gave me a discount because the stock is dented, but that doesn't affect its firing."

"Railroad." "Train." "Revolver." "Factory." I know none of this strangeness.

Mistral leaves the soup to cool and picks up knitting needles. She sits at the table with her yarn. "What are the worlds saying about us giants, dearie? Is there any plan for reopening our portals?"

I sense this isn't an offhand question, so I answer carefully. "Humans don't remember the triad war."

Corentine sets down her pistol. "What do they say about giants?"

"Very little. As you seem to know, it's been nine hundred years since the war ended. What little we recall has been put into storybooks."

"You hear that, Sister?" Corentine asks snidely. "We've been reduced to children's tales."

Mistral's knitting needles pause and then click faster.

Corentine saunters over to me, her slow steps pronounced. "We, too, were taught about your kind from childhood. Our elders tell of greedy, compassionless giant slayers who stole the land of our inheritance." The giantess hunches over me. "I hear ticking again. Are you carrying a timepiece on you?"

"No."

"I hear it too," Mistral says, setting her knitting in her lap.

Corentine grabs my arm so fast I've no hope of escape. She holds me while Mistral pats me down. The giantess feels the hard glass over my ticker and tears open the top of my shirt.

"What is that?" Corentine gasps.

"My heart."

"That isn't a heart, that's a clock." She leans away in repulsion. "Clocks aren't permitted in the Silver-Clouded Plain. They're talismans of he who betrayed us to the Creator."

Jamison's contract with the sea hag falls out of my breast pocket. Corentine holds me at gunpoint while Mistral scoops up the paper. I hope she cannot read, but to no avail.

"Who's Jamison Callahan, and what's a sea hag?" Mistral asks.

I refuse to respond.

Mistral passes the paper to Corentine. She tucks the contract in her pocket and nods at her sister. Mistral picks me up by the back of my shirt and places me on a chair.

"Friend of our brother's or not," says Corentine, "we cannot let a human wander around our world. It would be bedlam."

My feet hang over the floor as they tie me to the chair. I saw this once in a storybook. The giants mean to prop the chair over the fire and roast me. "Please don't do this. You don't want to eat me. You're right. I'm bony and tasteless."

"Eat you?" Corentine makes a face. "I'd rather eat a basket of artichokes."

Mistral appears wounded. "I like artichokes."

"Listen to me," I say. "I have to find the Bard before the prince does. You cannot hold me captive. The elven guard might come here looking for me."

"Really?" asks Mistral. "We could ask them to return our brother."

"Or we could trade the human for him," Corentine says. The sisters wear the same shrewd grin. "Let's put her in there. I cannot stand that obnoxious ticking."

Corentine gags me, and then Mistral sets me in the closet. I struggle against my bindings and mumble against my gag. Mistral pauses in the open doorway, her eyes marked with sympathy. Corentine wrenches the door from her sister's grasp and slams it shut.

The closet door swings open, and morning sunlight strikes me. I drop my face to the side to shield my eyes.

"Good morning," says Mistral, carrying a knitting basket full of green wool. "I hope you slept well."

My arms and fingers are numb. The throbbing in my side has become so insistent I've begun to think it will never heal. My fever simmers away. I need to relieve myself. And I'm so hungry I could eat the cloth gag in my mouth.

So no, I didn't sleep well at all.

"Corentine and I are off to work," Mistral goes on, unfailingly chipper. "If you behave while we're gone, I'll convince her to let you out for supper."

A whistle sounds in the distance.

"That's the train," Corentine says, handing her sister a cloak.

"Be good today," Mistral whispers.

She shuts the door again, and I hear them leave the cottage. A line of daylight pushes its way through the crack under the door, taunting me.

The next hour hurts. The Esen sisters must know even humans require a chamber pot from time to time. I count the minutes to distract me, but after another hour, I hurt so badly I can hardly think of anything except getting out of here.

My spirit rises from my body, jumping out in desperation. I look down at myself and wince. My hair is in tatters, leaves and sticks stuck in my braid, and my color pale. The bloodstains on my shirt have dried to brown splotches. I drift toward the door, and my side pangs. My cuts are visible on my spirit as shadowy slashes. I don't know what to do for them. Unlike other injuries, time hasn't helped them heal.

I pass through the closet door and float through the roof. Hovering over the cottage, I take in the sisters' vegetable garden. I stop myself from going higher and drop back down into the main room.

Now, to find my sword.

I poke through the cupboards, under furniture, and behind the row of carnyxes. The thing Corentine called a sewing machine is a marvel. I concentrate with some difficulty and crank the wheel. The needle runs a line of thread across the hem of some trousers. I finish the seam, astonished by its straightness, and move down the hall.

Two bedchamber doors are across from each other. I go through the one on the right. Knitted items are strewn across the dresser and wooden chest—hats, scarves, a man's green vest. This must be Mistral's room. I look about, but she has nothing of interest under the bed or in her wardrobe closet.

Across the hall, I enter the second bedchamber. Corentine's ophicleide sits on its stand in the corner. I skim the sheet music beside it—a battle song. A tapestry of a warrior giant holding a human head in one hand and a mace in the other hangs over her bed. The giant's ferocious yell is silent, though I can easily imagine his gut-shaking bellow. Straight out of my childhood nightmares.

No sign of my sword. I drift back into the main area of the cottage, then up into the rafters and chimney. Again, nothing.

My clock heart spins more slowly. I've checked everywhere. Maybe the sisters took my sword with them. Maybe they recognized the hallowed blade and realized what they held.

A vibrating sound comes from the kitchen.

I float over to the washbasin. The noise rises from under the rug. Concentrating, I solidify my spirit form, pull the rug aside, and lift the loose floorboard. In a shallow compartment lies the sword of Avelyn. I reach for it, and my fingers pass through the hilt. I'm soul weary, and my clock heart is spinning downward, the revolutions even slower. My spirit needs to return to my body.

Mustering my full strength of mind, I reach again and grasp the hilt. I waste no time returning to the closet. Opening the door takes two tries, but I get in and begin to saw myself free.

The sword wasn't made for sawing, and my tired strokes are inefficient. The blade slips off the rope and strikes the air beside it. The emptiness there breaks, like a cut in a sheet. Curious, I inspect the slit closer. The little indentation in the air shimmers, iridescent. I poke the end of my sword at it, and the front of my blade goes inside the slit. I yank the blade out again, the weapon still intact. The opening is bigger from shoving the blade inside.

I step closer to it, and my clock heart spins faster, as it does when I'm near a portal. I slip my hand inside the opening, and it disappears.

The shimmering hole pulls, trying to drag me inside. I jerk back and gape at the fading rainbow.

"Holy Mother of Madrona. Osric was right."

The sword pulses, and something brightens on its hilt, an inscription I've never noticed before. The symbol is from the tree alphabet—a centurion, the second largest tree in the worlds, following the elderwoods. Supposedly their seeds were pieces of broken stars that fell from the heavens and took root in the land. The centurions grow tall in an attempt to return to the firmament where they belong.

"Centurion? Was that your name when you were a star?" The sword warms and vibrates, which I take to mean yes. "Nice to officially meet you."

Someone pounds at the front door.

"Mistral? Corentine?" a deep voice booms.

I shut myself in the closet again. More pounding comes from the front door.

"It's Sheriff Ramiel. Open up or I'm coming in!"

I saw at my restraints, breaking one side of the cords. The front door bangs open. I poke my spirit head out of the closet through the wooden door.

A giant enters the house. He's enormous, bigger than the Esen sisters, and Neely, *and* Redmond. He ducks inside and straightens. His feet are clad in boots that would dwarf me, should I try to stand in them. His ear-length hair lies limp against his head, and he's wearing a uniform—charcoal trousers, a white shirt, and a black cloak. A silver star is pinned to his cloak, engraved with the word "SHERIFF."

He stomps around the main room, then helps himself to the fruit on the table and pockets a vine of tomatoes. He doesn't call for the sisters again, as though he knew he wouldn't find them here. Before he takes a bite of a plum, he lifts his chin and sniffs the air. His nostrils flare.

My clock heart slows, a heavy *ka-chunk, ka-chunk.*

The sheriff sets down the piece of fruit and sniffs the air again. He follows the scent he's caught around the room and pauses by the sofa where I lay last night. He bends to sniff the cushions, then straightens suddenly, and his gaze flies to me. I freeze halfway outside of the closet. His focus is on the door, but can he smell me?

The giant inhales a lungful of air and starts for the closet.

He *can* smell me.

I slide my head back inside and saw faster at the last binding. My body sags more and more, wilting in the chair, and my grip on my sword weakens. The ticktocking of my heart in my body drags, the mechanism on the verge of stalling.

Footsteps stomp closer.

I break the last binding. My body slumps sideways, nearly sliding off the chair. I set the sword at my side and fall back inside myself.

Sitting up, my ticker picks up in speed. The sheriff's footsteps stop outside the door. I grasp my sword with both hands as the doorknob begins to turn in a steady revolution. I lift my weapon, my nerves on fire, my vision drifting in and out, my side in excruciating pain. The doorknob hits the end of the revolution. A crack opens in the door, wider, wider—

"Sheriff Ramiel, what are you doing here?"

Corentine.

The doorknob quits moving. I listen as the Esen sisters stomp into their cottage. All three giants stand on the other side of the door, their voices clear as spring water.

"Have you been in our cupboards?" asks Mistral.

"Put down the revolver, Corentine," the sheriff replies gruffly.

"Be grateful I saw it was you before I unloaded my chambers."

"Why aren't you two working at the factory?" he returns.

"Mistral is a tad under the weather. Why are *you* here, Ramiel?"

"Elves have been spotted nearby. I know, I know, it's an unusual report, but I also saw odd canine tracks this morning, so I'm making the rounds. With you two living on your own out here, this would be a prime place for someone to hide."

I slide off the chair onto shaky legs and sidle up to the door.

"We haven't seen anything unusual," Corentine says.

"Keep an eye out," the sheriff answers. "I spoke to a chief deputy in Rackfort last night. Someone saw a man in the city. I thought that was hogwash, but the deputy swears the witness smelled a human. Your cottage smells strange too."

"My sister made cabbage stew last night," Corentine answers tightly. "You really should return to your rounds, Ramiel."

"If you see anything—"

"We'll praise Madrona that the portals have been reopened," Mistral says brightly. "What a miracle that will be."

Mistral starts to chitchat with the sheriff about the sisters' high yield of garlic in their garden, their voices moving away from the door. The sheriff declines to take a bushel and goes on his way.

"Sneaky fribble," Corentine hisses. "He didn't come for anything except the pocketful of tomatoes he pinched from our kitchen."

"He'll keep looking for the human," Mistral answers. "Such a discovery would surely earn him a promotion."

Footsteps thud closer. I raise my sword as the Esen sisters open the closet.

Mistral lays a hand against her cheek in surprise. "Well, look at that. She found her sword."

"She better be worth losing half a day's wages for," Corentine grumbles. "Put your blade down, woman. We aren't going to hurt you."

My feet tingle from the blood rushing back into them. My wrists are bruised from their bindings. "You'll understand why I don't believe you."

"We locked you away before we knew you were telling the truth." Corentine goes to the kitchen to pour herself a glass of water.

Mistral gives me a penitent smile. Neither one discourages me from stepping into the main living area.

"How did the sheriff know he'd smelled a human?" I ask.

Corentine finishes draining her cup. "He didn't know for certain or you'd be dead."

Mistral pulls out a chair for me. "Sit, Everley Donovan. Tell us why you've come to our world."

My side and head throb, and I still need to find the latrine, but I'm afraid the sisters will force me back into the closet if I disagree, so I slide into the chair. Mistral puts on the kettle and sets down a basket of tarts bigger than my hand on the table. Corentine hovers over me with squinty eyes.

"As I said," I start, "I need to find a luthier named the Bard before the prince of the elves does. All of Avelyn is at risk. Prince Killian has already destroyed the Land of Youth."

The Esen sisters swap glances of alarm. I decide against telling them that Markham seeks an artifact that can awake their ancestors. They may not be against such a notion, especially if it results in freeing the giants and taking back the land of their inheritance.

Mistral spoons herbs into a teapot sieve for stewing. "Why must you find him if the elven guard is here, dearie?"

"The prince killed my family. He's the reason I have a clock for a heart. I want to be the one who catches him and turns him in."

Corentine runs her nail across a groove in the table, making the indentation deeper. "Do you worship Father Time?"

"No." I rub at my temples, my head pounding. "Not anymore."

She stops driving her nail into the table and sits back, satisfied.

"We asked around the factory to see if anyone had heard about your luthier," says Mistral, steeping the tea. "The one you called the Bard has a shop in Rackfort."

I sit up straighter. "How far away is it? Can you take me?"

The sisters give each other another sidelong glance.

"Perhaps we will," Mistral answers, "if you promise to help us get our brother back."

Neely was captured for helping me. Of course, I won't let the elves keep him. "As soon as we have the prince, we'll find Neely."

Mistral pours our tea and sets the steaming cups in front of us. "This is for your fever."

My teacup is the size of a bowl, and it smells delicious—lemon and honey—but I ask to use the latrine. The sisters keep an eye on me from the window as I go outside through the back door. Upon my return, they promptly quit speaking to one another.

Corentine holds out a spool of cloth to me, bandaging for my injured side. "You're welcome to our tea and our latrine and our bandages, but I want to make something clear, Everley Donovan from the Land of the Living. I don't care about you or your human world. I care about our brother."

These giantess sisters will be my guides through their city, and that isn't much of a comfort. I could create a portal with my sword and leave this place. In seconds, I could be home, but Jamison asked me not to give up, so I accept the bandages.

"We'll find Neely," I promise.

The sisters exchange one of their we're-communicating-without-talking glances. I'm beginning to think they can read each other's minds, or perhaps this is how sisters connect, how my older sister, Isleen, and I would have communicated had we had more time together.

Mistral sets a basket on the table.

"What's that for?" I ask.

Corentine's lips peel back in a violent grin. "We're going to bury you."

Chapter Fourteen

I lie in the back of the donkey cart, buried under bushels of garlic. I would have preferred to hide among crates of lemons or a strong-scented wood to mask my smell, but the Esen sisters grew an abundance of garlic in their garden, so that's what they had to spare.

The big donkey, the size of a draft horse, stops the cart.

Corentine pokes me. "You alive?"

"So far."

The train platform is empty. Mistral explained while loading me down with garlic that giants go into the city in the morning and return in the evening. This is the final run into Rackfort before nightfall. The next train doesn't return until morning.

Our train whistles closer. As it pulls alongside the platform, the ground rumbles, and wheels screech to a stop. The front part of the train—what Mistral called the engine—puffs and hisses. Voices ring out, and footsteps pound past us as patrons exit the train cars.

The donkey cart begins to move. We go over a bump, up an incline, over another bump, and stop. A loud screeching, like a door shutting, fills my ears, and all goes dim. A few minutes later, everything starts to shake.

Mistral pulls bushels of garlic off me and throws off the cover. "You can come out now. It's just geese and sheep in the livestock car."

I sit up and brush off the papery garlic skins that fell on my cloak. We're inside a big metal cage rocking from side to side. I climb out slowly to protect my injured side and sit on a hay bale with my sword in my lap. I bandaged my cuts, and the tea lowered my fever, but I'm still babying my wounds.

Corentine scratches the donkey's head, and the donkey preens into her touch. The giant might have something in common with Neely after all.

"How long until we reach Rackfort?" I ask.

Mistral takes her knitting out of her basket. "About an hour."

Her sister slides open the side door of the train car. Wind pours in, and with it, the loud chugging. I marvel at the giants' ingenuity. They must be at least thirty years ahead of us in transportation and weaponry.

Mistral knits a shawl while Corentine chews on a piece of straw and scowls at the passing grassland. I fidget in my seat, unable to get comfortable. The geese across the way are bedded down in the straw, miserable in their confines. I fit right in.

The skyline changes in the distance, providing a glimpse of smoke trails in the sky. Fire from a pyre or more trains? I join Corentine near the door. "What are those?"

"Smokestacks from the factories."

"Factory . . . is that a type of shipping dock?"

She pulls the straw out of her mouth. "You don't know what a factory is? There isn't a giant in all the world who doesn't work in a factory or know someone who does."

"We've no railroads either."

"We've had factories and trains for twelve years or so. After the Creator took her power from us to build up our lands, we began using our gifts to make new contraptions and machines. The factories are where we do our production."

"When you did have your power, how did you 'build up the lands'?" I keep hearing this phrase, but I'm uncertain what it means. "You reshaped the lands how?"

"Music." Corentine's eyes gleam. "The Creator gave us dominion over the call of life. A piece of her voice dwells in us and also in the land. Our ancestors would drum their drums and play their instruments, and the land would respond depending on the tone of the song—a meandering tune sculpted meadows riddled with sweet-water streams or marshlands with gentle grasses. Bombastic brass medleys called up jagged mountains and chiseled away rough shorelines. Poignant melodies from string quartets smoothed out valleys and burrowed tunnels—the same tunnels that our warriors traveled to infiltrate your world in the war, woman." She points west. "They're still there, of course. Only, now, those who leave cannot come back." Corentine chews on the end of the stalk again and studies me.

"What?" I ask.

"Our historians say that humans once thought giants were big and dense."

"Interesting." I'm not about to tell her we still believe that.

"But look at us." Corentine sweeps her arm out to draw my attention to the train. "Giants have always been the smartest and most industrious of the triad. Humans are only good as helpmates."

My face warms. "That sort of thinking led to your curse."

"Hogwash," Corentine retorts. "We were betrayed by Father Time and abandoned by the Creator."

"Your ancestors nearly annihilated my ancestors."

"Woman"—Corentine scoffs—"if we had wanted the humans gone, you would be. We never intended to exterminate your kind. Nothor, the great warrior who led the attack on your ancestors, planned to relocate them here and take back the Land of the Living."

Corentine is repeating propaganda she heard from someone justifying their ancestors' actions. The Creator wouldn't have interfered and cursed the giants had Nothor's army been merciful. War is war, and what's done in a time of war is often indefensible.

A glimpse at the distance stuns me. The immense city comes into focus, its shape and size appearing to have been assembled by a god. A towering wall with straight-laid bricks surrounds inner rectangular stone structures that rise in height and progression, like a musical scale growing higher. It's as though someone chiseled a civilization out of a mountain, complete with roads, buildings, security walls, and passable raised archways.

"Is that Rackfort?" I ask.

"It is," Mistral replies from where she's still knitting. "Does it look like your cities?"

"Good gracious, no." Dorestand is a mishmash of structural designs that were built over decades. "This is a fortress."

"Rackfort was the first city our ancestors constructed," Mistral explains. "Our leader's eldest son, Nothor, built it to withstand an invasion."

Or Nothor was paranoid because he himself plotted to invade the human world.

The train chugs steadily westward toward the setting sun over the city of giants. Outlying boroughs, those not inside the fortress walls, are downtrodden and mucky, full of shabby lean-tos and shacks. Almost everything is twice the size of what I know back home. Metal sheets are laid down as rooftops and propped up as doors. Smells of rotting rubbish and air thick with the smog billowing from the factories stew over the hovels. Enormous gates stand open in the main city wall, the gatehouse guarded by lawmen. Countless giants depart through them to return home for the evening. The square ramparts and turrets atop the stone wall feel archaic next to the factory buildings. One after one, beacons are lit in the lookouts, illuminating the twilight sky.

The railroad tracks run toward a tunnel in the wall. We enter, everything goes murky for a few moments, then we exit again. The train runs parallel to the outer city wall, our pathway lit by the beacons. Here the city roads are clean and the buildings in good repair. Pixies dart about, disappearing rubbish dropped on the ground with their magical dust. I'd been told they're employed as rubbish collectors, but I'd only seen them in the Everwoods.

"I didn't realize pixies live here," I say.

"They work in the cities," Mistral replies.

"Ill-tempered vermin," Corentine grouses. "Stay clear of them and don't make eye contact, or they'll take that as a challenge."

"But pixies are inherently good."

"Maybe once upon a time, but not anymore." Corentine shoos me away from the door and closes it. "Get ready to disembark."

I climb into the donkey cart, and the Esen sisters pile garlic over me again. I stop them before they cover my head. "How far to the Bard's shop?"

"Stay hidden," Corentine warns, "or we might not make it."

Mistral clucks her tongue at her sister. "It's just a short walk, dearie. You'll be all right."

A loud screeching noise sounds as the train slows. The giantesses cover the last of me and hook up the donkey to the cart. The train stops and the side door rattles open.

We disembark the car, and familiar scents sneak under the canvas—unwashed bodies, discarded wash water, cooking meat—the smell of hundreds of people living closely together. I cover my ticker with one hand, my sword in the other. The cart bumps over cobblestones, jogging my teeth together.

"What's he doing here?" Mistral asks.

The cart starts to slow.

"Don't slow down," Corentine snaps. "Keep going or he'll know we spotted him."

A question burns on my tongue. Who is here?

"It's not working," Mistral says. "He's still following us."

I hear a gun hammer cock—Corentine loading her revolver.

I push my spirit out of my body and hover above us. The mighty city nearly knocks me right back down into myself. Everything about Rackfort is overwhelmingly enormous. Horses, wagons, and carts are all larger than I'm used to. The sheer size of the stone buildings, so tall they mask the sky, and the vast width of the streets packed with countless lumbering giants shrink me like a mouse hiding in a house.

A purple pixie, a different color than Radella, darts up to me. Her gossamer wings have ragged tears around the edges, and she has scratches on her legs.

"Hello, little one. Are you hurt?" I ask.

The pixie bares her teeth and snaps at me. I recoil and lift my sword to her. She trills crossly and zips off.

"Don't go too fast," Corentine says. She and Mistral guide the donkey-drawn cart farther up the street. I catch up to them and float along at their pace.

"He may not be here for us," Mistral whispers. "He may have business in the city."

I search behind us and spot Sheriff Ramiel in pursuit on foot about fifty yards away. A revolver is partially hidden under his cloak. I start to dive back into my body to warn the Esen sisters, but then I stop. I can do something.

Keeping an eye on the donkey cart, I fly to the sheriff and sink down in front of him. Only the pixies can see me while I'm in my spirit form, but they take no notice of me. Once he's closer, I solidify while lifting my sword and slice his belt in two. His trousers loosen and drop to his ankles.

"What in Avelyn?" The sheriff stops and grapples to pull up his pants.

Another giant pushing a cart piled high with fruit doesn't see Ramiel bent over and runs into him. Lines of plums spill out of the cart, rolling in every direction across the road. The vendor yells at the sheriff, and the two of them begin to gather the fallen fruit. Ramiel will be busy for a moment.

I float back to the donkey cart and the Esen sisters. After sinking back into myself, I uncover my face. "The sheriff's gone."

"Shh," Corentine snaps. "Be quiet and hide!"

"But she's right. Ramiel's not behind us anymore." Mistral peers down at me. "How did you know, dearie?"

"Clever guess," I answer. She gives an unconvinced "hmm" and takes care covering me back up. Her gentleness prompts me to ask, "Have you ever been married?"

"I was betrothed once," Mistral replies quietly. "He was killed in an assembly-line accident at a factory."

I don't know what an assembly line is, but I can guess. "Do you have children?"

"No. I would never bring a child into this Creator-less world. Living in a cursed world, locked away from the rest of Avelyn . . . I wouldn't do that to an innocent babe."

The cart slows to a halt.

"We're here," says Corentine. "You can come out now, but stay behind us."

I get out of the cart. We're in an alleyway off a courtyard with an old clock tower as the centerpiece. The timepiece's glass face has been shattered, and the clock gears are gutted or left to rust. The giants have been locked away for so long they've lost hope of ever getting out. Clocks must be a reminder of how long they've been held in purgatory.

The Esen sisters lead me out of the alley to the front of a building, shielding me with their hefty frames. A few strides later, we stop at a frosted glass-pane door embossed with fancy gold letters that read, *Nightingale Music*. Underneath, in smaller letters, it says, *Handmade since the beginning of time*.

Bells jangle as Corentine pushes the door open and shoves me inside. The reek of the city hovers a moment, then dissipates. In its place comes the pungent smell of drying lacquer followed by the light scent of sawdust. Shelves extend from the shiny black-and-white marble tile floor to the ceiling. They are packed with wooden creations, from marionette dolls to cuckoo clocks to jewelry boxes. Their craftsmanship varies from classically simple to ornately engraved and painted with elaborate designs.

"How has this shop been here all along and we've never seen it?" Mistral whispers.

"You've never seen it before tonight?" I reply.

The giantess shakes her head. "We found this place after you suggested we look for luthiers."

Petite wooden boxes are set out in a neat merchandise display around the clerk's desk. The layout of the storefront is not unlike my uncle's clock shop, except the space is filled with ceiling-high shelves.

One of the boxes by the desk is tipped open. Inside, a pixie figurine stands on her tiptoes, her iridescent wings outstretched. The lovely construction is highly detailed, with finishings that could only be done by a master carver. Just one of these boxes would take the maker several days to complete. The individuality of the detailed pieces alone astounds me. The accumulated hours spent to construct each creation in the shop must add up to a remarkable amount of time.

Music starts to play somewhere off to the right, behind more shelves. The hairs on the back of my neck stand on end. I haven't heard this song in a long while. It's the tune Carlin played for my mother on her birthday—the night they were murdered.

Mistral bumps into a table and nearly knocks over a lady marionette. She grabs the doll before it hits the ground, and her hands tangle in the strings.

"Put that down," Corentine hisses.

"I'm trying." Mistral starts to pull free and entangles herself more.

Corentine tries to help her, and I wander toward the sound of the music. The rows of shelves continue, the shop much bigger than it appears from the street. Finally, seven rows later, I find the box playing music on a middle shelf, its lid open. A piece of glass inside reveals the moving gearwork. A cylinder spins as a metal comb hits it, producing chimes in various notes. I look around to see who would have turned the lever, but no one else is here.

"Everley!" Corentine calls. "Where are you?"

"Coming." I bring the box with me.

Mistral has detangled herself from the doll and is now preoccupied with a hummingbird music box on the desk. The delicate painted bird dances from side to side and sings a lullaby, the same tune Jamison has struggled to remember, only in another key. His version is moodier, sadder than this sweeter melody.

As the music approaches the final stanza, the cylinder slows to a halt, and a small figure appears in the doorway of the unlit back room behind the clerk's desk.

"Hello?" I ask. "Are you the Bard?"

The figure walks out into the light. She's a human-size marionette doll with hinges in her arms and legs and a straight neck, with facial features painted on in a permanent, eerie smile. Her dress is painted on too, except for the bottom, which is cloth from the waist down. No strings move her. She walks on flat wooden feet that clack against the marble floor.

The marionette doll waves us forward.

"Sister?" Mistral says, her voice jumping nervously. "I think she wants us to follow her."

Corentine hesitates, glancing between the marionette and the front door. She wants to leave. They both do. I don't blame them. But I'm not afraid, not as much as I should be. Perhaps I'm not afraid because I think I know how the marionette was given life. Maybe because I've seen and done so many strange things in the past few days that this stranger thing doesn't frighten me. Or maybe I'm not deterred because my heart has begun to spin, a signal that whatever awaits me beyond this threshold is not of this world, and I must seek it.

This is a moment appointed by destiny, an event that will play in a glowing sphere on my timeline. Climbing the skystalk, hiking across the Silver-Clouded Plain, sneaking into the city of giants—these events were meant to happen. I was always going to follow this marionette doll.

"Wait here," I say to the Esen sisters, then go to greet my fate.

Chapter Fifteen

I step into the workshop. Tools and scraps of wood cover the work-benches, and crates overflowing with cogs and gears are stacked in the corners. I spent years of my life in and out of my uncle's workplace, listening to him hammer, chisel, and saw wood. Running my finger across one of the dented workbenches, I endure a fresh swell of grief. Elderwood Manor is a splendid home, but the estate doesn't have the same nostalgic ambiance as this simple workshop.

The marionette waits for me in the opposite doorway. My clock heart spins faster as I follow her out of the shop, down a short corridor, and into a grand theater.

Hundreds of seats sized to accommodate humans face the raised stage, and two tiers with viewing boxes line the left and right wings. Sconces flicker light across the damask-covered walls, and chandeliers brighten the stage. How can a hall of this size exist inside the storefront we entered?

In the center of the stage sits a man—a human—strumming a silver harp. He's seated on a chair, his fingers gracefully flowing across the strings, serenading the empty theater with the loneliest song I have ever heard. My bones ache from the simple yet moving melody. I go down the rows of seats to the base of the stage. The harpist is of variable youth, somewhere in his twenties, and wears an old-style three-piece suit with a dashing mustard-yellow necktie and a pocket-watch chain hanging from his vest pocket. His winsome good looks are traditional in taste, the arrangement of his features intriguing but not especially striking. He plays for so long I sit in the front row to rest my aching side until the last note hangs in the air.

"Please forgive me the indulgence," says the harpist, his voice musical in tenor. "It's been decades since I've had an audience."

The marionette reappears and offers me a cup of black tea, which I decline.

"Do you live here?" I ask the man.

"Yes, and except for my servant, Maisie, I am alone."

His marionette stands between us, her expression blank.

"How did you bring her to life?"

"Ah, but you already know the answer, don't you?" He strokes the strings of the harp again, playing a soft, ethereal scale meant to put me at ease. It doesn't. "A long, long time ago, I animated Maisie with heartwood."

I notice the piece then, the coin-size section of wood in the center of the marionette's chest.

"Maisie and I have been together here three hundred and fifty years or so, banished into hiding by the last Time Bearer."

"You're the Bard," I state, and he nods. "Then you're immortal?"

"Who can say what qualifies as immortality? Is immortality living endless months and years? Is it resiliency to those years? Or is it an absence of time?" He squints at me in question. "You've seen time cheated, traded, gifted, and stopped. Why not stretched?"

I have no clue what he's rambling on about, but he's the luthier I've come for. "Why do you stay if you're alone?"

"I was whisked away from the Land of Youth. Princess Amadara, my dearest friend and an honorable Time Bearer, watched over me. Her dastardly husband was quite displeased when he learned the Creator's luthier had been right under his nose and his wife never told him."

"You know Killian Markham?" I utter, my voice pitching in confusion.

"Know him? He's partly why I'm here." The Bard quits playing the harp and walks to the end of the stage, looming over me like the Esen sisters do. The two giants still haven't mustered the courage to leave the storefront. The Bard sits, his feet hanging over the edge of the stage. "I recognize the sword of Avelyn in your grasp. You're the Time Bearer, just as Amadara was. I loved her as a sister, whereas Eiocha is my heart and soul. Alas, our love was unequal. Oh, Eiocha cares for me, the same as any other creation, but I could never have her for myself. I was pushed from the womb of an acorn, born into worlds where I would die faster and age less gracefully than other creatures, where I would serve as a helpmate until I died."

His bitterness tugs at my own. "You're the firstborn man."

"I was the first. While the other humans embarked for the Land of the Living, I stayed at Madrona's roots and fell in love with Eiocha. I spent decades crafting a violin for her. She rewarded me with longevity, the ability to age so slowly that the cosmos would fall asleep waiting for my demise. I outlived my siblings, and for centuries I dwelled in the Everwoods, oblivious to the events in Avelyn—until the giants attacked."

"You were alive for the triad war?"

"I didn't take up arms. My hands create; they do not destroy. I put everything I am into that violin. My whole heart, my talent, my love went into that creation, and then Eiocha destroyed it." The Bard lifts his empty hands and balls them into fists. "Father Time hid me in a faraway kingdom." His hardened gaze rises to mine. "My location was discovered by Killian, so I was moved here. While in isolation, I have spent centuries trying to remake my masterpiece."

I lick my dry lips. "Did you?"

"I had enough scraps of heartwood saved for one more creation." The Bard rises and walks offstage. He returns a moment later with a violin case. He sets the case before me and opens the lid. Nestled on red velvet within is the most beautiful polished instrument I've ever seen. He lifts the violin bow. "Each string is a strand of Eiocha's hair—mare hair, from when she was in her mortal form."

Someone behind us starts to applaud. Markham strides down an aisle on the far side of the theater, clapping slowly. I draw my sword.

"Good evening, Everley," he says.

I eye his approach. "You're not welcome here."

"Your manners are still appalling, but it's always pleasant to see you. Alas, you're not why I'm here. I have business with the Bard."

The Bard places the violin bow back in the case. "Is it time already?"

"I'm early. Impatience got the better of me." Markham hops up onto the stage down the way and crosses in front of me to reach the Bard. "You received my message."

"It isn't often that I get a letter from someone who should be dead."

Markham gestures at the violin case. "Is this it?"

The Bard steps in front of him, blocking the instrument. "It's called Nightingale." He closes the lid and locks it. "Did you bring my payment?"

Markham pulls out a coin pouch and shakes a pair of blue skyseeds into his palm. "Plant them both, and they'll take you far away from here."

"I want the infinity sandglass as well." The Bard tips his head back, his gaze sharp. "Don't try to trick me, Killian. I feel Father Time's power on you. I know you have the mighty timepiece in your possession."

"The skyseeds will take you where you desire," says Markham.

"But I have to wait for them to grow. Like you, I'm impatient. This is our bargain: the seeds and the sandglass for Nightingale."

"Don't do it," I say. "Killian means to start a war and destroy my world."

"I've no loyalty to the Land of the Living," replies the Bard. "My home is in the Everwoods, and I'm no longer welcome there."

Emily R. King

Selfish blaggard. He cannot return to his home, so he doesn't care if my people keep theirs. Is this what becomes of us when we live too long? We lose our humanity?

The Bard holds Nightingale out to the prince. The two grip the other's treasure, and then the Bard yanks his hands back, taking everything.

The seeds fall from his grasp, hit the floor, and spill out of the bag. Markham lunges and knocks him in the face. The Bard's hold on the violin case slips. The prince grabs it and leaps from the stage in front of Maisie. He shoves the marionette at me, and we stumble backward together. The Bard jumps off the stage and pushes me aside to go after the prince, but Markham has disappeared through the workshop door.

I raise my sword and start after him. The Bard steps into my path.

"Father Time sent you to sabotage me," he snarls, hoisting the sandglass. "I heard the rhythm of your clock heart the moment you stepped into my shop. I sense the power of your heartwood in every ticktock, Time Bearer." The Bard pulls a carving knife from his pocket with his other hand, and his marionette moves closer behind me. He sets the infinity sandglass on the stage and starts at me with the knife. "Hold her down, Maisie. Best not to let her heartwood go to waste."

The marionette grabs me around the middle. I twist left and slice down, severing her arm. Wrenching free, I swing around while sinking low and cut her across the knees. She crumples to the ground, twitching.

"No!" The Bard rushes forward and kneels beside her, cradling her wooden face. "My dearest pet."

I grab the sandglass and sprint up the aisle, through the workshop, and into the storefront. Several shelves have been knocked over, the Esen sisters trapped under them. Corentine groans. I go to her and help her push off the shelf. Together, we unbury Mistral.

Mistral sits up, her head bleeding. "We heard a noise and went to look," she explains. "Someone pushed the shelves on us."

142

"Prince Killian, I assume." I move out of the way as the giantess stands. "He stole an artifact, and he's getting away."

Corentine draws her revolver. "I'll kill him for making my sister bleed."

I hope I get to see her try.

I slip the sandglass into a pretty box I found in the shop and close it. The music box that plays the song haunting Jamison is on the floor. I stuff it into my pocket, hug the sandglass against me, and hurry outside with the sisters. A noise echoes from a nearby street—the barghest's howl.

"What in the Creator's name is that?" Mistral asks.

"The elven guard," I answer. "Their bloodhound is hunting its mark."

The barghest howls again, farther away. Commander Asmer must be tracking the prince. If they catch him first, Queen Imelda will have Nightingale.

I sprint toward the barghest, darting around carts and horses and wagons. Giants release exclamations of surprise. Corentine raises her revolver over her head as she barrels through pedestrians, and Mistral carefully shuffles between them after us.

"Sorry," she says as she bumps into others. "So sorry. Please excuse us. Oh, pardon me."

Another howl. I slow down to listen, and Corentine charges onward.

"This way!" she says.

"How do you know?"

"Their hound smells like dog, a delicacy for giants."

Mistral runs behind us, huffing and puffing. More howling from ahead, and then a train whistle. The platform comes into view. The elven guard is there, and the guards and their barghest are causing a commotion. Ahead of them, Markham runs into an open passenger car, and the elves load on seconds after. The train starts to pull away from the station.

"I thought trains don't run at night," I say.

"This one travels north of the city," Corentine answers.

Someone shouts from behind us. "Esen sisters, stop!"

Sheriff Ramiel chases us, his revolver ready, his trousers tied with a section of rope. We run onto the platform after the moving train. Corentine jumps onto the back of the last passenger car and hauls Mistral on beside her. I sprint after them, my hand outstretched for theirs, my other hand on the sandglass box.

"Human, halt!" calls the sheriff.

I run faster, and he fires.

A bullet strikes the ground beside me. I leap for Corentine, and she swings me up and sets me next to her. The sheriff runs to the end of the platform, where he's forced to stop, the last train car out of his reach. He fires a couple shots that bounce off the metal exterior of the car in sparks. The three of us duck inside the back door, and passengers gasp.

Corentine raises her revolver. "The human is with me."

Everyone backs away from the armed giantess as we rush down the aisle. Outside, we step across the hitch from one car to the next. Again, we go inside another passenger car, and Corentine wards off the alarmed passengers. As soon as it's determined I'm human, giants jump on their chairs as though they've discovered a rat.

Outside the front door, screams come from the next passenger car, followed by barking. I look up and see Markham leap over the top of the third train car to the second, hefting the violin case. The elven guard charges through the car in front of us. Corentine and Mistral have a better chance of stopping the elves than I do.

"Give me your revolver," I say.

"Are you mad, woman?" Corentine asks. "You can't fire this."

"The prince is getting away!"

Mistral wrenches the revolver from her sister, takes the sandglass box from me, and slams the revolver into my hands. "Go, dearie."

I climb the ladder. When I'm halfway up, Commander Asmer throws open the back door of the next passenger car. Her guards aim their arrows at the giants. I mount the top of the ladder, slipping out of their view. The whines of the barghest can be heard over Corentine's growls, then the wind deafens me to the skirmish below.

Markham stands at the opposite end of the train car, preparing to jump.

"Stop!" I aim the revolver at him. Holding the firearm requires both hands. I hate to think what the recoil will do.

He turns around slowly. "You need to learn when to leave well enough alone!"

"Stop this, Killian! I'll never let you wake the giants. Put down the violin and go home to your sister!"

"I cannot," he yells. "You aren't the only one who is trying to live up to the memory of their father, Evie."

My chest pounds, my ticker sprinting. "Put down Nightingale! I will shoot!"

He opens his arms wide, daring me. His sleeves ride up, and instead of the bandage I saw on his forearm before, he has a mark—*a scar?* But he's impervious to injury.

I squint harder to see across the distance, my eyes burning from the wind, and Commander Asmer steps onto the roof of the train car behind me. I stand between her and Markham.

She aims her rapier at me. "Stay out of this, Everley! Your part is over. This is between me and the prince."

Markham smirks and turns to leap across to the other train car.

I pull the trigger.

The recoil flings me back. I land on top of the moving train car and slide to the edge. Commander Asmer grabs me by the leg and pulls me back before I go over.

"Stay there," she shouts.

She makes her way to where Markham has fallen and places her rapier to his throat. I cannot hear what she says over the wind, but he drops his head to the side and doesn't get up. I rise to my knees, cradling my bandaged wound. The cuts on my side are bleeding again.

More elves climb onto the roof of the train. Corentine appears at the top of the ladder next and crosses to me. She picks up the revolver and helps me to my feet.

"What were you thinking, woman? The recoil could have thrown you off the train!"

"I'm here, aren't I?"

She snorts. "Well, at least you got your prince."

Commander Asmer binds him, and her comrades seize Nightingale.

Finally, finally, *finally*, Markham has been captured.

But I don't have him. Not at all.

Chapter Sixteen

I pace back and forth in front of the door. Four days. The elves brought me to the Land of Promise and have held me captive for four long days. They locked me in this chamber that's furnished with an enormous bed, fine rugs, a glittering chandelier, a wardrobe full of fashionable ladies' clothes, and a quaint sitting room that overlooks acres of orchards. So this grand room smells of lemon and verbena? So the silk bedsheets feel like bathing in starlight? They cannot buy my silence with comforts.

Still, this *is* the finest prison I've been held in.

I haven't spoken to anyone except the surgeon who visited me the first day. The homely young elf placed a mushy green salve on my cuts and left. Service gnomes deliver my meals. Three times a day, they bring me a plate stacked high with delicious raw vegetables. When I demanded to know where they are holding Corentine and Muriel, they bared their teeth at me. Worst of all, the elven guard confiscated the infinity sandglass, my sword, and the music box I took from the Bard's shop.

They will regret taking my sword.

For some reason I haven't puzzled out, I cannot spirit jump. I have tried but travel nowhere. I go to the window and run my finger over the millwork. The elves could have left me something to do, let me carve wood to pass the time. Mostly, I stare out the window at the field-workers, an assortment of elves, spriggans, and trolls who go out at dawn and return at sunset.

I had never seen a troll before. The short, rangy green creatures live up to their reputation. Large square noses, spiky ears that stick out from the sides of their heads, and extra-large hands and feet, with really long fingers and toes for grasping tools. Their thin lips hardly close over their jagged teeth, a leer that gives them an air of surliness.

Beyond the orchards, vineyards line the rolling hills in rows of groomed vines. A wide, swift river runs between the farmland, and off far in the distance, white-capped mountains loom. The late-day sunlight gives a dreamy haze to the scenery, as if bits of glitter hang in the air.

The view is nothing short of spectacular. I could gaze at it for hours, and have done so, for a lack of anything better to do. The Land of Promise is a suitable name for this haven. Since my arrival, I'm less tired, my ticker has not skipped a beat once, my skin has softened, and I feel more rested than I have since I last slept in my bed at home in Dorestand under my uncle's roof. I only hope Corentine and Mistral are so comfortable.

Commander Asmer let them come along to bargain with the elven queen for Neely's release. We arrived through an exit portal in the middle of the night, so I saw little of the chateau except for lanterns, worn cream walls, octagonal towers, and a slate roof. Then the guard ambushed the Esen sisters, taking them away, and brought me here.

A rap comes at the door. If that's another gnome come to snap at me, I'll—

Osric opens the door. I run to him, and he pulls me in close. He has his color back, and his leg is healed.

"When did you get here?" I ask.

"I'll tell you later. The queen has summoned you. Be wholly honest with her, Evie."

"About what?"

Commander Asmer appears behind him and clears her throat.

"We have much to discuss later," Osric says. "Remember you're a human in the elven world. Many still believe your kind are servant folk." His gaze bores into mine, warning me to behave.

"I understand."

Asmer leads us down the corridor, additional guards trailing behind. Every gold doorknob gleams, and the mahogany floors shine. Oak beams run along the ceiling, and fluted pilasters frame the doors. Hand-painted murals of leafy branches laden with red apples and flowery vines border the top and base of the walls.

"What is this place?"

My inquiry is meant for Osric, but the commander answers. "The queen's private chateau. This was her childhood home."

I peer around at the gilded doors and sconces. This looks nothing like the world we came from. "Do you have trains and factories here too?"

"No, no industrialization. The Land of Promise is a place of purity. We have altered the world only where necessary, thus maintaining the integrity of its original beauty and divinity. We work with the land, not against it."

Asmer opens the door to a circular two-story grand salon. Towering lattice windows overlook an elaborate garden of green boxwood and yellow roses. A chandelier hangs above the center of the room, glittering and silver. The hearth holds birch logs untouched by fire. Over the mantel hangs a ceiling-high gilded mirror, and on the opposite wall, the mounted head of a centicore. The antelope-like creature, with tusks and curled horns, stares ahead with glassy eyes.

Ornate furniture decorated with precious antiques is arranged around the glossy white piano by the window. Queen Imelda sits there, pounding out a cascade of notes. Strands of her fine hair have fallen loose from her sparkling crown, the damask-silk bell sleeves of her sapphire-blue gown draping over her lap. No one speaks until she strikes the last chord and lifts her hands from the keys.

"Your Majesty?" says the commander, flanked by guards. "Miss Donovan is here."

Queen Imelda's focus cuts across the room to me. "How are you feeling, Everley?"

"What did you do with the giantesses?"

The queen tugs down her sleeves. "I will answer your questions once you answer mine. The cuts on your side. How did you get them?"

"I was attacked."

"By what?"

Her interest confounds me. "I don't understand why it matters. I was hurt and now I'm healed. Thank you for the salve."

"The salve was a potent mixture of the same enchantment we spread on our apple seeds before we plant them in the ground to grow charm apples. What harmed you was not of our worlds." She swivels on the bench, shifting her knees toward me. "Your skin was split, but also your spirit. Only one beast I know of has that power, and the elves rarely speak of her."

A servant steps forward with a thick old book opened to a marked page. The queen runs her finger over the fade page and stops to read aloud. "'A beast hails from the nothingness between the stars, a craven and vicious monster, bred from the coldest night to disrupt the light. The cythrawl, known by Madrona's children as the Destroyer, dwells in the farthest recesses of Avelyn. She wormed her way in between the stitches as Eiocha sewed the worlds into the heavens with her song. The cythrawl is a venomous light-eater, a devourer of creation power—spirits. If bitten by a cythrawl, the poison will spread to the victim's heart. Only highly concentrated creation power may heal them.'"

She slams the book closed and stares at me. I have never explained that I can spirit jump. My ability is private, a skill I won't discuss with a room full of people.

Osric steps to my side. "Remember to be honest. Trust me, Evie. You can tell her the truth."

"I don't know what attacked me," I answer loudly and clearly. "A shadow came at me while I was spirit jumping from the Silver-Clouded Plain. I'd never encountered it before."

"The cythrawl is not something you encounter. She's something you run from. She's a kreacher, a corrupted creation." Queen Imelda picks up my music box from behind her on the piano bench. "We found this among your possessions. Where did you get it?"

"The Bard's shop."

The queen winds the lever, and the music starts. "An interesting selection."

"Do you know the song?"

She gives me a quizzical look, as if she doesn't understand why I took the box without knowing the tune it plays. "This is a sample of the everafter song, the very lullaby Eiocha played on her violin to stitch the worlds into the cloth of the eternities. Eiocha played this piece in another key to put the warrior giants to sleep and end the triad war. No one remembers that rendition of the tune, though, for that would be very dangerous." The queen holds the music box carefully in her palms as it plays. "I'm aware of my brother's intention to wake the warrior giants. Commander Asmer spoke with him, but he would not say why he wishes to do this."

"He wants to undo a wrong. Something to do with his—your—parents."

Queen Imelda holds down the turn lever of the music box, strangling the lullaby to silence. "He killed your family. Will you testify against him?"

I exchange a big-eyed glance with Osric. "Yes."

"Good." The queen sets down the music box. "My council has agreed to hold his trial tomorrow. Killian still has supporters. Their loyalty goes back a long time, but he has finally done something they cannot forgive him for. Elves are allies with the Land of the Living. An act against humans is an act against us."

"What about my sword and Nightingale?"

"Nightingale is locked away safely." Imelda sweeps her voluminous skirt behind her on the bench and faces the piano again. "Your sword and the infinity sandglass will be delivered to you upon the completion of the prince's trial and sentencing." She begins to play a slower, moodier song. I sense she has nothing more to say, and we have been dismissed, but I stay.

"Your Majesty, did you notice a scar on Markham's right forearm?"

"I haven't seen or spoken to my brother since he's arrived." She glances at Asmer, who shakes her head. "Why?"

"No reason," I mumble. "What will happen to Markham if he's found guilty? He cannot be executed."

"You mortals have a morbid preoccupation with death. I suppose I would, too, if I lived less than a century." She sighs tersely. "Death is too easy a punishment for destroying a world. Should Killian be found guilty, our judges will impose an equal punishment. For the safety of Avelyn, my brother will never leave our world again."

"But the Realm of Wyeth is looking for him. He's wanted for—"

"Everley, Killian will pay." Queen Imelda bows her head slightly, her diamond crown shifting forward and sparkling in the sunlight. "I swear by the Creator by whom my people swear. If I break my oath, may the land open to swallow me, the sea rise to drown me, and the moon fall upon me."

Her pledge was unnecessary, something that as queen, she doesn't owe me, a foreigner no less, and a human at that. I interrupt her playing one more time. "You know what he did to me, but I don't know what he did to you."

The queen strikes an aberrant chord and stills. "He left me." She waits for a breath and then resumes playing the same gloomy tune.

Commander Asmer ushers me into the corridor. My legs have turned to wax. This doesn't seem real. Markham will stand trial, and I will have my chance to tell everyone what he did to my family.

The commander leads Osric and me down a spiral stairway into the bowels of the manor. At a steel trapdoor, she pounds her foot and backs away. An eye slot opens in the door and shuts again. The latches click, and the trapdoor swings inward to reveal steep steps leading underground.

"This isn't eerie at all," I mutter.

"This is an oubliette," Asmer replies.

I have never heard that word, but as we descend farther down the stairs, I make out barred nooks containing detainees and realize "oubliette" is a fancy word for prison.

In the next cell, a blond woman with delicate features sits near the bars and tosses a bean sack up and down.

"Everley," she says, smirking. "You've finally made it."

"Harlow, I've wondered where you were. Enjoying yourself?"

Her eyes gleam, fiery yet cold. "I thought you got your sword back?"

"The elves have it for now."

She chuckles, a breathy sound brimming with spite. "It's a good thing your clock heart is attached to you, or you would have lost it by now too."

"How are you enjoying prison?" I counter. "You're looking haggard."

She rests her hands behind her head, her pose nonchalant. One would think this was her chateau. "I've been in worse places. The streets of Dorestand weren't a quaint little clock shop, but I always make do."

My teeth grip down hard. Harlow had a difficult childhood, I will give her that, but she let her life harden her, whereas Laverick, Claret, and Vevina had hope and relied on each other. Harlow depends on no one except Markham. When will she see him for what he is?

With nothing more to say, I continue down the block. Near the end of the row, I spot Neely and Redmond in one cell, and opposite them, Corentine and Mistral. All the giants are seated to avoid hitting their heads on the low ceiling. Asmer unlocks their cells. Neely beams at me and rises too fast, whacking the top of his head on the stone.

"Neely," I say. "Your foot is better."

"The surgeon healed it." He hauls me against him in a mighty hug. "My sisters told me what happened. You did well, Everley Donovan. You did well."

He sets me down, and I notice Jamison seated behind Redmond. I push past the giants and help him up. He's in need of a shave and clean clothes, but unharmed. He pulls me against him in a quick squeeze.

"How did you and Redmond get here?" I ask.

"The spriggans were guarding the skystalk on behalf of the elven queen. They brought us here after they caught us." He leans back to look at me. "The giantesses told me you caught Markham."

"I shot him. The elves seized him and took him captive."

One corner of his mouth turns up. "You did your part to put a stop to his wicked ways, Evie. More than your part."

I would feel happier had I turned him over to our queen, but Markham is no longer on the loose, and that's a feat worth celebrating. "Commander Asmer, where *is* the prince?"

She points at a big iron door down the hall. "He's never getting out of there."

The door is secured with so many bolts and locks that I lose count. But the commander must not know the prince very well, or she wouldn't make such a guarantee. Escaping is what Markham does best.

Chapter Seventeen

Dishes of colorful fruit and vegetables are set out on tables in the garden. The celebration of the capture of the prince is a strange way to follow up our imprisonment. On our walk from the oubliette to the garden, Osric explained that his queen held us captive in preparation for being witnesses in the trial, so we wouldn't flee. The dinner spread is magnificent. Gnomes push serving carts laden with pastries and cakes and place them opposite dishes of herb potatoes and savory pies. Redmond and Corentine nearly trip over one another to get to the custard tarts first. Mistral strolls after them, her arm through Neely's, basking in their reunion. Jamison bypasses the food to pour us glasses of whisky. We sip drinks as the sun sinks over the orchard.

"Queen Imelda asked me to testify," I say.

Jamison finishes his drink in one swallow. "She asked me too."

"I'm nervous."

"All you have to do is tell the truth."

"The truth has never made a difference before."

Jamison guides me to sit on the ledge of the fountain. The stone centerpiece, a sculpture of Eiocha cradling the seven worlds, trickles clear water into the base. "You're worried Killian will get away?"

I keep seeing him on top of the train car, daring me to shoot him. "Markham has never been bested, Jamison. It's unlike him to get caught, at least not intentionally."

"You think he wants to stand trial?"

I pull my shoulders up to my ears and hold them there before dropping them again. "I don't know."

The magenta sky reflects off the snowcapped mountain, turning the ivory peaks the same soft color. Jamison frowns at the stunning view. Is he thinking about his bargain with the sea hag? When will he tell me what Muriel showed him? I want to give him the chance to tell me on his own, or at least wait until we're alone to ask him.

"How long do you suppose we've been gone from home?" he ponders aloud.

"Time passes the same in every world except the Land Under the Wave."

"So, a couple of days," he concludes.

I can guess he's concerned about the happenings at home, about whether word of our nuptials was discovered. I wonder if the Fox and the Cat and the others can manage to stay in hiding until after the trial.

Across the way, Osric speaks to Dalyor. He touches the guard's shoulder, attentive and engaging. He's answering with words instead of his customary grunts. A pair of guards bring a bushel of green apples to the greenway behind the fountain. A couple of elves choose a piece of the fruit while others ready their bows and arrows. Jamison and I watch Osric join them and set an apple on his own head. Dalyor backs up and cocks an arrow in his bow.

"Osric isn't going to . . . ?"

Jamison answers, his voice low and bemused. "I think he is."

The giants lumber over to watch the game. Osric is so still I dare say he isn't breathing. Dalyor pulls back on the arrow and lets it fly. The arrowhead pierces the apple straight through and tosses it off Osric's head. Osric picks up the impaled fruit and takes a bite. The giants cheer and laugh.

Queen Imelda strides into the garden, and their laughter dies off. The air fills with a tenseness that puts an end to the festivities. The guards quit playing the game with their arrows and disperse. Imelda reclines in a red cushioned chair that the gnomes carried out for her and picks grapes off a platter.

A moment later, Commander Asmer announces that it's time to take the giants home by way of the infinity sandglass. Jamison and I go to give our farewells.

Corentine crosses her arms over her chest and glowers at me. "You could have told me the prince meant to wake our warrior ancestors."

"I didn't know if you would agree with him or not."

"Why would we want to repeat our ancestors' mistakes? We must look forward to a day when the curse is lifted." Corentine pulls a paper out of her pocket—Jamison's contract with the sea hag—and hands it to him. "I believe this is yours."

"Oh. Ah, thank you." He quickly tucks it away. "Where did you find it?"

"My sister and I took it off Everley."

I evade eye contact with Jamison; otherwise, I may not be able to stop myself from demanding he tell me what the sea hag showed him about his future. We will speak about this later, when we're alone, so he can explain in private why he would do something so stupid as to agree to give away a month of his life for fortune-telling.

Mistral thuds over and drapes a red wool shawl she knit over my shoulders. The color matches my gloves. "For you, dearie. Visit us at any time. You'll always be welcome in our home."

"It's beautiful, Mistral. Thank you."

Neely scoops me up in his constricting embrace. "I'll miss you, poppet. Will you miss me?"

"How could I not?" I croak.

He sets me down, and I spot Captain Redmond waiting off to the side. He tips his head at me in farewell, and I march over to him.

"What? No goodbye?"

"You appeared to have plenty already. I didn't want to overtax you."

I start to turn away, then stop. "Why did you collect clocks when they're forbidden in your world? Everyone else there despises them and what they stand for, yet you sought them out and brought them aboard your ship."

Redmond presses his lips together and glances down. "My father never thought Father Time was to blame for our banishment from Avelyn. He blamed our own kind."

"So, you love clocks because of him?"

"You could say so, or you could suppose that I'm not a very good giant." His eyes glint with mischief. "Or maybe I've learned the importance of time."

"Are you baiting me, Captain?"

"I wouldn't think of it, Ticker." He nudges me with his elbow, nearly knocking me over, and thuds away.

Commander Asmer escorts the giants out of the garden. Jamison and I wave farewell until they're out of sight. Then I scan for Osric, but he has left too. Coincidentally, or perhaps not coincidentally, so has Dalyor.

A string quartet files into the garden and sets up in front of the fountain.

The queen waves us over. "I've arranged a private recital for you." She lies back on her chaise and pops another grape into her mouth while the string players set up. "Lord Callahan, have you reconsidered my offer about selling your pianoforte?"

"I haven't, Your Majesty."

"Pity. Do you play?"

"I play the violin."

"Perhaps you can perform for me." The queen flourishes a hand, and the string quartet begins the everafter song.

Jamison falters a step, then walks to the fountain in a daze and sits, his attention fixated on the musicians. I join him and watch his total captivation with the haunting music. Queen Imelda shuts her eyes and hums along with the melody. Unlike the prior times I heard this song, I no longer find myself allured. The music feels sinister, infectious, almost parasitic with how it clings to the soul and coaxes an unnatural sense of relaxation, dulling one's awareness. I'm glad when the players reach the middle of the tune and trail off.

"I'm afraid that's all they know," Imelda says. "Exquisite, though, isn't it?"

I give a noncommittal nod. Jamison's attention remains far away, still tied up in the song.

"Are you all right, Lord Callahan?" asks the queen.

He doesn't respond. I touch his knee, and he jolts slightly.

"Thank you for the private recital," he says softly. I don't know where his thoughts have gone, but I grow impatient to speak to him alone.

"We've had a long day," I say, rising. "We should rest."

"Yes, of course." Imelda signals, and Commander Asmer reappears, returned from taking our giant friends home. "The commander will show you to your quarters."

We return inside and travel quietly through the hallways to our doorways. Jamison's room is next to mine. I loiter in the corridor outside, waiting for him to divulge something—anything—about his contract with the sea hag or his moment in the garden with the queen, but the commander also lingers. Giving up, I bid Jamison good night. He kisses me on the cheek and goes into his quarters.

Asmer motions at my doorframe. A white light flashes by her hand, then disappears. "You're free to move about the chateau," she says. "Don't bother looking for your sword. I cast an enchantment to hide it, and I can hear what you're doing from down the hall."

"An enchantment . . . ? You're also a sorceress?"

"We call ourselves enchantresses. Our powers are tied to the Land of Promise, which emanates more creation power than any other world." The commander leans against the wall and points out a marking of a hemlock tree on the floor by my door. "Our runes ward off evil. The symbols come from an ancient alphabet—"

"I've heard of the tree alphabet."

She cocks her head. "The enchantment I just removed was to prevent you from spirit jumping. Did it work?"

"I suppose so. How did the queen know I can spirit jump?"

"All Time Bearers can. Queen Imelda likes me to keep an eye on them for her."

"You've been watching me?"

Commander Asmer grins, then pushes away from the wall and strolls off.

I slide into my softly lit bedchamber and stare out the window for I don't know how long, my emotions and thoughts bouncing around. My mother used to say that when you don't know what to do, stay still until you do. But stillness isn't going to fix my apprehension. I kneel in the middle of the room, choosing a position of humility for the importance of what I'm about to do. Ideally, I would wait until I have my sword, but tomorrow's trial will not wait. What happens to Markham will affect everything. Our futures are tied.

My breaths match the cadence of my clock heart. Each ticktock softens as my spirit rises out of my body. My soul doesn't burst out as it once did, jumping to sky-high levels, but peels away little by little. I hover over myself, watching my body's quietness, and soar through the wall into Jamison's room.

He's lying in bed, gazing at the ceiling. I float over to him and drift down closer, my body parallel to his. His breath catches.

"Evie?"

I gaze into his eyes, seeking a connection, evidence that he can see me. He stares in my direction but doesn't fasten on me. Having him here, close yet disconnected, uncorks my fears.

"I saw you die," I whisper. "You were on a battlefield, alive one second and gone the next. Did Muriel show you? I want to ask you, but I'm afraid you'll say yes."

His lips part, his gaze pensive.

"I wanted to tell you about my spirit jumping, but I don't wish to worry you. You have so many responsibilities now. This should be my burden to bear."

He frowns, and our stares connect for a second. The moment is fleeting yet long enough for me to feel seen.

"Jamison?"

"I . . ." He shakes his head at himself and rolls over into his pillow. I hang over him as he drifts off to sleep.

I float up through the ceiling and into the night. Moonlight casts shadows into the orchards and vineyards. I float higher, the ground shrinking and shrinking below me, and search the heavens for a path to the Everwoods. My spirit remembers the way and quickly leads me there. I land on the pathway of daisy petals and hurry down the line of lighted globes, straight to the end.

No one else is around, no pixies, sprites, or gnomes. No Father Time either. I'm alone as I look into the final sphere.

Within the light plays a picture of these very surroundings. I see myself in the Everwoods, bleeding on the ground. Markham stands over me, holding a burning torch. He touches the torch to the lowest branch of the nearest elderwood tree. A fire ignites in the boughs and races upward and outward, leaping from treetop to treetop and raining down flames that set the undergrowth ablaze. Soon, the prince and I are ringed by an unstoppable inferno.

I stumble back. This cannot be what's to come. I bump into an elderwood tree and lay my palm against the velvety bark. The trees' collective voice, said by one, said by all, rumbles through my mind.

The forest will burn.

My clock heart spins faster. I succumb to its momentum and let my ticker lift me up and away from the Everwoods, into the heavens. Every burning star reminds me of the blinding flames I saw devouring the sacred grove of elderwoods, destroying creation power hungrily, mercilessly. I flee from them, from the light. Away from the constellations, the comets, the searing radiance of the cosmos. At last, the soft glow of my spirit is the only light I can see. I hold a hand over my spinning ticker and tarry in the expanse of nothing for so long I lose track of where I am, which direction I came from, how long I've lingered.

Shadows move in front of me. I reach for my sword and remember too late—I'm unarmed.

A long, rounded figure wriggles out of the night, slithering toward me. "Are you lost, little clock? Can I help you find your way?"

Her gravelly voice sends tremors through me. "I'm not lost. I'm on my way home."

"Home," the cythrawl hisses, winding her wormy body around me. "Why would you go back to your world where time wages a war against your body, barraging you with age and decay? Stay here with me where time cannot harm you."

Her tail hits my shoulder. She's so large and long, snakelike, I cannot discern her total length, but her outline resembles a mammoth worm. "I know who you are."

"Oh?" She sounds pleased. "Did they tell you I am older than the worlds? I have seen the beginning and will bear witness to the end."

"You're the Destroyer."

"We are all part creator, part destroyer. Eternity is not sameness and stagnation. Eternity is molding what once was into what will be." The cythrawl slides closer. "The end of your life is nearing. Will you let someone else decide when you are born, when you will die? Or will you stay here and choose for yourself what becomes of you?"

"All I will become if I stay is your next meal," I state.

"Such a death would hold more purpose than your corpse rotting away in the ground, feasted on by maggots. I can give your death meaning, little clock. Let me take away your worries and pains. No more time beating against you, wearing you down, tick by tock. Rest with me, and time will accost you no more."

The cythrawl lunges. I drop down beneath her coils, and she snaps after me. I dart right, then left, her jaws closing behind me. She cuts me off. I pull back, but she's behind me as well, her long, winding body encircling me.

Her teeth sink into my arm. Icy heat shoots through my spirit, so cold it burns. I pull free, cradling my throbbing wound, and spot a tiny beacon in the distance.

I fly toward the light. The cythrawl charges and chomps after me. My wound turns cold, then numb, the icy poison spreading out from the bite mark.

Up ahead, the beacon becomes a cluster of stars, and within them, the worlds of Avelyn. The cythrawl pursues me with relentless snaps and hungry growls. She nears the lights and shrinks away. I go faster toward them, and she falls behind.

My arm has lost all feeling, the numbness crawling toward my chest, toward my spinning clock heart. The Land of Promise comes into view. I dive, spiraling faster, picking up speed as I drop. My spirit pitches through the roof of the chateau and lands in my bedchamber.

My body kneels on the floor nearby, eyes closed. I drag my spirit across the carpet and roll over into myself. Gasping awake, I clutch my wounded arm and fall onto my side. My spirit brought the injury into my body. My arm bleeds, the flesh around the bite gray from decay.

The door flies open, and someone rushes in. Only when they bend over me do I see it's Asmer. But she is not a she. The commander no longer has a womanly body. All except her feminine face and long red hair is shaped like a man. She has a boxy upper body that tapers down to a square waist and a flatter chest and bottom.

Asmer leans over me and inspects my wound. "What did this?"

"Cythrawl," I wheeze.

She grabs the clumpy paste the surgeon used on my side off the bedside table and smears a handful over my bleeding arm. A warm, tingling sensation chases away the numbness and returns feeling. In seconds, the wound begins to close, and color returns to my skin.

Asmer sits back on her heels. "Not many souls survive an encounter with the cythrawl, especially not twice."

"I wish I felt lucky. How did you know I was injured?"

"I was with Her Majesty, and I felt a threat breach the protective enchantment over the chateau. I must have sensed the cythrawl's poison in you." Asmer lifts me to my feet and helps me lie down on the bed. Her female face on the male body feels less surprising the longer I look at her. "Would you like me to fetch Lord Callahan?"

"Let him rest. The salve is working."

"You shouldn't be alone tonight. The salve will take full effect by morning, then you should be out of danger of the venom reaching your heart."

I collapse into the pillows. "Send Osric. He'll come."

Asmer pulls the blankets up to my chin. "You must wonder why I look this way."

"You don't have to tell me."

"It isn't a secret. I was born male. That's who others saw, but that's not what's in my heart. Every morning when I wake up, I glamour myself. The charm wears off in the late hours of the evening." Asmer picks at a hangnail with rapt intensity. "As a human, you must think I'm strange."

"I think you should look however makes you happy." I glance down at myself. "I would glamour my clock heart if I could."

Asmer waves her hand over the front of me. "Like this?"

I pull aside the top of my shirt to reveal smooth, bare skin. My scar in the middle of my chest and my ticker are gone. Though I can still hear the timepiece ticking, tears of astonishment sting my eyes. I have not seen myself whole in so long I didn't think such a thing was possible.

"The glamour won't last long, but it feels good to look how you feel inside, doesn't it?" asks Asmer.

"It's remarkable. Thank you."

She steps back from the bed. "I'll send for Osric. Try to rest."

The commander goes, and I wipe at my tears. Markham's stains have been on me for so long I have forgotten what it's like to look at myself and not see him. To only see me.

Osric hurries into the room. His shirt is untucked and his hair mussed, as though he was woken from a deep sleep. "Asmer told me what happened. Evie, why would you do something so dangerous?"

I pull the blanket up to my chin. "I didn't mean to meet the cythrawl. I went to the Everwoods first, then I got scared. I walked to the end of my timeline to see my future."

Osric's eyes grow wide as he sits beside me. "And?"

"It was awful." I sniffle back my tears and sag against him. "What's the point of Markham's trial if he's bound to win?"

"Is that what you saw?"

"No, but his freedom was implied."

Osric rests his head against the headboard. "So that's it, then. The prince wins and we lose. Our fate is doomed."

"Yes. No. I don't know. The Evermore timeline showed me something I'd never seen before, something Father Time has never mentioned. How could the timeline be wrong?" Osric lapses into silence and drapes his arm over my shoulder. I lean against him and notice tiny lines around his eyes. More wrinkles? I sit up to look at him closer. "I haven't seen you eat a charm apple or drink cider since we've been here."

"I quit." He drops his chin shyly. "I was waiting for you to notice."

"Osric, that's grand!"

"Do you think so?" He turns his head from side to side to show me his profile. "Am I aging gracefully?"

"You're still unbelievably handsome, if that's what you mean. How did you quit? I thought you were depending on the charm apples to heal more quickly."

"I came home to replenish my supply, then thought about what you said and decided to let myself grow older. I've lived hundreds of years, and I'm proud of my age and wisdom. Asmer gave me cleansing tablets to ease my thirst if I have any cravings for another apple. Being home helps as well. Every creature who visits the Land of Promise reaps the rewards of its mighty creation power. I know you have a negative view of the humans working for elves, but many of your kind came to live here willingly to ease their ailments and illnesses."

"This place is a wonder," I admit. My clock heart turns smoother here, seamlessly moving time. "I'm proud of you for coming home, Osric."

"I'll find out tomorrow if it was the right choice." His tone turns apprehensive. "My parents will be at the trial."

"They will be glad to see you. You're their son." Markham's comment about living up to the memory of his father returns to my mind. Added to the queen's grudge against her brother, I'm still confused. "Why is Imelda upset with Killian for leaving? I thought she would be angrier about the other things he's done."

"You should ask her," Osric replies. "Imelda rides every morning. Meet her at the stables at dawn."

"I don't think she likes me very much."

"Imelda doesn't like anyone, except maybe Asmer."

I consider not saying anything, but Osric may already know. "Asmer told me she was born male."

"She has always been female at heart. The glamour charm reveals her true self." Osric shoves a pillow under my sore arm to prop it up, and I smell an unfamiliar cologne on him. Either he's wearing a new scent or the cologne isn't his.

"I saw you speaking to Dalyor," I say, watching his nonreaction from the corner of my eye. "Where did you two go?"

"I went to his practice. Dalyor sings tenor in the royal choir. We met there long ago when I was a member as well. He asked me to come along for old time's sake."

I was expecting something more scandalous, a passionate tryst in a garden shed perhaps. "It's sweet that you went to listen to him sing."

"My father was the royal minstrel for years, then he was promoted to royal choir conductor. I thought he might be there, but he retired while I was away."

"You must have inherited his talent for music. Why haven't I ever heard you sing?"

Osric nudges his foot against mine. "Do you use all *your* talents?"

He means his question lightly, but I respond in earnest. "As a lass, I wanted to explore the high seas like my father. But I love carving wood and creating things. I hoped to become a clockmaker like my uncle."

"Hoped? Evie, you can still dream."

"I cannot think beyond tomorrow."

"We must, or what's the point in fighting the prince?" Osric kisses the top of my head and pulls away. "Get some rest."

He takes a quilt and pillow over to the sofa. I adjust my bedcover and notice my ugly chest scar and clock heart are back again. Asmer's glamour has worn off, and the wound on my arm looks terrible. The salve is healing the bite mark, but the attack is still fresh in my mind.

"Osric?" I whisper. "Would you mind sleeping beside me?"

"If that will help you rest." He settles next to me and starts to turn down the lamp. I stiffen at the loss of light. He leaves the lamp shining dimly and opens his arm to me. I fit myself against his side and try to fall asleep, but my dread holds me awake.

Osric begins to sing softly in his native tongue. His rich tenor eases into me, soothing away my concerns about the morrow. I shut my eyes, exhaustion pulling me down into sleepiness, and his gentle music sweeps me away.

Chapter Eighteen

Queen Imelda's head snaps around as I enter the stables. "Everley, you're up early. I hope you slept well."

"I did, thank you, Your Majesty. May I join you on your ride?"

She hesitates, then bats a flippant hand. "If you wish. My stable hands will prepare you a horse. My mare Berceuse is tolerant of new riders."

Two spriggans teeter on their ropy legs to a stall—they're the stable hands? The long-faced, twiglike creatures are less intimidating when they aren't trying to trip me, but I still dislike them. The spriggans lead a white mare out of her stall. I blink fast, not believing what I'm seeing. Berceuse has an ashen diamond between her eyes, the same as the mare I was riding in my vision of the battlefield.

"Is something the matter?" asks the queen.

"No, no. She's a pretty mare."

"Meet me in the warm-up yard." Queen Imelda mounts her gray-speckled stallion and rides out of the stables.

My nerves jitter as the spriggans saddle the mare. I brush the diamond on her nose. So, the horse is real? This doesn't mean the battle I saw is imminent.

I launch into the saddle. All that's left of the cythrawl's bite is a bruise, but my arm is still sore. Taking up the reins, I ride Berceuse into the yard where the queen's stallion is walking laps. Another spriggan opens the gate, and my horse and I saunter out into the vineyard. The field hands are arriving for work, trolls and elves in sun hats and loose clothing. They touch each tree and bid it good morning.

"What are they doing?" I ask.

"These olive trees have been here for generations. They were planted around the vineyards as protection for the fragile grapevines. Some of them are a thousand years old. They greet them out of respect for their longevity."

Our horses trample over fallen grapes. The food has been left on the ground to spoil, something I rarely see in my world. Too many people would starve with such waste. "You could feed a lot of mouths with the fruit on the ground."

"We don't have enough hands to pick our vines clean," replies the queen. "In the days when we had human laborers, these vineyards and orchards were pristine. Now, whatever our field hands cannot get to falls off to rot." Imelda exhales swiftly, expelling all discussion of their crops. "You and Berceuse are well suited for one another. You've ridden before?"

"My father and older brothers taught me."

"I taught Killian how to ride. Along this trail, in fact." The queen ducks her head as she leads us between heavy-laden apple trees. "The first day we rode, he loved the freedom. He begged me not to go back. We had lessons and music practice yet to do, but we stayed out almost the whole day. My father was furious with us for wandering about unsupervised. As the oldest child and his heir, I was to blame. He took away my piano privileges for a year."

"A *year*?"

"I understand that's a long time for a human, but for elves, it's a fair punishment to deliver upon a disobedient child." Queen Imelda's voice softens. "Taking away my piano lessons was the same as taking away my favorite toy. Killian would play his violin close by me so I wouldn't miss my music as much. Our impromptu riding excursion is still the freest day I've had."

I shift in my saddle, her story about her and her brother sitting uneasily with me.

The vineyard ends, and we set down a wider dirt path. More daylight expands our view of the region to reveal crisp mountains lit with hazy morning light. Queen Imelda and I ride side by side through peach trees.

"Markham mentioned your parents to me," I say. "What happened to them?"

Her face falls, her tone dull. "Our parents, like many elderly elves, lost hold of their minds. After countless decades of living, an elf's memory often declines and our minds erode. It's a long, difficult, demoralizing death. Forgetting your family, not remembering your own name. Mother showed signs first, then Father. I had my duties as queen, so Killian cared for them. He was with Mother and Father so often it was as though I'd lost all three of them." Her lips turn downward. "Killian still has a loyal following. He's revered for his devotion to our parents and his musical talent."

I've never seen or heard Markham play any instrument, not even a single note on a pianoforte. "What did he play?"

"Everything. He's an exceptional musician, the greatest of his time. No instrument is beyond his skill, but his favorite to listen to and play is the violin." The queen's voice thickens with begrudging admiration or prideful jealousy. Maybe both. "Music is very important to elves. We rely on musicians, minstrels, choirs, and operas to tell our stories. We rejoice, mourn, teach, and worship through music. Killian made his audiences' souls sing with the call of life. In the eyes of our people, he could do no wrong."

"I'm sure your people revere you as well. You've been their ruler a long while."

"I made a misstep that they haven't forgiven me for. One of the disadvantages of living a long life is having more time to hold a grudge."

"May I ask what it was, Your Majesty?"

Imelda pulls back on her reins, stopping her horse. "Show me your clock heart, and I'll tell you."

"Pardon me?"

"I've a curiosity for your curiosity. So I will share my most private secret if you do the same for me."

I stop my horse and slowly undo my shirt buttons. I reveal my chest scar first and then pull aside the cloth to show her my ticker. "Killian gave me the one in the middle, which is why I need the clock for a heart."

"Impressive, Everley. Your resiliency is uncommon for a human." Imelda starts off on her mare again, leading me toward the outside of the orchard. "Now, for my secret. One day, when Killian and I were in our early adolescence, we snuck out at night to pick charm apples. The section of the orchard that grows them is under guard all day and night to deter thieves. We planned to draw the guard away by setting a small fire to the branches the gardener had trimmed off the olive trees and set in a burn pile. I lit the flame, and the guard came running. Killian and I took off for the orchard and stuffed our pockets full of the apples. Neither of us ate them, but their seeds always fascinated Killian. He would cut them out and store them in a vial he kept in his pocket. He liked carrying the potent creation power, 'like a god' he would say. We were returning to the chateau when we heard the shouts and saw the flames. The fire had jumped from the burn pile to the grass and spread to the olive trees. Three of our oldest, most precious trees perished."

Imelda stops before a wide gap in the line of olive trees. "Killian and I were found missing from our beds and pulled into our father's study for questioning. Killian had the idea to set the fire as a distraction, but I was the one who lit the flame. The blame of our escapade fell entirely on me. I was the heir, and future rulers are not allowed to make such reckless mistakes. The world heard about the terrible loss. Our people have thought less of me since."

"And your brother?"

"Killian's guilt was soon forgotten." Imelda sets our horses into a walk again, away from the olive trees. "My brother has done terrible things, and I take responsibility for what he's become. He's my kin."

"What will you do with Nightingale?"

"Destroy it. The elven council of justices won't allow me to touch the instrument yet, as it's evidence for the trial, but the threat must be eliminated."

I would think twice before destroying the heartwood of an elder-wood tree, but such a decision is for a queen to make, I suppose. "What do you plan to do with Harlow?"

"Miss Glaspey refused to answer questions about Killian. As his accomplice, her punishment could range from expulsion to execution. The decision depends on his proven guilt." We ride in silence toward the training yard. The queen pulls in front of me, blocking my way to the gate. "I won't relish this trial. Killian is my blood, but that won't prevent me from inflicting the punishment he deserves."

She rides ahead of me into the yard to complete laps to cool down her horse. I return to the stables and dismount the mare.

"Thank you for the ride, Berceuse," I say, patting her side. "I hope I never see you again. Believe me when I say that would be for the best."

I turn the mare over to the spriggan stable hand and stride outside. Jamison is standing by the fence around the training yard, watching the queen ride.

He passes me a large orange. "You missed breakfast."

"I appreciate it." I drop my gaze to the fruit in my hands, not at all hungry.

He jams his hands in his pockets and hazards a smile. "Would you like to go for a walk?"

"Yes." I slide my arm through his, and we take a pathway into the garden.

Jamison stares up at the crooked branches of the trees, the little green leaves dancing in the breeze. "This place is out of a storybook."

"I think the elves' secret to their long lives may be in their soil and sunshine."

"Maybe so. My knee doesn't hurt, and the food and water taste better. The call of life has a fullness unlike in any other world." Jamison directs me to a bench under a tree with a view of the vineyard and river, and we sit together. "I have news from home."

I set aside the orange and try to guess whether the news is good or bad. His tone gives nothing away.

"Osric visited Elderwood Manor before coming here," he says. "Secretary Winters sent me a letter, and the Fox and the Cat opened it."

"The secretary found proof of our marriage," I say, more a statement than a question. A statement I hope isn't true.

"He did. The captain's logbook did indeed include mention of our nuptials. Upon my return, I will be stripped of my title."

That is not all. His estates and wealth will be absorbed by the Progressive Ministry—the queen's preferred recipient of charitable donations—and he will never again be permitted to serve in the navy. Every part of this feels like a kick to the chest, yet he does not sound upset. "Did you know this yesterday?"

"Osric visited me while I was in the oubliette. I asked him not to say anything to you until we spoke. I want you to know that this changes nothing. Everything I said about our wedding vows before still stands. Let them have my title and wealth. I lost them once before and survived. I can do it again."

"Jamison, this is your entire life they're taking. Tell Winters I blackmailed you or put you under an enchantment."

He shakes his head. "I won't put the blame on you."

"I've lost my home and my family's legacy. I know what you're giving up. I cannot let you lose what you have left of your family." I rein in my anger, for I'm not upset at him. I'm angry with myself for thinking we could ever start over and build a life. "The queen and council already think I'm heinous. Tell them I enchanted you to marry me and you had no choice. The secretary will believe you. He's on your side."

Jamison sets his jaw. "I won't lie, Evie."

"Then you will lose everything!"

"I'm not losing anything I cannot live without. I thought I'd lost the most important things in my life when my father disowned me. I can survive without my fortune and manors, but I've seen my life without you, and that void was bigger and emptier than any title or wealth could fill." He takes his hands in mine, his grip firm, warm. "You're my wife, Everley Donovan. I thought I lost you once. I won't lose you again."

"But you love your homes. They're the places of your childhood. Your mother's heirlooms, your grandmother's library. Your father wanted you to have those things and pass them on to your children."

"I won't be happy with all those things if I can't share them with you." Jamison lifts the back of my hand to his lips and kisses it. "Embracing my duties to Elderwood Manor wasn't for myself. I wanted to give you a real home, a safe place."

"You did."

His expression turns pained. "I'm sorry I'm asking you to give up your home again."

"Jamison Callahan," I say in all seriousness, "I don't love you for your land or your title. You wanted to create a home, and you have. My home is with you." He pulls me in close against him. A tenseness runs through his body that soaks into mine. "About your contract with the sea hag . . . were you planning on telling me?"

"Muriel advised me not to, but now that you know, I will explain everything *after* the trial." His blue eyes bore into mine. "Let's get through today, and then I promise I will answer all your questions. I don't wish to hide anything from you, Evie."

I've waited two days already. Another few hours won't hurt.

Osric appears down the pathway. "There you are. Commander Asmer wants to prep you both for the trial."

"We'll be right there." Jamison rises and offers me his hand, pulling me to my feet. "My mother used to say that life is a blank storybook. You and I are only partially through our story, Evie. We have pages and pages yet to fill. Today is just one day in the many to come."

As we set off for the chateau, I think of the final image I saw on my timeline of the Everwoods burning. I wonder if we are indeed authoring our own story and how much of what's to come has already been decided.

Chapter Nineteen

Our cavalcade leaves the chateau at high noon. Jamison and I ride with Osric in our own carriage, staring out the windows at tidy rows of grapevines.

Markham was moved to the prison wagon as we were leaving. The door was shut before he spotted me, but I saw him shackled and unadorned. I also saw the field-workers kneel to him. Countless elves sank to their knees and removed their grass sun hats and laid them over their hearts.

I'm still sickened by the sight.

Queen Imelda warned me that the prince has supporters. I didn't think too much of her claim—until they kneeled. Now I think of nothing else.

A wind curls in through the window, carrying the perfume of the lavender meadows. The clean lines of intense purple stretch into the distance. Past the lavender are lemon and orange groves, and even blueberry fields.

"Osric, what *can't* elves grow on their land?" I ask. He sits across from Jamison and me, staring outside. "Osric?"

"Hmm?" His attention jumps to me. It's another moment before he realizes I'm waiting for an answer. "Sorry, Evie. I didn't hear you."

I leave my first question alone and ask another. "How long has it been since you've seen your parents?"

"Almost four hundred years. Do you think they've changed?"

He's certainly changing. Even since last night, Osric has aged. The slight lines around his eyes and mouth reflect an inner wisdom that was hidden before. He looks more distinguished, less perfect and untouchable. "A lot has happened since you left. Give them a chance to welcome you. They're still your parents."

"That's my concern." Osric pops a small white tablet into his mouth, the herbal remedy Asmer gave him to take as his body weens off of the charm apples. He's been eating them all morning. Osric mutters under his breath. "I cannot wait for this trial to end."

Nor can I.

The carriage takes us through blossoming poppy fields, then the land drops away to cliffs. We travel by the river, alongside a dramatic, craggy riverbed and past perpendicular limestone ravines. Commander Asmer and the elven guard ride on horseback between the carriages in single file down the narrow road. The cavalcade plods away from the snaking water, and the noise of the rushing river is replaced by music.

"Do I hear an orchestra?" Jamison asks.

"An opera," Osric corrects. "The music celebrates the creation of the worlds. Before we hold trials, this opera is performed to remind us of our sacred heritage and duties. After the opera is finished, attendees stay for the trial."

Jamison and I trade looks of astonishment.

"You think that's peculiar?" Osric asks. "Before an execution, the royal choir performs the creation-day song."

"Ironic," Jamison remarks. "And morbid."

I would listen to the elven choir sing a schoolhouse alphabet song if it ended in Markham's comeuppance. "What do you think will happen to the prince if he's found guilty?"

"I can think of only one suitable punishment for him." Osric's gaze chills. "His limbs should be severed from his body one by one to symbolize his excommunication from Avelyn."

"But his body will heal."

"Then he will be dismembered again and again as necessary."

I should be eager for Markham to be punished, even hungry for it, but a brutal sentencing feels excessive. We mustn't make a martyr out of him.

Our carriage rolls up to the rear of the outdoor theater. The flag of the Land of Promise, a crown of ivy wreathing a red apple, flutters above. We climb out of our carriage just as Queen Imelda alights from hers. She straightens her skirt and adjusts the sleeves of her all-black dress. The worshipful music from the opera swells in triumphant resolve, an elf warbling the lyrics to an aria in their native language. Commander Asmer rides her horse over to her ruler.

"Your Majesty, the opera company should conclude shortly."

"We'll wait here," Imelda replies.

The prison wagon rolls to a halt. Two guards open the back door and haul Markham out. He ducks his chin to shield his eyes from the sunshine. The elf prince has been stripped of his glamour charm. His pointy ears and nose give his wolfish appearance an even more feral look.

"My dearest queen, you look tired," he says, feigning concern. "Were you up late pacing the floor? I do hope I've caused you at least one sleepless night."

"Little Brother," she answers tightly, "I'd been told you haven't aged a day."

"Envious?"

"Oh, my, no." Imelda strides up to him, her eyes hard. "You revolt me for cheating time."

"We both know I didn't cheat time—I outsmarted it."

Imelda yanks up his sleeves one at a time and checks his skin. She twists his forearm to show me a scar. "Is this the one you asked about?"

"Yes," I say. "Weeks ago, I cut him and he bled."

Markham's expression turns murderous. My sword left a mark on him, but how? Why did this wound leave a scar when so many others haven't?

Imelda leans in close to his ear as though to whisper, then speaks at a normal volume so everyone can hear. "I will figure out how to make you bleed again, Brother. I intend to spend the rest of my life using your immortality against you."

He stares right past her at me. "Did Imelda tell you how our parents died?"

I draw back in surprise at his out-of-place question.

"How dare you mention Mother and Father," Imelda says. "You shame our family name."

"I've a long way to go before I'm as shameful as you," replies the prince.

"Show respect for your queen!" Asmer hits him over the head with her stave, and he stumbles to his knees. "Gag him."

The guards drag Markham back to the prison wagon and gag him.

"Please forgive this unpleasantness, and for Creator's sake, ignore his lies," Imelda says on a tired sigh. "Deflection is one of Killian's greatest weapons."

The opera within the theater crescendos to an epic finale. All the instruments blast the last few notes, building and building in volume and intensity, then sustaining the enormity of the sound to the last breath.

Applause follows, a groundswell of thunder. A guard opens the door to the backstage area, and the opera company files out. Queen Imelda boosts her chin, and with the applause still roaring, she glides onto the stage followed by her guard.

Osric motions for Jamison and me go to the door. We peer out at the enormous theater packed with elves, every seat full. Even the musicians have stayed in the orchestra pit, as though expecting their conductor to lead them in an encore. In a balcony overlooking the front of the house, the elven council is seated. Ancient looking, with their thin skin and white hair, the justices will officiate from above in their matching green robes.

The queen signals for us to step out onto the stage. The weight of thousands of stares lands on Jamison and me. I stand tall, my gait unwavering, and continue following Osric. Members of the audience whisper while others lift their noses and glare in contempt at us humans. Osric leads us to the far left stage, a couple dozen paces away from the queen and the justices who are high above in an elevated box overlooking the stage and theater.

Runes from the tree alphabet have been carved into the floor in a circle. A guard tells Jamison and me to stand in the middle. As I step inside, the heartwood of my clock heart warms. The power of the runes—symbols of oak trees—is believed to offer protection to those who stand within the circle.

A lute player hits a high note, silencing the audience. The sun beats down, squeezing perspiration from my back. The queen looks to the council. An elderly justice seated in the middle of her colleagues, slightly forward from the rest, nods, and the proceedings begin.

"Prince Killian has returned home," announces Imelda. The acoustics in the theater carry her voice far and wide, unnaturally so. Either the structure or stage has been enchanted to amplify voices. "This is not a joyful homecoming. Our prince must answer for egregious accusations against him. Guards, bring the prisoner forward."

Commander Asmer and another guard appear at the rear door with the prince. The audience bows their heads as Markham, bound and gagged, is led to the center of the stage. My nerves pop and rattle. I have dreamed of this moment for years, but I never imagined anyone attending his trial would treat him with awe and respect.

"The prince has been accused of violating and exploiting creation power for gain," Imelda continues. "As elves, we sanctify the longevity of life. Every creation has worth. The corruption or abuse of creation power is a dire offense. The charges against Prince Killian are as follows: manslaughter, assuming a false identity, blackmail, the obliteration of one of the seven worlds, and treason by way of plotting to usurp the Land of the Living, our protected territory. What say you to these charges, Your Majesty?"

Markham gazes into the crowd, his expression proud but trembling, displaying a sliver of vulnerability. "I'm innocent, Your Honors."

His plea is absurd. He has so much blood on his hands they should be dripping.

"The prince's plea has been noted," Imelda says. "In preparation for this trial, the council has listened to testimonies of creatures from all over the worlds who have witnessed the prince's various attacks and corruptions against Avelyn. The two main witnesses here today will conclude these testimonies."

"The justices will vote after the end of the trial," Osric whispers. "Should they tie six to six, Imelda will act as the deciding vote."

The austere justices reveal nothing about their opinion of the prince or us thus far. My insides roil, my anxiety rising to a simmer.

"First," says the queen, "we will hear from Everley Donovan of the Land of the Living. Please come forward to the witness box, Miss Donovan."

I wipe my sweaty palms against my trousers. The surreality of this moment seems to drag time to a halt. This is the day I have been waiting for. I cannot fail my family.

Jamison squeezes my elbow. "You can do this."

I'm not sure if I can, but I will try. Because, someday, when stories about the wicked prince of the elves are chronicled, I want it written that I did not shirk my duty to put him away.

Osric escorts me to the middle of the stage. Another circle of symbols—birch trees—is etched into the floor. I cannot recall their meaning. As I step into the center, the runes pulse with a soft glow that pushes into every cog of my heart.

"The witness circle coerces honest testimonies," says the main justice. "While standing in its bounds, you are held by truth. Do you accept these parameters, human?"

"I accept," I say.

"Then we shall commence. Queen Imelda will moderate these proceedings. You may start, Your Majesty."

"Thank you, Your Honor," Imelda replies, and launches into her first question. "Everley Donovan, were you present when Prince Killian trespassed into the Everwoods and infiltrated the Land of Youth?"

"Yes, I was in his expedition party."

"What was the condition of the world when you arrived?"

"The Land of Youth was locked in time. The only people we saw— soldiers; patrons; and their princess, Killian's wife, Amadara—had become wooden."

"How long were you there?"

"Time was stalled, so I cannot say for certain, but it cannot have been more than an hour. Our entrance into the world compromised the hold on time." The queen appears mildly displeased with my response, so I clarify. "Entering the Land of Youth was akin to walking across thin ice. Our presence disrupted the tear in time, which led to instability and, very quickly, the collapse of the world."

"Did the prince try to stop this collapse?"

"No. In fact, he trapped my husband and me and left us there to die while he left for the Land of the Living. We barely escaped."

Murmurs break out in the crowd.

"Thank you, Miss Donovan. You may leave the circle."

My brows turn down over my eyes. "That's all? But I didn't answer any questions about my family."

"Your testimony has been very helpful," the queen replies. "We've no more questions for you at this time. Please leave the circle."

Markham wears a smirk, little but sharp, like a thorn in my insole.

I address the justices. "Her Majesty said I would be given the chance to testify about my personal experiences with the prince."

"And you have," Imelda answers, her gaze darting to the council. Every one of the magistrates dons a scowl of irritation or impatience.

"Everley," Osric whispers, "you've done all you can."

"I haven't told the council what Markham did to my parents and siblings," I reply just as quietly. "This is why I'm here. This is why I've come all this way. I've waited for this trial since I was a child. I cannot step down, Osric."

"Miss Donovan." The councilwoman's stern announcement of my name booms through the theater. "The court orders you to leave the witness circle this instant. We require no further testimony from you. You are dismissed."

The circle of birch-tree runes around me pulses a glow. I open my mouth to speak, and an invisible tightness binds my tongue. My eyes gape as I clutch my throat. I can breathe, but my voice is strangled.

Osric gently clutches my arm. "Now that the council has dismissed you, the runes will prohibit you from speaking as long as you're in the witness circle. You're finished, Evie. I'm sorry, but your testimony is done."

But I'm not done. Not anywhere close.

I try to compel my voice to come out, but the binding spell grows tighter, choking me. I stumble out of the circle and gasp. My ability to breathe returns, but my tongue remains bound.

Markham stares ahead, his eyes laughing. Only after I cross the stage back to Jamison does the binding leave my mouth. I lean forward and rub my aching throat.

"Evie, what happened?" Jamison asks.

"I don't understand," I rasp, my tongue thick and heavy. "Imelda said the justices wanted to hear from me. I thought I would get to speak about what Markham did to my family."

Jamison speaks quietly, his voice lower in pitch than usual. "I knew she couldn't be trusted."

"Give her time," Osric replies. "The queen is focusing on Killian's most significant offenses because she wants a quick conviction."

"Are you saying the slaughter of Everley's family is insignificant?" Jamison asks.

"I'm saying be patient."

Queen Imelda's voice carries across the stage. "We will now hear testimony from Jamison Callahan, who also hails from the Land of the Living."

Jamison pulls upright and strides to the witness box. The birch-tree runes pulse a glow as he steps inside and faces the council.

The queen begins. "Jamison Callahan—"

"*Lord* Callahan."

The audience whispers. A smirk tugs at my lips. He's using his lord-of-the-manor voice.

"Pardon me?" asks Imelda.

"I'm the marquess of Arundel, a nobleman in my world, and that remarkable woman"—Jamison points at me—"is Lady Callahan, my wife. The court shall address her as such."

"The court has taken note of this correction," the queen replies dryly. "Lord Callahan, were you in attendance when Prince Killian trespassed into the Everwoods and entered the Land of Youth?"

"I was with the prince and Everley." Jamison stares coolly at the council of justices. "Everley's older brother Tavis was also with us. Prince Killian murdered him before our eyes."

Louder whispers sound in the audience.

"Lord Callahan!" snaps the councilwoman. "You must only answer the question asked of you. Queen Imelda, control your witness."

"My apologies, Your Honor." Queen Imelda hurries her interrogation along. "Lord Callahan, did the prince construct a tale known to humans as *The Legend of Princess Amadara*?"

"Yes."

"And did this elaborate fabrication conceal the prince's true identity as an elf?"

"The tale did that and more. Prince Killian wore a glamour charm to appear human so we would not suspect he wasn't of our world."

"I must remind you to answer the questions plainly," Imelda replies. "Or we will switch to yes-or-no replies. Is it true that you served under Prince Killian's command while he was posing as a human sailor in your queen's navy?"

"He was an admiral, but that wasn't good enough for him. The prince wanted more control, more access. He lied to earn our queen's trust, and she appointed Killian—"

"Prince Killian to you," interrupts the justice.

"He's not *my* prince," Jamison counters.

"That is true, Your Honors." Queen Imelda looks to them for how to address this statement.

The councilwoman purses her lips. "Proceed."

"Lord Callahan, please explain the nature of Prince Killian's assembly into your queen's royal navy."

"My queen appointed Killian as governor over a penal colony located on the cursed isle where the gates to the Everwoods are hidden."

"Did you know the prince was an elf?" asks Queen Imelda.

"No one did. As I said, he was hidden by a glamour charm. He wanted us to believe he was human so he could lie to us—and lie he did. He persuaded Everley's brother against her, against their father, who he murdered along with her mother and two siblings in a failed effort to steal the sword of Avelyn."

Outrage erupts across the theater, momentarily drowning him out. Markham dons his mask of martyrdom, a mixture of humility and devastation.

Jamison speaks louder, near to shouting. "Killian tried to murder Everley too. She was just seven years old at the time of her family's assassination. She has a clock heart now because of what he—"

"Lord Callahan is ordered to step down!" the lead councilwoman bellows.

Jamison opens his mouth. His throat bobs as he tries to speak. The noises in the crowd simmer down, the air fraught with tension.

Queen Imelda's face and neck are flushed. "This concludes the final witness testimony," she says. "Lord Callahan, you will step down."

"Why is she doing this, Osric?" I demand. "Why won't Imelda let us speak?"

"I fear the queen is under instructions from the council. They may have decided to hold Prince Killian accountable only for the offenses that adversely affect the Land of Promise or Avelyn as a whole. The death of your family was terrible, but our justices will not condemn their prince over the death of a few humans."

A wall of fury hits me. "You're saying their deaths *are* inconsequential."

"*I* don't think that." Osric speaks quickly, his breath hot and his tone sharp. "I would never think that."

"Your council does. I can tell by their sour expressions that they don't want us here. Jamison and I are nothing but servants to them, helpmates to pick their fruit and clean their manors."

"Evie, you must open your mind," Osric pleads. "Proving that Killian is responsible for the ruin of a world is our truest way of convicting him. Don't let Imelda's means of doing so blind you from what's happening here. Killian's punishment won't just be for the Land of Youth. He will pay for all the blood he's shed."

My family's blood is just a drop in a very large bucket, lost in a sea of silence.

Jamison returns to us and steps into the circle. The second he regains control over his tongue, he speaks. "I'm sorry, Evie. I tried. I tried to tell them."

"This isn't your fault," I say dully. The fault is mine. I naively thought that today would be the day of Markham's total reckoning.

The queen stands below the balcony of justices and quietly converses with them. Her hands move wildly, her motions adamant. Imelda shakes her head, and the lead justice glowers, as though she has asked Imelda to do something and Imelda refused. Imelda's shoulders slump, her arms go down, and she nods. The queen has lost whatever argument just ensued.

"The day isn't over yet," Osric utters, his tone dismal.

But Jamison and I were the final witnesses. No one else has come to testify.

Queen Imelda returns to face the audience. She smooths down the skirt of her black dress and squares her shoulders, her delicate chin held high. "The justices summon the accused to the witness circle. Prince Killian, please step forward."

Chapter Twenty

Markham steps into the witness circle, the chains around his wrists jangling. My clock heart ticks so violently each beat echoes across the open theater.

The prince's shoulders curl forward, his chin lowered in false humility. He's chosen to play the victim of his sister's cruelty and vindictiveness. According to the audience members' pity-filled gazes and sympathetic frowns, they believe his act.

"Why does Killian get to speak?" Jamison demands. His voice carries across the stage and out to the rest of the theater. "A world has been destroyed. The people of the Land of Youth have no voice. Why should he get one?"

Osric gestures for him to calm down. "The accused has the right to speak. You must stay quiet or they'll remove you from the stage."

"Maybe I should let them," Jamison says. "Then I wouldn't have to listen to whatever hogwash Killian is about to tell everyone. He hasn't even spoken yet, and I can already tell they believe him more than us."

All of the justices and countless members of the audience scowl at Jamison. I slide my hand into his and glare back at them.

"We've come this far," I say. "Let's see it through."

Jamison squeezes my hand, and together we stare out at the crowd.

"Prince Killian," starts the head councilwoman. "I will be addressing you during this portion of the trial." The justices must have determined

Imelda is unfit to interrogate her brother or thought it inappropriate given their blood tie. The queen stands off to the side, ready to jump in if given the chance. "Your Majesty, the council is troubled by the witness testimonies that have been given about you this day. We have many questions for you."

"I'll do my best to clarify, Your Honors," Markham replies.

"According to both humans' testimonies, you located the gate to the Everwoods on an isle in the Land of the Living. Is this true?"

"Yes, but I could not have done so without Everley Donovan's help. She guided our party and me to the gate."

The justice sits taller. "The *woman* led you to the Everwoods?"

"I couldn't find the way on my own. Miss Donovan, pardon me—Lady Callahan—offered to assist me, and I accepted."

"What's he doing?" I whisper.

Jamison boosts his chin. "Deflecting."

"What was your agreement with the human woman?" asks the justice.

Markham bows his head in regret. "She was to guide me to the Everwoods and into the Land of Youth. I warned her the world was unstable, but she insisted we go, and I was desperate to see my wife, Amadara."

I clench my teeth so hard my jaw aches. That isn't what happened on the expedition. Markham blackmailed me into helping him, and then, when we scaled the castle tower in the Land of Youth, he plunged my sword into Amadara's chest and cut out her heart.

"You went into the Everwoods, where only the elect may enter?" the councilwoman asks.

"All the portals leading into the Land of Youth were frozen, so we had to pass through the Everwoods to enter the world," explains the prince. "My wife and every other creature in the Land of Youth had turned to wood, just as Lady Callahan testified. Amadara herself was entombed in an elderwood tree. The castle was indefensible. The humans in my party preyed on the opportunity and stole coins from the collection plate in the chapel."

"That's not true," Jamison whispers hotly. "Why isn't the witness box binding his tongue? How is he able to lie?"

"He isn't lying." I shut my eyes, remembering our visit to the castle. "Laverick and Claret pinched coins from the chapel, and candlesticks, I think."

"That foul nidget," Osric swears. "The runes don't detect falsities when they're based on the truth."

Markham knows he can exaggerate all he wants. He will edge up to the line between truth and falsity, and his efforts are bearing fruit. The crowd is captivated. Their looks of sympathy nauseate me.

"Then what happened, Prince Killian?" prods the lead justice.

"I'm reticent to say, Your Honor."

"You must answer the question, Your Majesty."

Markham sends me an apologetic glance. "I'm sorry, Everley. I know this must hurt you, but I owe my people the truth." He puts on a fake brave front and speaks to the council again. "Lady Callahan's older brother, Tavis, harvested the heartwood from my wife. When I tried to stop him from taking it, he fought against me. My blade was true, and he fell by the sword. Everley sought revenge against me, so I left her and Lord Callahan in the Land of Youth and escaped to prevent the heartwood from falling into their hands."

"Liar!" I yell. "Tavis harvested the heartwood to help you, and you killed him!" I try to step out of the circle, but the protection runes knock me back.

"You see her fury?" Markham questions. "The woman will say anything to take her revenge. She has pursued me and harassed me and plotted against me for months."

"You murdered my brother," I growl.

"Silence," orders the councilwoman. "Lady Callahan, you may not speak out of turn again, or we will be forced to remove you from the trial."

Commander Asmer hustles over to me. "Everley, you need to be quiet."

"Markham is twisting the truth," Jamison replies. "He killed her brother."

Asmer drops her voice to a whisper. "Killian wants them to believe Everley is an impulsive, hotheaded woman. Her outbursts only give him credibility. Evie, do you understand?"

A large lump forms in my throat. I manage a nod, tears burning in my eyes. The commander warns Osric to keep me under control and then strides away.

"Your Honors," Markham says, becoming bolder every minute, "I suffered through this woman's and man's inaccurate testimonies without a word. Today they have shown you their bias against me. Emotions clearly cloud their judgment and compromise their renditions of the events in question."

Heads bob in agreement across the audience. Even a councilmember or two let their facade of impartiality slip to nod along.

Queen Imelda goes to stand beneath the council's box. "Your Honors, the prince mustn't be permitted to defame my witnesses. It's only fair that I be allowed to redirect this line of questioning and regain the confidence of the court."

The justices discuss this among themselves for a moment, and then the head councilwoman grants her permission.

The queen marches over to the testimony box and starts in on her witness. "Did you cause the destruction of the Land of Youth? Yes-or-no answers, please."

Markham struggles to speak, fighting against the power of the runes. "Nnnnnnnn—yes."

Everyone in the hall hushes.

"At the beginning of these proceedings, you uttered a plea of innocence," Imelda reminds him.

"If I may explain, I did indeed trespass through the Everwoods and enter the Land of Youth, but I only wanted to find my wife. Everything I did, including lying to the humans and disguising myself, was to see her again. I thought I could wake her and break the curse, but once I saw her, I knew that could never be so. Had I the chance to do it over again, I wouldn't have gone." Markham's eyes mist. "It was never my intention to collapse a world."

Jamison recoils in disgust. "How is he able to lie? He knew the Land of Youth would fall."

"I don't think he did," I reply. Markham couldn't have known for certain what would transpire when we entered that time-stalled world. Still, the consequences remain the same. The world has fallen, and the casualties of the collapse are countless.

Imelda chews the corner of her lip in consternation. Every attempt to trap the prince has led to more sympathy for him and less for us. I've no doubt the audience is convinced his real wrongdoing was his selfless need to see his wife again. The queen starts to walk away, then pivots on her heels. "Did you kill Princess Amadara?"

My ticker skips a beat. This is it, the question I've been waiting for.

Markham seeks approval from the council. "I thought I was on trial for the fall of a world?"

"This speaks to his charges of treason," Imelda explains.

"Answer the question, Your Majesty," says the councilwoman.

Markham clasps his bound hands together as if in prayer. "No, I did not kill my wife. She ended her life when she tore time."

"Weren't you angry with Amadara for hiding the Bard from you?" Imelda asks.

"I was upset with her for lying, but I loved her."

"You planted skyseeds, grew a skystalk, and infiltrated the Silver-Clouded Plain, all so you could find the Bard, who had been moved before Amadara's death, so you could locate Nightingale, wake the giants, and restart the triad war."

"Is there a question coming?" Markham asks tautly.

Queen Imelda stomps over to him, right up to the runes. "You violated our mandate to oversee the Land of the Living when you gave away jurisdiction of their seas to the merrow king in exchange for the location of the infinity sandglass, something you had no power to do. Why?"

"Because that's what our father would have done!" Markham yells. "Because that's what *you* should have done!"

Imelda recoils as though struck.

"Humans are lost without us," Markham proclaims. "They've forgotten their place. They need us to guide them, and we need them too. Our crops are rotting in our fields. We could bring them here, and they would be happier, healthier. Yes, Nightingale would have brought about a war. Yes, a battle would have been terrible, but in the end, the triad would have returned to their true order and all would be right again in Avelyn."

Markham breathes hard, his voice ringing out and echoing back. His unraveling should be more satisfying, but his reasoning, his justifications, is alarming, particularly because he's still in the witness box, still under the control of the runes.

This is what he believes. His truth is horrifying.

Imelda steps away from her brother, slightly dazed. "I'm finished, Your Honors."

The justices don't move, the lot of them frozen in astonishment. Markham has shown his true self. He wishes to defy the Creator, and the elves could never, ever side with him against the goddess.

The council holds a private discussion in their box. Imelda watches them intensely. I wish I could hear what they're saying, and yet I don't. Again, Markham has me standing on a hinge with him, and depending on which way the pathway bends, my future will unfold.

Jamison and Osric say nothing. The prince has lowered his chin, resuming a stance of meekness. Little noise comes from the audience. We are all held in this moment of waiting.

At last, after a million forevers, the head justice signals she's ready to speak.

"As elves, we have received a charge from the Creator to watch over not only our human brothers and sisters but every living creature. Our sacred responsibility to uphold creation power has led us to leave our portals and hearts open. However, we are disturbed by Lord and Lady Callahan's participation in the demise of one of Eiocha's precious worlds. We cannot rightly penalize our prince and excuse them. Therefore, we will reconvene in private to discuss a proper and just consequence for their involvement. Prince Killian will remain detained under our guard, and Lord and Lady Callahan are to stay in the Land of Promise until we have reached a decision. This trial is dismissed."

Cheers rise from the audience. Markham bows his head low, hiding what I am sure is a huge smirk. I have no binding on my tongue, yet I have lost the strength to speak.

"What does this mean?" Jamison asks.

"The council has yet to determine what actions should be taken against the prince," Osric answers solemnly, "and you and Everley."

"We did nothing wrong," Jamison counters, his tone incredulous. "Markham coerced us to go to the Everwoods. That was his mission."

"Regrettably, in offering your report, you admitted to many of the same offenses as the prince."

"We weren't on trial!" Jamison rejoins.

Osric grunts in agreement. "I'm sorry. I've been gone too long. I thought they would see Killian for the monster he is and condemn him. There's still a chance they will."

"What if they don't?" I whisper, my voice hollow.

"You aren't citizens of the Land of Promise. The justices will likely call for a short prison sentence or expulsion from our world."

The orchestra launches into an upbeat song. I forgot they were there. The tone of their tune borders on celebratory, grating at every raw nerve in my body. Osric may reserve hope and faith in his people, but I have none.

Imelda storms over to us, flushed and glistening from perspiration. "Your testimonies were a disgrace. My brother made you out to be fools."

"You didn't portray yourself well either, Your Majesty," Jamison retorts. "Nor did you prepare us for that abysmal questioning. You told us this trial would be Killian's reckoning. Justice is fair, but nothing about that was just."

"My brother is a brilliant manipulator." The queen sets her jaw, angry tears clouding her eyes. "You two will never understand the burden he is to me." She strides off to Commander Asmer, who is stationed at the door leading off the stage.

Noises of the audience departing and the orchestra music drift far away, as though I have tumbled down a tunnel. I stand at one end of the stage, and the prince is at the other. The sensation of being far away lingers as I watch two guards escort him offstage. I note how careful their grips are on him compared to when he was brought out. One of the elves is Dalyor. The prince exchanges words with him, and they share a split-second smile. I am too deadened from shock to ask if Osric noticed.

Jamison and I follow him to the carriage. Elves have gathered at the back of the theater for a view of their prince. They shout his name, clamoring for his attention. A line of guards holds them at bay. Markham steps onto the back of the wagon, getting higher up so they can see him, and waves. The crowd presses against the guards to get closer to their prince. He finishes waving and goes inside the wagon.

"He's going to get away," I mutter vacantly to myself. "They're going to set him free."

Osric grunts, more of a growl. "He will not go free. Killian has admitted to grievous crimes. The council could never look the other way."

Members of the mob seeking a view of the prince begin to dissipate. A voice calls out for Osric from the other side of the guard line, and an older married couple approaches. They are dressed in fine clothes, well groomed, and handsome. Osric goes to them, and the guard lets them pass to our side. The couple stands close together at a distance, scrutinizing him and us.

"Mother and Father," Osric says, his tone cautious. "How are you?"

"Well enough for two old elves," his mother replies. "You know these humans?"

Osric lifts his chin. "I do. They're my friends."

"They're deceivers." His father's tone is colder than his mother's. "Humans belong in our fields, not giving testimony against our prince."

Their discussion draws the attention of those around us. Dalyor steps away from the prison wagon and wanders closer to his friend.

Osric speaks slowly and annunciates clearly, as though seeking patience. "The prince spirited away your only daughter unto death."

"Brea knew better than to consort with the prince," his mother snaps. "She was brazen to tempt him."

Osric's face turns steely. "She was charmed by Killian, just as you have been."

"You should show respect for your prince," his father replies.

Osric guffaws, a broken, humorless sound. "To think I believed you might have changed."

"You shouldn't have come home," says his father. "Why couldn't you have just stayed away?" He wraps his arm around his wife and leads her back in the direction in which they came.

Osric tremors, on the verge of snapping into a rage or dissolving into tears. Dalyor and I reach for him at the same time. Osric pulls away from us both and bounds into our carriage.

Emily R. King

"I'll talk to him." I climb into the carriage after him. Osric wipes his eyes and stares at the floor. Jamison joins us, and the carriage begins to roll out with the cavalcade. "Your father shouldn't have said that. You've every right to be here. This is your home too."

"Why do they defend Killian over their daughter?" Jamison asks.

"My parents think he should have been king. For a time, Killian had so much outside support there was talk that his father would buck tradition and favor him over Imelda for the throne. After the king and queen passed away, the speculation lessened, but some of Killian's supporters still think Imelda is unfit to govern."

"Why?"

Osric sighs deeply and slumps in his bench. "I'm not certain you would understand."

"Give us a chance," Jamison replies.

Osric looks around the carriage for possible listening ears, then drops his voice to a whisper. "Queen Imelda . . . Queen Imelda killed her parents."

Chapter Twenty-One

Osric refuses to say anything else until we return to the chateau. He leads Jamison and me away from the manor, past the boxwood garden, and into the orchards. I am bursting by the time he sits on a bench overlooking trees full of shiny red charm apples. The second he notices them, he starts to sweat. I almost suggest we go elsewhere, but he starts in.

"What I tell you can never be shared."

Jamison and I both nod in agreement.

"Long ago, when Killian and I were friends—before I realized he was a supreme nidget—he confided in me about the night his parents passed away."

Jamison waits to see if I will take the last seat on the bench. I'm too restless to sit, so he does. "How did they die?" he asks.

"Prince Killian was performing with the royal choir in a special concert for Queen Thora and King Markham's six hundred and fiftieth wedding anniversary. It had rained for many days leading up to the show. The weather had cleared in time for everyone to come from far and wide to celebrate. Halfway through the second part, during the prince's performance with the choir, Queen Thora became tired. Imelda left early to see that her parents made it safely home. Mudslides had washed out the main road back to the chateau, so they took a lower road in the ravine by the river. The water was running high and fast that night. Their carriage tipped over on loose rocks and slid down the embankment into the rapids. Imelda escaped with a few scratches, but the king and queen . . ."

Osric picks up a fallen charm apple and rolls it in his hands. "Brea and I were at the theater when the news reached us. I had been singing in the choir. Killian was thanking my father, the choir director then, for our wonderful performances. My sister ran to tell them what happened. Killian left straightaway for the river and was there all night and day. The carriage driver was found alive but died hours later. The king's and queen's bodies were recovered four days after the accident."

"That's terrible," I say. "But how is Imelda to blame?"

"There was speculation as to how she was the only one who survived." Osric sounds somewhat suspicious himself, or at least uncertain. "Killian went into mourning. He blamed himself for not leaving the concert early with his parents. He hasn't played music since. When he finally emerged from his seclusion years later, he was harder, more serious . . . driven. He had a plan to smuggle charm apples to the Otherworlds to sell for profit and asked me to work with him. Before, his life revolved around music and spending time with his family. But since the king and queen died, most everything he's done has been to hurt Imelda."

"All because he blames her for their accident," Jamison concludes.

"Killian doesn't just blame her," Osric says. "He's convinced she killed them."

Imelda is spoiled, self-important, and dismissive, but a murderess? After being accused of hurting my own uncle, I'm hesitant to brand anyone such a thing without proof. "Why would Imelda want her parents gone? What did she gain? They were incapacitated by their failing health, so she was already ruling in their stead."

"That's where things get tricky." Osric stares at the apple in his hands. "Imelda and Killian were close in their childhood years. She was never as well liked as he was. His musical talent cast a shadow over hers, and then there was an incident where sacred trees were destroyed. But Imelda adored her brother, and Killian was devoted to her and their parents. When the king's and queen's minds began to fail, Markham took care of them without complaint."

I side-eye Osric. "You think he was a good son."

"I *know* he was a good son. Killian wasn't always bent and warped. He was a talented, bright, capable young prince with a brilliant future ahead of him. That's no excuse, of course."

"You pity him for losing his parents," Jamison says.

"Or something else?" I ask. "Why did Markham confide in you and ask you to start a smuggling racket with him?"

Osric clutches the charm apple harder, his color rising. "There was a time when I had lofty aspirations. I came to work at the royal family's chateau to manage their orchards and get noticed. Killian and I met. He was so damn charming."

He starts to lift the apple to his mouth, his focus far away.

"Osric," I say sternly, snatching the apple from his grasp. He jolts into awareness and wipes his hands on his trousers to erase the sensation of the apple from his hands. "You fancied Killian?"

"What do you want me to say, Evie? I was a young elf who, like many others, dreamed of falling in love with a handsome prince."

"But it's Killian!" I say, my nose wrinkling.

"It was a foolish fantasy. Nothing ever came of it. Killian favors females, and I . . . I moved on." Osric pops one of his remedy tablets into his mouth. "As I said, that was a long time ago."

"Then why are you defending him now? After all he's done? I don't care what he did. I only care that he's dangerous."

"Everley," Jamison says, his tone reasonable, "Osric isn't denying that Killian has done awful things."

I bite down on a groan. Jamison should take my side or, at the very least, be as repulsed as I am. Osric was taken in by Killian in more ways than one. I don't know if I can ever look at him in the same way. "I'm done listening to excuses. I don't care how musically talented Markham was or how good he was to his parents. He's a monster. Whether monsters are born or made doesn't change the fact that he is one."

I kick the apple at my foot, sending it rolling, and march off. Jamison and Osric call for me to come back, but I maintain a swift pace out of the garden via a leafy arbor and through a back door into the chateau.

Commander Asmer spots me stomping down the hall. "Everley, supper will be served—"

"I want my sword. The queen said I could have it back after the trial. I want it sent to my room *right now*." I continue into my chamber and slam the door.

Staying in this world was a foolish waste of time. Our friends are at home hiding from soldiers while we're waiting on a group of narrow-minded elves to punish a spoiled prince. The justices want to blame Jamison and me for the fall of a world, a world we barely spent any time in.

They're going to let him go. Maybe not now, but eventually he will weasel his way out of here. He's already begun to charm the guards and drum up support from his people. They will be glad to see him rise to power again, and he has all the time in the worlds. He only has to wait us out.

I cannot spend another day with him, or near him, or in the same building as him. He's always there, like a nightmare waiting for me to fall asleep so it can torment me.

The elves have failed, and I have nowhere else to turn.

Pressing a hand over my chest, I seek the power of my heart. *Father Time, I know you're close, and I know you're aware of everything that's happened. You and I need to have a conversation.*

My clock heart begins beating smoother, calmer, the bangs easing to soothing whispers. The scent of daisies billows in from behind me. I turn around and eye Father Time from his shiny top hat down to his polished shoes. He's leaning heavily against his cane, propped against it more than when we last met.

"Everley," he says by way of greeting, those solemn eyes devoid of any gladness at my summons, "you're speaking to us again."

"I need your help. Markham exaggerated during his testimony and confused the justices."

"Killian is a habitual creature."

"He's a menace. You told me once that my sword can stop him." At my reminder, Father Time's gaze intensifies. "I cut his arm before, and he bled. It left a scar. How do I do it again? Only this time, I'll make sure my aim is true."

"There is a way. You must be in spirit form when you wound him, and you must strike him down with the sword of Avelyn. No salve is powerful enough to heal a blow from the immortal sword when she and her victim are in spirit form."

I rock back on my heels. "Centurion *can* stop him."

"Centurion was her name when she was a star, before Eiocha forged her into a blade. She is immortal; thus, she can kill an immortal."

"Then I'll get my sword and the infinity sandglass, and I'll spirit jump with Markham and finish this once and for all." I hurry to the door.

"Merely ending Prince Killian will not correct the fracture in the timeline," Father Time says, halting me. "Certain measures must be taken to do both. We can tell you how to be rid of him *and* repair the timeline."

"Repair it in what way?"

"It would be as though Killian had never existed." Father Time's words pierce my soul, cutting down to the wick of what I desire. "Such a change has a cost. You would grow up never having known Prince Killian."

I arch a brow. "I'm not seeing the problem."

"You met Jamison and your friends while hunting for Markham. Without him to bring you together, you wouldn't have had reason to meet."

My chest pumps faster. I could be free of Markham. We all could. But I would not know Jamison, or Claret, or Laverick. I would never have met Osric or Radella. I wouldn't know Vevina, Dr. Huxley, or Quinn.

Father Time removes his hat and holds it over his cane. "Your friends would still have their lives, but you would not be in them. The sweetness and the bitterness of the life you have now would be gone, as though it never was. Such an attempt to repair a fracture in the timeline this immense has never been made. Every Time Bearer has held the power, but it is risky; thus none have tried. You must want to alter the timeline more than anything in all the worlds. If even the tiniest shred of yourself wishes for this life and this existence over Killian's departure, you would rend the timeline, and Avelyn would stall forever."

"So I give up everything or he wins?"

Father Time exhales. "This is your choice, Everley."

My arms drop, hanging loosely at my sides. "I cannot wish for none of this to have ever happened."

"Prince Killian will not stop," Father Time replies. "He will continue until he makes himself a god over all the worlds."

A picture flashes through my mind of the Everwoods burning. Of course, I want to prevent that from happening, but not by giving up this life. My uncle sacrificed his last years for me. I owe it to him to make the most of the life I've been given. "What if I don't correct the timeline? What if I just kill Markham with the sword?"

"Then Prince Killian would be gone, but his wake of pain would continue to ripple out into the eternities. The power of one soul, one life, is immense. Choices are made; consequences follow. This is the law of agency."

I'm not responsible for fixing Markham's choices, but I can make this world better by removing him from it. I throw open the door. The exit is blocked by chains of daisies hanging from the doorframe to the floor. I part the vines, and the flowers disintegrate, white petals drifting to the ground in a pile of silken snow.

Jamison stands on the other side of the door, my sword in hand and his eyes wide. He spots Father Time, hands me my sword, and steps inside. I shut the door behind him, and they stare at each other for so long I lose count of the seconds.

"You're Father Time," Jamison says at last. "You know me."

"We know you, Jamison Callahan." Father Time tips his head back and evaluates him shrewdly, without gentleness. "You have been waiting to speak with us."

"Do you care what happens to Everley?"

Father Time nods, a staid drop of his chin. "We care about every living spirit."

"But do you care for her more than you did Amadara? More than her father? More than her uncle?" Jamison takes a charged step toward him. "Do you care enough about Everley not to let her lose against Killian?"

Father Time sighs and bends over his cane. "Muriel showed you your future."

I frown back and forth between him and Jamison. "What did the sea hag show you?"

Neither replies.

"We cannot promise what you seek, Jamison," Father Time says. "But with time, all things are possible."

Jamison rests his fist over his chest. "Promise me that the last thing Muriel showed me will come true. Swear to me the sea hag was right about how this all ends."

I pull my sword in close to my hardening belly. "Jamison, what did Muriel see?"

Father Time returns Jamison's penetrating stare with his own. "Muriel warned you that she could not assure you what was to come. The future is uncertain."

"But you're Father Time," Jamison says, his desperation gnawing at my own. "You can promise me that Evie will be all right."

Father Time rubs his chin. "This is why we don't tamper in matters of the heart. Muriel was too loose with her projections."

"Then she was wrong?" Jamison presses.

Father Time offers him an apologetic half smile. "You have a stalwart heart, Jamison Callahan. You have proven time and again that you are steadfast and bold, admirable qualities that will continue to preserve you. Your heart will not fail you."

Jamison turns pensive, all his questions and demands spent.

Father Time bows to me and then puts his hat on. "Think on our words, Everley. We haven't much time." He stamps his cane against the floor twice in a row—*tick*tock—and disappears.

The scent of daisies remains. Jamison drops onto the edge of the bed and buries his face in his hands. I sit beside him and wait. An eternity passes, though, in all truth, it's probably just a few minutes until Jamison ends his silence.

"We were in the Land Under the Wave," he says, speaking through his hands. "You had left for Everblue to get your sword from the merrow king. Radella and I stayed behind with Muriel. The sea hag offered repeatedly to show me what was to come. I was hesitant to give up any time to pay her for her reading, so she promised she would take just a year from me."

"The contract said you exchanged a month for her prediction."

"Muriel asked to take a year from me before she saw that just over three months was all the time I had left." He lifts his misery-marked face from his hands. "She showed me things, flashes of scenes. I saw you and me returning to the Land Under the Wave, both of us climbing the skystalk, the two of us standing on a stage before thousands of elves. They were just pictures, but they felt real. Then she showed me a battlefield surrounded by fallen trees, and two armies charging each other. Giants and elves and men all fighting. Carnage."

I am too stunned to move or speak.

"You were leading the charge on a white mare, the same horse I saw you riding this morning. Our friends were falling by the sword. One by one, they were gone. I tried to fight my way to you, then a mace flew at me." Jamison's voice breaks. "I saw myself on the ground. I don't know how, but I was outside myself, looking down at my body. I was dying. Muriel said that would be my fate unless . . ."

"Unless what?"

He doesn't answer.

Muriel told him he had just over three months left to live. She took a month as payment for her fortune-telling, and that was more than a month ago. If she is right, that leaves Jamison just weeks.

He runs his tongue over his bottom teeth. "For a while, I thought the visions Muriel showed me were dreams. We were doing fine, you and I, at Elderwood Manor. I wanted the sea hag to be wrong. Then the things she showed me started to occur."

"Father Time didn't confirm her predictions."

"He didn't disagree with them either. And I know what I saw." Jamison covers his face with his hands again. I pull them down so he will look at me.

"Is that everything Muriel showed you?"

"There was one last picture." A bit of light returns to his countenance, a spark of hope. "You and I were in your uncle's clock shop. The store was full of clocks again, and you were smiling. I thought the scene was from the past, from the day we met, but everything else she showed me was of the future."

I release a breathy snort. "This has to be of the future. I didn't smile at you for a long time after we met."

"She never clarified the timing." Jamison shakes his head at himself, dismissing his doubts about the conflicting visions. "But I did see us in the clock shop. I did."

"Then there's hope."

Chapter Twenty-Two

Night has fallen. The hour has grown late, creeping toward a new day. I slip out of bed and pause. Jamison is sleeping on his stomach, one arm tucked under a pillow, the other strewn across the side where I just lay. He fell asleep in his clothes. The longer I watch him, the more I want to slide back in with him, so I quickly slip on my boots and collect my sword.

"Are you ready to finish this, Centurion?"

The sword warms in my hand. Father Time may call her by her new name, but Centurion was a star first. Just because she may have another purpose doesn't mean her past should be forgotten.

I tiptoe down the corridor. Someone is playing a lullaby on the pianoforte in the double parlor. I look in through the open door and freeze. Markham sits at the piano, his fingers flying over the ivory keys, a revolver on the bench beside him. The infinity sandglass and Nightingale are on a sofa table. Queen Imelda is tied to a chair, her crown askew and her hair hanging limply around her face. Asmer lies motionless on the floor by the draperied windows, her head bleeding, her stave beside her. No other guards are in sight.

"Come in, Everley," says Markham.

I hover in the doorway. "I was on the way to your cell. How . . . how did you get out?"

"A guard released me. He's a member of the royal choir and a huge admirer of my music. Back in the day, we performed together. He's felt unappreciated by my sister."

While Markham plays the quiet melody, he nods toward a pair of feet behind the piano that I didn't see before. I edge into the room, and a body, a gunshot wound in the chest, comes into sight—Dalyor.

He couldn't have released the prince. He's Osric's friend.

Yet there he is on the floor, dead.

Imelda's eyes are puffy from crying. Markham switches musical numbers to an eloquent melody. The prince's music has a finesse, a fluid constraint I've rarely heard, a refinement that comes from innate talent and a diligence to achieve perfection.

"It's been too long since I last performed," he says, swaying his head from side to side. "One never forgets the joy of creating beauty. You carve wooden creations, Evie. You understand how it feels to put your heart into something." He plays foreboding, sinister chords. "After my parents died, I swore I wouldn't create music again until I avenged them."

I sidestep farther into the room, keeping a distance from him while edging toward the queen. "Imelda, are you all right?"

Markham plays at a softer volume, background music. "Tell Everley what you did, Imelda."

"I don't know what you mean." She blows a loose strand of hair from her eyes. "You're angry about something long in the past."

He picks up the revolver and aims it at his sister. "I remember that night as well as if it were yesterday. Start with when you left the theater with Mother and Father."

Imelda's mouth bobs open. "You won't shoot me."

"I would, but this would be more effective." He aims the revolver at the commander still unmoving on the floor.

"Don't!" Imelda cries. "Killian, Asmer has done nothing to you."

"Someone told you about my relationship with Brea, and it wasn't one of my guards."

Imelda's lower lip trembles. "The night Mother and Father died was a tragedy. Our carriage tipping over was an accident."

He laughs and lowers the revolver to his lap. "Convenient, isn't it? Everyone else died in the accident, yet here you are."

Imelda drops her gaze. "I loved Mother and Father. Unlike you, I wasn't given time to mourn and disappear for years. I had to serve our people."

Markham rises from the pianoforte so fast the bench falls back. "Don't lie to me, Imelda! I spoke to the driver after he was pulled from the river. Before he died, he told me he had warned you the carriage wheel was loose. You ordered him to leave it alone."

"You're blaming me for the driver's incompetence?"

"You walked away from that accident with every hair on your head!" Markham strides to her and levels the barrel of the revolver at her temple.

I ready my sword. I have one strike, one lunge to land a blow, or I will be shot.

"Tell the truth," he says.

Imelda begins to cry. I dare not urge her to speak.

The prince presses the gun against her temple. "Three seconds. Everley's ticker will count down for us."

Tick . . .

Tock.

"Mother and Father could hardly remember their own names!" Imelda cries. "Their bodies were here, but the parents who raised us were gone."

He pushes her head to the side with the firearm's barrel. She cringes, crying harder. "You wanted them gone," he snarls.

"Their deaths were merciful. They were shells of who they once were. You spent all your time with them. You were too close to see what was happening. They hardly remembered you, and they completely forgot their own daughter."

Markham's hand trembles, rage pouring off him. "You were jealous they remembered me and not you."

"I was jealous of *them*! They had *you*!" Sobs overcome Imelda, tears rolling down her face. "I adored you, Killian. The day you were born, you gave me a greater purpose. I wasn't just to become a queen—I was your older sister. I was more than my royal title. I played with you, rode horses with you, lied for you. Then when Mother and Father began to lose their memories, you abandoned me. You gave them all your time and left me alone."

Markham rocks back in astonishment.

I shuffle closer to them, my sword at the ready. "You're brother and sister, Killian. Your parents wouldn't want you to harm her."

"You have no idea who our parents were," Markham snaps. "Everything I've done, I have done to honor their memory."

He leaves the revolver at his sister's head and whistles.

Harlow enters the room with Jamison, holding him at gunpoint. He surveys the room, his gaze latching on to the gun in Markham's hand, still aimed at the queen's head, and then landing on me. I could grab the sandglass, get a hold of Markham, and spirit jump us out of here, but I cannot outrun shots from his revolver.

"What did you do with the others?" I ask.

"Thanks to Dalyor's help, the rest of the guards—including our dear friend Osric—are locked in the oubliette. All it took was Dalyor holding their precious queen at gunpoint, and the guards acquiesced. You've gained in popularity, Sister. At least in your close circles." Markham strokes her hair away from her tearstained face. "Our father's greatest regret was letting our human laborers go. You weren't there for his final days, Imelda. You didn't hear him, didn't see the fire in his eyes. In between the moments when he would stare off at nothing for hours, he was lucid and more honest than ever. He warned me you were incapable of restoring order to Avelyn. He said you were weak."

"I believe all life is hallowed," Imelda rasps.

Markham straightens the crown atop her head. "You think everyone exists for you. Even my birth, my life, was to give you a greater purpose. But I'm not beholden to you. My life is mine."

Imelda's chin quivers. "I love you, Killian. I always have. You're my little brother."

He shifts in front of her, lowering the gun to her chest and pressing his lips to her forehead. "I never loved you like I loved them."

He fires.

Imelda's eyes expand, her chest blooming crimson. He catches her as she slumps forward and hugs her against him. "I held Mother and Father when I found them in the river," he whispers. "You shouldn't have done it, Imelda. You should have told me you were lonely."

"I'm sorry." She gasps. "You. Were. My. Everything."

"I know." He kisses her forehead and repeats, "I know." He rests his lips against his sister's skin, holding them there as her eyes go blank.

My sword arm gives way, my blade slowly dropping. Jamison gapes in astonishment, and Harlow . . . Harlow is grinning.

"Change comes through sacrifice." Markham pushes his sister back against the chair and rises. "Callahan, I believe you have something I need."

"My fist in your jaw?"

"Something much more powerful. I overheard you playing the everafter song the morning I visited your manor. For years, that song came to me in my dreams, but I could never hear the ending." Markham gestures at a quill and piece of sheet music on the table near Nightingale. "Write down the final measures of the song. I've written the rest."

Jamison doesn't move.

"He doesn't know the whole song," I say. "Tell him, Jamison. Tell him how it's been eluding you."

"He told you that to protect you," Markham replies. "He knows the song. Being around you, Time Bearer, has sharpened his awareness. He hears with spiritual ears."

"But he—"

"I was afraid to tell you, Evie," Jamison says. "This was my burden to bear. You had so many worries of your own already."

I said the same to him just last night about my spirit jumping when I was in his quarters . . . "You saw me last night in your room?"

His gaze searches my face, skimming over every feature with care. "No, but I would recognize your voice anywhere."

"You two warm my heart," Markham says with mock sweetness. He picks up the quill, strides to Jamison, and presses it into his hand. "Now, finish that composition and I'll be on my way."

Jamison stares back at him, unmoved. The prince waits another moment and then kicks him in his bad knee. Jamison pitches forward on a pained groan.

I swish my blade at the prince. "Touch him again, and I'll take off your head."

"Threaten him again, and I'll blow *your* head off," Harlow counters.

Markham lifts his revolver to Jamison's face and runs the barrels across his chin. When Jamison does not flinch away, the prince redirects his aim at me. "I will shoot her, Callahan."

"Please do," Harlow says.

"Go ahead." I hold myself firm, my feet planted. Dying for the good of Avelyn is a worthy death. It was my father's death. My uncle's death. If it was good enough for them, it's good enough for me.

Markham squeezes down on the trigger.

"All right!" Jamison replies, standing tall again. "I'll do it."

"You can't," I breathe.

"I cannot lose you. Trust me, Evie."

Jamison hobbles over to the sheet music and jots down the ending of the everafter song. My clock heart booms like thunder. Harlow smirks the whole time. At the finish, Jamison sets down the quill and steps away.

Markham skims the composition and grins. "Thank you, Callahan. You've been very helpful. For this, I'll let you live to see what becomes of your world."

He waves his revolver at the two of us, herding us into the corner. Harlow holds Jamison and me at gunpoint while Markham rolls up the composition and slips it into the violin case with Nightingale. Harlow takes several slow steps backward to him. They stand on either side of the infinity sandglass, and each sets a hand on the timepiece.

"See you on the battlefield, Evie." Markham salutes me with his revolver, then twists the dial on the sandglass. He and Harlow are whisked away.

I release a shudder I've been holding in, then run to Imelda and search her for signs of life. She's gone. Dalyor didn't make it either, but Asmer is breathing. I pat her cheeks and shake her awake. As I help her sit up, she sees her queen.

"Oh, no, no, no." Asmer crawls over to Imelda and kneels before her.

"The prince shot her and took Nightingale," I say.

Asmer sags where she sits, her head hanging between her knees. "He's not our prince. He's our king."

Markham has bathed another room in blood. More lives lost. More futures destroyed. And he isn't finished.

Jamison won't meet my gaze. Because I cannot decide which I am— more outraged than disappointed or more disappointed than outraged that he gave the prince the song—I settle for neither.

"I'm going after Markham."

"Everley," he says, "we're lucky he left us alive."

"Don't thank luck." Asmer raises her head bleakly. "Killian left you alive because he needs something from you."

Markham told me he wouldn't kill me or destroy the infinity sand-glass. It's insulting that he put me in the same category as a timepiece, but Asmer is right. I am a tool, and he's not done with me yet.

"Grand," I say. "I'm not done with him either."

"You aren't going alone," Jamison replies. His weight is on his good leg. He cuts a piece of cloth from a drapery and wraps his bad knee for support.

"You must stop Killian before he finishes playing the everafter song," Asmer says.

"I will," I promise. "Release Osric from the oubliette. Tell him we'll meet him at Elderwood Manor as soon as we can."

I stand back, facing the windows, and slice my sword across the air twice in a big X. At first, I see nothing, and then iridescent tears appear. My clock heart starts to spin. Centurion is proving herself to be much more than just a star or a sword. She's a lifesaver.

"That's a new trick," Jamison remarks.

"Let's hope it works." I take him by the hand and walk toward the windows, straight through the flimsy rainbow opening and into the dark.

The drop is long and filled with streams of light that fade away to crooked ashen shadows. We land deep in a coppice of sky-high trees. I willed my sword to bring us to the Black Forest, and here we are, standing on the mossy undergrowth in the thick, damp brush.

Jamison bends in half. "Every damn time."

I give him a moment to recover from his nausea and take in our bearings. Markham must be somewhere, but which direction? I aim my sword at the woods and turn in a circle, waiting for Centurion to signal which way to go.

"Evie," Jamison says, "I'm sorry. I didn't want to lose you."

I clench my teeth. Doesn't he realize he might lose me regardless? I suppose I *am* more outraged than disappointed, and until that changes, I'll hold my tongue to keep from saying something I'll regret.

Far off in the distance, a single note on a violin pierces the quiet. The hairs stand up on the top of my head, and my sword begins to vibrate. Markham is tuning his instrument.

"This way."

I run through the trees, leading with my sword. Jamison limps a little but keeps pace with me. The music begins, the strains of the everafter song—serious, somber, beckoning. If the song were a person, it would be an old hag singing an entrancing lullaby to her next victim.

Jamison lags behind as I tear through the woods.

"Keep going!" he says. "I'll be right behind you!"

I push myself harder. My clock heart rises in rhythm to meet my demands.

Music saturates the forest like a heavy mist, stirring up the air and awakening the trees. Branches sway and roots heave from the soil as the foliage comes alive in a maze of swinging boughs and rustling leaves. I leap over a rising root and catch my toe, tripping to the ground and tearing a hole through my red glove.

The land roars under me. Everything sways, but not because of wind. Something silent but strong pushes the branches, a power older than the worlds. I pull myself up and race onward.

Time, be on my side.

I feel a burst of vigor from my clock heart and sprint faster. The song is nearing its middle. The old hag has cast her enchantment on the forest, and this place of serenity has fallen wholly under her command.

Birds dart up into the predawn sky. The rising sun has begun to lighten the heavens to a soft gray. Little animals scurry from their burrows and skitter away from the roiling dirt and snapping roots. Boughs catch my cloak and hair. I untangle myself and tumble forward, narrowly avoiding falling in a snag of roots.

A gap lies in the trees ahead. I fight my way out and into a field.

Markham stands in the middle, playing the transcendent song on Nightingale, distending the air with a leaden pulse.

A gun goes off, the bullet whizzing past me. Harlow steps into my line of sight, positioning herself between him and me.

She keeps the revolver aimed at me and plants her feet. "Give me a reason to shoot you, Everley. I have four more shots, and I will empty them all into your gut."

"Stay out of this, Harlow." I step forward. She fires again, nearly hitting my boot.

"Three shots. Next time I won't miss."

"Yes, you will. Markham wants me alive."

Her eyes shoot daggers.

The music surpasses the portion of the song that's familiar to me, the part Jamison played and hummed, and continues into the final section.

"Harlow, step aside," I say. "Markham means to enslave humans. This is your world, and these are your people."

"*My* people?" Her face screws up in malice. "These people abandoned me when I lost my parents. I was forced to live on the streets and steal table scraps from rubbish bins and sell secrets for coin. Only Killian cared what became of me. Now I will sit on a throne at his side while *your* people serve me as their queen."

A soft glow radiates from Nightingale and spreads out, the texture granular, like sand pouring from an hourglass. The sand flows off the violin strings in delicate waves, threads of light that sweep out over the trees. The grains of light rain down on the forest, pattering to the ground where they shimmer, and soak into the dirt.

The ground shakes stronger. Dirt ruptures in heaving knolls, tearing up roots and toppling trees. I look for Jamison, but he still hasn't come out. A tree falls into the clearing, landing between me and Harlow with a crackling crash. I glance at Markham. Then the trees.

I run back into the forest.

The land is buckling, the ground rising in swells, showering me with dirt and leaves and twigs. I dodge big holes and blink filth from my eyes.

"Jamison!"

A tree starts to drop toward me. I jump and roll. Lying on my back, my sword tight in my grip, I gaze up at the trembling treetops. A massive hand bursts out of the ground near my head. I scream and crawl away as more hands and arms push out of the land.

"Everley!" Jamison calls.

"Over here!"

He clambers over a fallen tree, his face streaked with dirt and sweat. A hand shoots up from under the ground and scares him so badly he falls backward.

We sit on the ground across from each other. A giant pushes his head above the ground. Then one arm, then the next. The giant gasps and pulls his torso into the air.

Behind me, another giant unburies himself. We scramble to our feet, and Jamison crosses to me on the other side.

"Follow me," I say.

Both of us are already running.

We lunge over and around more giants rising from the land. More trees snap and crack as they fall over. We break out of the forest, and Jamison pulls up short, grabbing his knee. The binding came off while he was running.

"Killian is almost done playing the song," Jamison pants. "Go!"

I sprint across the field. The last of the golden sand flies from Nightingale into the forest. Harlow shoots at me. I zigzag away, her next shot closer.

Markham draws out the last note, his eyes closed in rapture. The sand hangs in the air a moment longer and evaporates.

A beat of silence swoops in, and everything falls quiet.

Then, from deep in the woods—a roar.

Figures emerge from the craggy sea of slashed flora. They start as silhouettes in the shadows and thud out into the clearing. The giants carry heavy maces, long poles, and battle-axes. I already see a few dozen of them, and more keep coming. They are bigger than those of the Silver-Clouded Plain. Over time, their kind must have lost height, or these beings were selected as their warriors because of their exceptional size.

One of them emerges ahead of the others and slams the end of his battle-axe into the ground, scaring away the last of the birds. He's a mammoth, easily twice the size of Sheriff Ramiel. This is the giant from the tapestry over Corentine's bed. Nothor, the leader of the warrior giants who attacked the Land of the Living centuries ago.

Jamison hunkers down behind a fallen tree. I run for the high grass and skid to my knees. Markham calmly puts Nightingale back in the case and picks up the infinity sandglass. Harlow stays close to his side, almost behind him.

"Who are you?" Nothor booms.

Markham lifts the infinity sandglass for him to see. "I am Killian Markham, helmsman to time and king of the Land of Promise. I have come to do what none other could or would. I have woken you and your warrior brothers from your unjust rest and brought you back to finish the mission you began nine hundred years ago, here on this forgotten battlefield."

The giant sniffs the air and curls his lip. "You're an elf."

"Much has changed while you've been asleep. The Land of the Living has become populated with humans again. After Eiocha put your army to sleep, she cursed your kind, locking them away in your world, and charged us elves to look after the humans and their land. I have worked for many centuries to wake your army so we may restore proper order to Avelyn."

Nothor sneers. "You speak too prettily, King. Elves are devious, lazy. You only want humans so they can do your work for you."

"As I said," Markham answers, forcing calm into his voice, "humans no longer serve us. Eiocha forbade us to retain them as our helpmates."

"Then who is that?" Nothor gestures at Harlow with his battle-axe. "She's human. I smelled her sweet blood from across the field."

Harlow steps out from Markham's shadow, braver with only one bullet left in her revolver than I would be against these warrior giants.

"Harlow is my queen. She is only half human." At his nod, Harlow waves a hand over herself, and her already stunning features peel away to reveal pointy ears, nose, and chin.

Harlow has been wearing a glamour charm? She's an elf?

"We woke you, and now we ask a favor in return," Markham says.

"What do you want from us, Elf King?" Nothor squints at them in distrust. He may be big and scary like the giants from my children's storybooks, but he is not stupid.

"Any humans who surrender will be mine. So you don't think this is a trick, I have a show of good faith. Your army must be hungry after centuries of hibernation. A village lies just east of here. Go. Feast. Replenish yourselves and return here by noon tomorrow so we may march on the city."

Nothor stomps closer to Markham and squints down at him, as though deciding whether he can be trusted. He lifts his foot and stomps down, crushing the violin case and instrument inside. The crunch of him smashing Nightingale into the ground is grisly, like bones crushing.

Nothor steps back, satisfied. "We have a bargain, Elf King."

The wind blows past me and continues their direction. Nothor's head turns my way. I press myself lower to the ground.

"I smell humans," the giant snarls.

Markham points. "Yes, the village is that way."

Nothor sniffs the air once more, then slams his battle-axe into the ground three times. "Soldiers, move out!"

By now, his army must be in the hundreds, all of them gathered behind him in the wreckage of the forest.

The giants march east, their footsteps vibrating across the land. I stay low as the rumbles from their departure fade, then pull myself up. Markham and Harlow have gone, swept away by the infinity sandglass. They left a disaster. The field is littered with debris from the forest—branches, bushes, leaves, sticks. I scale the largest tree trunk I can find near me to look out. As far as I can see, the Black Forest has been felled.

Jamison limps over and stares up at me from below.

"It's gone," I say. "The whole forest is in tatters."

"I know you don't want to hear this right now, but I have to tell you why I gave Killian the song." Jamison peers up at me, begging me to listen. "Muriel told me that for you and me to survive this together, I had to give Killian what he asked for. At first, I didn't know what that would be. Then the string quartet performed the everafter song, and something turned on inside my mind. I heard voices singing from the sky, like a divine choir serenading me from the heavens. My heart burned upon hearing the full piece of music, memorizing it forever, and I knew that as long as I gave Killian what he wanted, everything would be all right. Because, you see, the question I asked Muriel to show me, the one I had her look into the future to answer, was whether you and I would have a long, happy life together."

I slide back down the tree and land beside him. "How does this destruction help us? Wouldn't Markham waking the giants be detrimental to our future?"

"Sometimes to win, first you have to lose. That's what Muriel said when I asked her what Markham would want from me. I know this looks bleak—it *is* bleak—but this was a chance I had to take for us." He rests against the tree, shifting off his bad leg to give it a rest. "Muriel showed me how wonderful our future could be. As I told you, I saw the two of us together in the clock shop, but that isn't all. I left out the biggest part. Everley, we weren't alone. The city was celebrating the summer growing season in the streets. People were openly worshiping

Mother Madrona. Everything was different. Our whole lives were better; everyone was happier."

This is all well and good for the future, but what about right now? I pull away from Jamison. "We have to warn the villagers."

"We'll never get there ahead of the giants."

I pull off my torn glove and shove it into my pocket, leaving the other one on. "What would you have us do? The giants are out there. We cannot put them back to sleep. Nightingale was crushed."

"Then we fight and win. We end this war."

My belly pangs at the thought of the defenseless villagers. We cannot stand up to the giants on our own, but we can enlist help. "We need to speak with Queen Aislinn."

"You're a wanted criminal, Evie. The palace guards will have orders to kill you on the spot."

"We have to warn the army those giants are loose in Wyeth."

Jamison gives a panicked look.

"What?" I ask.

"One of the visions Muriel showed me was of a giant smashing apart Elderwood Manor. The image was so fleeting I'd forgotten."

The Fox and the Cat are watching over the manor still, and Osric is supposed to meet us there.

I lift my sword and slice a hole in the sky. "We need to get home."

Chapter Twenty-Three

We emerge from the portal into Jamison's study. No fire is burning in the hearth. Northern Wyeth is chilly even in the summer. The absence of flame-covered logs in the fireplace first thing in the morning sets me on edge.

I listen at the door while Jamison goes to the firearm cabinet. His small arsenal has been raided. He grabs a candlestick for light, and we creep into the corridor.

No sound comes from anywhere, and there's not a servant in sight. I start up the stairway. At the top, the echo of a door shutting sounds from down the corridor, from Jamison's room.

We tiptoe over squeaky floorboards and pause outside. Jamison twists the doorknob, pushing in, and we're greeted by the end of a musket.

"Everley?" Claret breathes, lowering the firearm.

Laverick sits in a chair by the window, another musket laid across her lap. She rushes over and grabs me up in a hug. "How did you get in the house?" she asks. "Did the soldiers see you?"

I look around. "Soldiers?"

Claret whistles toward the door. "Vevina, Alick, and Quinn are here. They came in from the coast earlier this morning. Forgive us being in your room, Jamison. We have the best view of the soldiers' blockade from up here."

"No need to apologize." Jamison peers out the window at the soldiers positioned at the far end of the carriageway.

"More soldiers are stationed out back and on each end of the manor," says Claret.

Jamison closes the curtains tight. "How long have they been here?"

"Since soon after Osric left us to go to the Land of Promise," Laverick replies. "We had to sneak the others in through the hidden passageway. All the servants left because they didn't feel safe."

Footfalls sound down the hallway. Quinn dashes into the room with her cat, Prince, in her arms. She sets down the feline and hugs Jamison. Alick comes in after her, a bandage around his head. He settles for patting my shoulder when he sees my filthy appearance.

Vevina enters and looks me up and down. "Hard day?"

"I'd rather not discuss it." I sink down on the bed to rest my feet. "Why aren't the three of you at the coast?"

"The merrows came. Those damn water vixens were singing off our shoreline last night. I thought I was dreaming until this one"—Vevina thumbs at Alick—"got out of bed. I had to knock him out so he couldn't go to them."

"The merrows?" I ask. "But Queen Imelda told them not to—"

"The queen is dead, Evie," Jamison says gently. "King Dorian must have known Killian intended to dethrone her, or he gambled and infiltrated our seas anyhow."

"We packed up our belongings and left for here," Vevina says. "Quinn tied Alick to the wagon until first light."

"Good thinking, Quinn," Jamison replies. Her cat rubs against his leg and purrs. He picks up Prince, pets his head, and passes him to the lass.

I go to the desk and jot down a few names on a piece of paper, then I pull off my filthy cloak. "I'm going to Dorestand. When Osric arrives, tell him to get to the Silver-Clouded Plain. He has to find Captain

Redmond and tell him to bring as many giants as he can by tomorrow morning."

Jamison fetches me a clean cloak. "You shouldn't go alone."

"I'm making a stop on the way for help. I'll return as quickly as possible."

Claret peeks out the window at the soldiers again. "How will you leave?"

I flourish my sword, cutting a portal into the air. Everyone except Jamison gasps. I wish I could stay behind to listen to him explain to our friends what I'm doing, but I step through the gossamer opening. Seconds later, I arrive in the Everwoods. A gnome sees me and ducks into his hollow under the tree. Sheathing my sword, I glance around at the sprites and pixies whizzing about.

"Radella?"

A blue light flies at me. Radella spins around and trills excitedly.

"I'm glad to see you too. I need your help. Will you come with me?"

She starts to nod, then stops and frowns.

"You're not allowed to leave?"

She nods once slowly.

"We'll see about that. Where's Father Time?"

She waves for me to follow her. I dash after her, in between trees, past a gurgling brook, and through a curtain of flowering vines into a thicket I have never been to before.

The elderwood trees are so massive they would dwarf the warrior giants. Father Time kneels among the roots of the largest tree of them all. The base of her trunk is wider than one of the giants' train cars, and some of the knobs on her exposed roots are taller than me. Immense branches, dense with satiny leaves, fill the sky. Around the base, the elderwood's velvety russet bark has begun to peel off in thick chunks.

"I gave them life," a woman whispers, "you gave them time, and Eiocha gave them worlds. Why are they discontent?"

"That's the way of mortality," Father Time answers. "Mortals rarely appreciate what they are given. They seek more. This is their greatest strength, and their greatest weakness."

"I am weary." The woman's croaky voice doesn't come from a person. She isn't a woman at all. She's the tree Father Time is kneeling before.

Radella flies ahead of me and perches on his top hat. I shuffle into his view.

Father Time pushes himself up with his cane. "Madrona, our knight has come."

I walk to the ancient elderwood and rest my hand on her trunk. Her anguish throbs up my arm. "What's wrong?"

"She's wounded. She has seven main root systems that extend to the worlds. The collapse of the Land of Youth has hurt her."

Another feeling emanates from the tree. "She's sad."

"And heartsick. The loss of the Black Forest pains her. Many of those trees were her friends." Father Time sits on a lower root. He looks so young yet moves like a frail old man.

"Are you sick too?" I ask.

He releases a measured breath. "The fracture in the timeline grows worse. It must be repaired."

"Bring the prince to the Everwoods," whispers Madrona. "End his life with the sword here, where all creation was born, and all the wrongs he committed will be righted and Avelyn will be whole again."

Her promises are unfathomable. "How?"

"'Should they die where they are born, they will die forever,'" Mother Madrona replies, reciting a decree I don't recognize. "This is not a fate a mother wishes for her child, but my son does not have a penitent heart. His life must be taken to spare others."

Radella flies to me and perches on my shoulder. Her closeness is the comfort I need to see this conversation out. "What will happen to him?" I ask.

"It would be as though he had never been born," replies Father Time. "His soul would go to the farthest part of the eternities. All that he did would no longer exist. His entire life would be erased. You would have the life that was meant for you, Everley."

My ticker spins, a continuous loop turning me around. "But you said I wouldn't have met Jamison and my friends without Markham."

"Killian's actions rippled throughout the worlds," Father Time answers. "His choices have touched everyone in your life. They would all benefit from this restoration. Deaths will be reversed, sorrows will be healed, pains will be forgotten. We would not recommend something so drastic if we saw another way."

I want to help Madrona and Father Time, but to give up Jamison and my friends? This choice is impossible. Either option is too painful to consider. "Markham says he's restoring the worlds to help humans fulfill our purpose as helpmates. Is that all we are? All we were made to be?"

"'Helpmate' is another name for human," Madrona rasps. "Humans are powerful leaders and protectors. You will only be beneath another if they convince you that's where you belong."

Father Time's solemn gaze pushes into mine. "You and Centurion can finish this. Your hearts are tied together. What becomes of you becomes of her."

"I want Radella at my side."

"Soon, we will send defenders of the Everwoods to aid you," he says. "She will lead their way."

Radella darts into the air, her wings fluttering eagerly to fly out.

I rest my hand upon Mother Madrona's velvet bark again. "Can you reopen the entry portals to the Silver-Clouded Plain? The giants have done remarkable things in seclusion, but they're running out of hope and feel forsaken."

"You have your father's heart," whispers Madrona. "Brogan visited me when he came to the Everwoods. He was everything I hoped humans would be."

I shut my eyes to collect myself. "I miss him."

"His spirit and the spirits of your family members rest with me. They are with you."

Father Time ambles to my side. He looks even more fragile than last time we met, alarmingly so. What will happen to my clock heart—to time everywhere—if his power continues to decline? He holds out a daisy, then tucks it behind my ear. "We will speak with Eiocha about reopening the exit portals from the Silver-Clouded Plain. Go. Prepare for war."

The portal drops me outside the palace into the middle of Dorestand within view of the onyx river reflecting the late-day sun. Cool, damp air pours off the water and presses upon me. I climb the front steps to the door and approach the two entry guards.

"Tell Queen Aislinn that Everley Donovan is here to see her."

"The queen doesn't take visitors," answers the first.

I open the top two buttons of my shirt. My shirt slides to the side, sunshine reflecting off the glass face of my ticker. I draw my sword from under my cloak. "Tell the queen the sorceress with the clock heart requests an audience."

The second guard pushes open the door. Leaving my blade aimed at the first, we pass through the entry hall.

I have not been to the palace since I was a little girl. My father brought me once when he was delivering maps of his most recent exploration. He was proud to serve his homeland. His success as an explorer was due in part to his loyalty to the realm. For all the queen's faults, she appreciated his service, which is probably why she dislikes me. My clock heart represents everything she stands against—the existence of power beyond her own.

The throne room is empty. Another guard sees us and rushes off the other way, presumably to sound the alarm.

"Where is the queen?" I demand of the one I hold at knifepoint.

"Her Omnipotence is in a council meeting."

"Take me to her. Quickly!"

I prod my sword at him. He leads me through an antechamber off the throne room, then down a corridor to a set of double doors. More guards run toward us from down the corridor. I kick the double doors open and enter the hall.

People rise from their chairs around the long table. The heads of the navy and the army are present, along with the treasurer, Secretary Winters, and the queen. Her Omnipotence has lost weight since I last saw her, when I decided against shooting her. Her thin face ages her. At the sight of me, her eyes flash in fury.

"Someone should teach your men to pay better attention to your wanted criminals," I say.

Secretary Winters sits back down in his chair. "We'll take that into consideration. Lady Callahan, please come in."

The palace guards burst into the room and aim their swords and crossbows at me.

"I mean no harm," I say, lowering my blade. "I bring urgent news from the north."

"Is Lord Callahan all right?" Winters asks.

"He's safe, for now."

Winters gestures at the guards. "Leave us."

"But, Secretary," the queen blusters, "she's a dangerous criminal."

"Yet she came into our hall and disturbed our meeting, risking herself to deliver news. We'll hear her out, and then we can arrest her." Winters leans back, too relaxed for someone who thinks I'm a sorceress.

Most of his comrades have yet to move. I seize this moment to address them.

"The prince of the Land of Promise—better known to you as Governor Killian Markham—has slayed his sister, Queen Imelda, and awakened the warrior giants that were sleeping under the Black Forest."

I must sound insane. Humans think the Otherworlds are a legend, just like the giants and elves and merrows. I thought the same for most of my life. Only recently did I come to believe in the Creator or Mother Madrona, and belief in the latter could get one hanged in Wyeth, thanks to our queen and her inability to share attention with more than one god.

"The army of giants has set upon an eastern village," I say. "They're man-eaters. The prince wants them to defeat our kind so he can enslave those of us who surrender, starting with our realm. You must deploy troops and send them northward to meet them."

Queen Aislinn paces away from the table in a haste of rustling satin and petticoats. "She's a sorceress! She should be hanged!"

"There's more," I say, speaking over her. "The merrows from the Land Under the Wave have invaded our seas. The legends are true. Merrows sing to lure men into the water and drown them for sport. No one along the coastlines is safe."

"Preposterous," scoffs the queen.

"Perhaps not," replies the admiral. "One of our ships was found abandoned at sea this morning. All the men are missing. We thought they had been taken by pirates."

"I'll speak with the merrows." I don't know yet how I will convince them to leave our world, but I will. "In return for my help, you will remove the watch guard from Lord Callahan's manor and turn your attention to the merrows and giants, or Wyeth will fall."

"You dare threaten us?" Queen Aislinn demands. "Your father would never disrespect the council."

"You will not speak of my father." I lean across the table toward the queen, my grip tight on my sword. "Anyone who knew Brogan Donovan remembers an honest, faithful husband and father. Don't trust me, trust the man who raised me. My parents were good people, and so was Holden O'Shea. I loved my uncle and could never hurt him. He's dead because of Killian Markham. All the pain you want to punish me for was caused by him."

A messenger hurries into the room and bows before the general. "Sir, we've received an urgent report from the north. Giants are attacking the northeastern villages. No word yet on how many casualties."

Several gazes fly to me.

"Is that all?" the general asks the messenger.

"No, sir, the Black Forest is gone."

"Gone?"

"Torn apart."

The general blusters out another inquiry. "Is there anything more?"

"I've news for the admiral," replies the messenger. "Reports are coming in from all along our coastlines. Husbands and sons are missing. Their wives and daughters recall hearing melodies in the middle of the night. Their men went out to investigate and haven't returned."

"Don't send any more men to the coast," I tell the admiral. "Bring in your fleet and evacuate the coastline until I tell you it's safe."

To my, and probably everyone else's, surprise, particularly the queen's, the admiral nods and the messenger rushes off to deliver the orders. The council begins talking all at once. I could slip out now, but I have one last issue to discuss.

"Secretary Winters, I require a word with you on the matter of my husband. Jamison only lied to protect me."

"He hid a sorceress," Queen Aislinn hisses.

"I'm no more a sorceress than you are a proper queen."

"You're a debased Child of Madrona!"

I remove the daisy from my hair and slam it down on the table. "Do not speak ill of the Mother of All or I will tell everyone the real reason you want Killian Markham found."

Queen Aislinn sets her jaw and sits down in her chair.

"I will turn myself in," I say. "After the merrows and giants are gone, I'll surrender. In return, you must pardon Jamison and all the names on this list. They're good people who were only helping me."

I pass the paper to the secretary. He opens the list of names: Laverick Driscoll, Claret Rees, Vevina Laurent, Dr. Alick Huxley, Quinn Huxley, and every servant of Elderwood Manor.

"Whose word do we have that you'll return?" snipes the queen.

"The word of a Donovan and an O'Shea." I back away from the table. "Deploy every man you can spare to the Black Forest by noon tomorrow."

"We cannot move our army by then," replies the general.

"Killian Markham murdered my family in cold blood. If your men aren't in place by that hour, he will slay yours as well. Don't be late."

I slash my sword at the sky, opening a portal, and take my leave.

Chapter Twenty-Four

None of the lights are on inside Elderwood Manor. The windows are as dark as the night that has fallen. I plod up the steps to the front door, keen to go inside and rest, brush my hair, exchange my stockings for clean ones, kiss Jamison, eat a meal, drink a glass of whisky, and shed some of the tension from my travels. I might even put on that silk robe.

Stopping on the stoop, my gladness to be home mingles with a sobering thought. I have lost all the homes I have had. Each one was taken away by the same person. I stare up at the manor, and resolve sets my jaw. Markham will not take away this one.

A thudding noise sounds nearby. I glance over my shoulder and go still, my clock heart skipping a beat. The soldiers have gone. I didn't think of it before, but it's too soon for them to have received an order from the general all the way in the city.

The thuds approach the manor. I back into the doorway and draw my sword.

A giant lumbers around the side of the house from the back, dragging a mace alongside him that rips up grass and gravel. I quietly open the door behind me with my free hand. The giant sniffs the air, and his head jerks toward the front of the house.

"Hello, rabbit."

I back into the manor and slam the door. Hurrying across the foyer, I call up the stairway. "Jamison? Laverick?"

Thudding comes closer, rattling the chandelier. I run up the stairs and down the corridor to Jamison's room. The place is empty.

More stomping shakes the house. A shadow fills the window and falls over me. "I can smell you, rabbit."

I sink to the floor and crawl for the door.

His mace crashes through the window. I scream and scramble out the door. In the hallway, I stay low on my hands and knees and start back to the stairwell. Windows smash behind me. The mace demolishes room after room that I pass. At the last room—my room—the giant's hand bursts through the window, stopping just shy of grabbing me.

I hunker in the stairwell, glass shards covering my clothes and hair. Nothing moves in the quiet except for my ticker.

The giant kicks the front door open. I scream as he shoves his big shoulders through, mangling the entryway as he pushes himself inside.

He straightens in the two-story-tall entry hall. From the top of the stairs, I am level with his face. Ropes of bushy hair hang about his hulking shoulders, his expression mangled in a ferocious sneer. My every instinct shouts at me to run.

I lift my sword at him. "Get out of my house."

"The sword of Avelyn," he rumbles.

"I'm the Time Bearer. The hallowed sword chose me."

The giant roars, rips the banister from the floor, and throws it at me. I duck as the banister crashes through the wall behind me.

"Father Time betrayed us!" he growls. "He defended the weakling humans that stole our world." The giant bares his big, square teeth. "So we will eat you like the scared little rabbit you are."

"I'm not running." I slash the sky between us in big, wide arcs.

The giant swipes at me, and his arm goes through the portal.

"What is this?" he growls.

I run down the stairs and cut more arcs between us, closer to the floor. The giant pulls his arms out of the portal and chuckles. "Stupid rabbit."

He steps forward, and his foot goes into the opening of the portal. He teeters half in our world and half in the portal while I slide behind him.

"You belong in a pile of rubbish," I say. "I hope you like the pixies' treasure trove."

I stab the sword into the heel of his foot. He howls and pitches forward, falling through the portal. One moment, he's here, and the next, he's gone.

My hands are covered in scratches. I sink against the wall, winded. Jamison appears at the front door, squinting into the shadows and aiming his musket inside.

"It's me," I say.

"Evie?" He lowers his firearm and maneuvers around broken glass and wood. "I heard screaming—and roars."

The manor will need repairs, but our home is still standing. "I had to show an uninvited guest the door. Where is everyone?"

"We needed to move. The manor is too big of a target. Even the soldiers abandoned their posts. The giants are all over the countryside. I was keeping an eye out for you, but apparently not a close enough one. Come on."

Jamison lifts the musket to his shoulder. We check that our path is clear outside and then dash across the greenway. He directs me away from the carriageway and the manor, and down to a corner of the property I haven't been to before. Through the leafy trees, a pond glimmers in the moonlight. Crickets chirp in chorus, tucked in beds of grass, and an owl hoots from somewhere in the treetops. We turn away from the water and head into the brushwood. A wooden shack with a sod roof is hidden in the foliage. Jamison knocks three times in quick succession, then twice slowly.

Alick yanks the door open. He lowers his pistol and lets us in.

Everyone is crammed into the small space, all of them except Quinn carrying a loaded firearm. Claret and Laverick are together, and across the room, Vevina sits with Quinn and the lass's cat, Prince.

"What is this place?" I ask.

"My father's hunting cabin," Jamison replies. "It hasn't been used in decades."

"It smells like old potatoes," Quinn mutters.

Jamison pulls up an empty ammunition crate and sets it out for me. I don't get the chance to sit. Alick notices the scratches on my hands and begins cleaning them with a cloth and a bottle of whisky. He tends to me while Jamison informs me about what I've missed.

"Osric has come and gone. He wasn't optimistic about convincing Neely and Mundy to join the battle, but he went anyway. He said he would meet us outside the Black Forest tomorrow at noon. How was your visit to the palace?"

"Queen Aislinn was her usual delightful self, but the council was more receptive than I anticipated. They should be sending troops, but it depends on how quickly they can get here. I made them a promise, so I have one more place to go tonight." Before Jamison can offer to come along, I hedge, "I need female volunteers."

Quinn's hand shoots up. "Me. I'll go. Take me, Evie."

"I don't know," I say. "This will be dangerous, Quinn."

Alick finishes wrapping my hand with a bandage. "What's this about, Everley? Where are you going?"

"I need to speak with the merrows. I told the council I would send them back to where they belong."

Claret sinks lower in her seat.

"I'm sorry, Evie," says Laverick, sliding her arm around Claret. "We're not going with you this time either."

"No," the Cat replies. "I want to go."

"I don't think that's a good idea." Laverick touches her knee in an offer of support. "I know you want to put what happened with the merrows behind you, but it may be too soon."

"I'm tired of being afraid. Even the pond out there frightens me. I don't want to be fearful of water for the rest of my life." Claret pushes to her feet. "I want to do this, Lavey. I *need* to do this."

Laverick's gaze darts across the cabin to Vevina. "Are you going? The three of us should stay together."

Vevina gives a look of surprise, and her lips slide upward. "I wouldn't let my darlings go without me."

"Now I *have* to go!" Quinn exclaims, setting down her cat and rising. "You cannot let me be the only woman left behind."

I open my mouth to object that we aren't leaving a woman behind, but Quinn isn't a lass any longer. She has grown up right before my eyes. "All right, Quinn. You can come, but I'm going to need the pearl brooch back."

The ladies check their firearms and hike up their petticoats for travel.

Jamison pulls me aside, over to the corner. "Do you think now is the right time to go off and do this?"

"Now is the only time." I kiss his cheek. "We'll be prompt."

I face the middle of the room and strike out with my blade several times. Lines shimmer where I cut slits, more visible in the dim cabin than in daylight. I extend my hand to Quinn, and we link hands. The rest of the women join us, the five of us forming a chain. They tense for the jump, but no one balks as I lead us into the portal.

We land hand in hand. I glance down the row of women. Quinn's eyes are wide with wonder. Vevina has hers shut tight, and the Fox and the Cat are surveying our surroundings. A silver trail of moonlight shimmers across the inky sea. We let go of each other, except for Vevina, whose grip remains firm on Laverick's.

"My hand, Vevina," she says.

"We're here already?" Vevina pats the side of her short hair, collecting herself. "Is that all portal jumping is? I was expecting more fanfare. Sliding down rainbows or riding on comets."

"Maybe next time," I say. "Let's spread out."

The women venture down the rocky shoreline past piles of seaweed and mounds of driftwood. I climb onto a rock raised over the tide line and scan the watery horizon.

"Now what?" Vevina asks.

"Shh," says Quinn. "Do you hear that?"

A merrow serenades the night, her enchanting melody meant to summon us to slip into the sea for a deadly swim. Whereas Jamison and Alick would be waist deep in the waves by now, women require more than one merrow's voice for their song to persuade us into the water. I spot the creature singing just off the craggy rocks. She side-winds closer, her body from her chin down concealed below the surface.

"We wish to speak to Princess Nerina," I say.

"My princess isn't here," the merrow replies. "But you can come for a swim with me. The water's cool and welcoming."

Laverick levels her pistol at the merrow. "Go get your snotty little princess or I will shoot you in the gills."

"Vicious beast," snaps the merrow.

"You've no idea," retorts the Fox. "Your kind enslaved my companion. Be glad we need you or you'd be a floating corpse already."

The merrow hisses and dives underwater.

"We have pearls!" I call after her. "Tell Nerina I'll wait!"

All of us stand poised on the shoreline for several minutes, scouring the water for movement or any sign of the merrow's return. Time chugs onward in my chest. Maybe this won't work. Maybe this wasn't the most ideal time to come. Maybe reasoning with a merrow is lunacy.

A head rises in the water near my rock. Just as I hoped, the merrow princess cannot resist pearls.

"Hello, Nerina," I say, crouching down closer to the surface. "Remember me?"

"Do I remember you?" Her voice arches to a screech. "I was stuck in your wretched body for a whole night. Have you fixed that pathetic clock heart of yours?"

"As if you care."

She feigns a yawn. "What do you want, woman? I have men to summon."

Quinn lifts the pearl-and-diamond shell brooch above her head so the merrow can see it. The princess's eyes glitter hungrily.

"I want you to deliver a message to your father," I say. "Tell King Dorian to evacuate your kind from our world and leave us alone."

"You don't tell the merrow king what to do," Nerina rejoins.

I lift my sword for her to see. "Your father returned the sword of Avelyn to me because he sensed Avelyn was bound for war. Prince Killian has dethroned his sister, Queen Imelda, and awakened the ancient giant warriors from the triad war. The Land of the Living is under attack."

"Are you fishing for sympathy?"

"I expect your caution. This turmoil will only worsen, especially if the giants are successful in usurping our world. King Dorian would be wise to stay far away."

"We aren't threatened by your war," the princess says proudly. "We merrows can summon giants into the water the same as your men."

"Not these giants. They're twenty feet tall and mean as sin. They would snap your neck and slide you down their throat like a sardine." The princess narrows her eyes. "Above all else, your father longs for more time with his deceased wife. I cannot give him that, but I can send him away with his daughters where you will be safe and far away from Eiocha's wrath."

"You don't belong here," Claret says, her pistol steady on the princess. She bites her lower lip to hide the slight tremor. "Leave us alone."

Princess Nerina bares her teeth, her sharp canines and pointy ears eerily inhuman on her mostly human face. "Don't threaten me, woman."

I take the brooch from Quinn and dangle it over the water. "This belonged to a powerful marchioness. If you don't want it, I'll just put it in my—"

"Fine," says Nerina. "But I cannot make any promises. My father thinks for himself. He will do what's best for our kind."

"That's all I ask." King Dorian's daughters are his most precious treasure. I doubt he will disregard my warning.

I drop the brooch into the waves. Princess Nerina dives under and comes up again, clutching it to her chest. Her expression transforms into an ugly grin, then she swims off, splashing us with a slap of her tail.

"She's a darling," Vevina drawls, wiping off her wet cheeks. "Is she always so well mannered?"

"Do you think the king will listen to you?" Quinn asks.

I sheathe my sword. "I don't know, but at least we've bought us some time."

Claret reaches for Laverick's hand, then Vevina's. The three of them stand linked together and watch the princess swim out to sea. Quinn runs at them and jumps on Vevina's back. Laverick picks up a long, skinny piece of driftwood and pokes the lass on the bottom. In seconds, they all have sticks in their hands and are swinging them around like sparring swords. I stroll over and watch Claret and Laverick dance around each other, teaching Quinn swordplay tips.

Vevina comes to stand beside me. "The Fox and the Cat haven't lost their touch."

"They survived the streets because of you, because of each other."

"And we will survive this as well. Are you ready?"

I link my arm through Vevina's and smile. "Let's give them another moment."

It's another hour before everyone settles down in the cabin. No giants have been heard or seen or felt since our visitor surprised me at the manor. They must be resting up for the battle tomorrow. We should be doing the same, but I'm like a mechanical bird in a music box, chirping as my gears spin and spin.

"Vevina," Alick asks from where he sits in the corner. "Would you trim my hair, please? I'd like to look myself tomorrow."

She rises from where she was resting near the Fox and the Cat and goes to him. Her hand trails across his shoulder and caresses the long hair by his neck. "How short would you like it?"

"The length it was when we first met."

Jamison makes eyes at me and nods at the door. We slip outside into the mild night and fill our lungs with country air.

"This way," I say, tugging him along. "I have something to show you."

We go toward the pond and follow the marshy bank to the other side. Across the water is a freshly whitewashed gazebo.

"How did you . . . ?" Jamison hurries along the path. I trail him around the fishpond to the outdoor structure. He steps onto the open-side gazebo and does a big, slow lap around. He touches the latticework and faces me. "How?"

"Claret and Laverick. As soon as I told them about this place, they wanted to fix it up for you." I peer up at the domed roof. "They polished it up beautifully."

"It looks just like it did when I was a child."

"Hopefully it will stay this way." I step into his arms and rest my head against his shoulder.

"Everley, whatever happens tomorrow, remember I saw us in the clock shop."

And I saw the Everwoods burn.

"Would you have come into the shop on your own?" I ask.

"Pardon?"

"The day you saw me seated at the clerk's desk. You were there on assignment because of Markham. Say he hadn't given you a reason to go into the store. Would you have come into the shop on your own?"

Jamison leans back to read my expression. "Why are you asking?"

"I was thinking about what my life would be like without Markham." I gently skirt around my worries and the choices I must make on the morrow. "I met Laverick, Claret, and Vevina because I went to the docks to learn swordplay. I met Quinn and Alick on the ship. I met Radella and Osric during our journeys through the Otherworlds. And I met you because you came into the clock shop on an errand for the navy. All of you came into my life because of Markham."

Jamison pushes my hair out of my face. "I would have visited the shop on my own."

"How do you know?"

"Because Markham changed your life the same way you changed mine. One look at you—"

"And choirs of pixies sang."

He chuckles, then lifts my hand and lays it over his heart. "*You* changed my life. Not Markham."

We lean against each other, bracing each other up, and gaze out at the fishpond. The two of us relax into one another, letting ourselves breathe from our worries of the morrow. As I rest against him, my spirit starts to tug off my body. Before I can sink back down, I notice Jamison's spirit is lifting out of himself too.

He is mesmerized by the pond and doesn't appear to notice—he would certainly yell or show alarm if he did.

I am doing this. Somehow, I am drawing his spirit up with mine.

I pull us back down again so he doesn't realize what's happening. We stay together, holding each other and listening to the frogs and crickets for so long I forget we cannot return to the manor. We have to sleep in that shed.

Jamison yawns, which sets off a round of yawns from us both. We disentangle ourselves from each other and stroll back to the cabin on heavy feet. Laverick sits outside on an empty ammunitions crate, a shawl draped across her shoulders and a musket in her lap. Jamison thanks her repeatedly for her work on the gazebo and goes in. I pause to stay outside with her.

"The gazebo is perfect."

"Gave us something to do." Laverick rises to shake out her legs and kicks a rock, sending it into the weeds. She punts two more before she speaks again. "I know the constable is dead."

"H-how?"

"I heard the stars sigh." She sets down the firearm and draws the shawl around her shoulders. "When my mama got ill, she gave me the job of slaughtering the ducks. I hated holding them down and swinging the cleaver, but she said death would sneak into my life many times and I shouldn't be afraid of it. Death is a silence you can hear, she told me, like the stars are taking a collective sigh. A sigh is what I heard when Mama fell asleep by the fire one afternoon. I heard it again from the constable in the alley." Laverick stares in the direction of the hooting owl. "I've always wondered why the stars sigh. Do you think it's a sad sigh? Or a contented sigh because one of Madrona's spirits has gone home?"

I roll a few answers around in my head before settling upon one. "I think death is only one part of life. We shouldn't let it stop us from living." I take off the key necklace I've been carrying. "I want you to have this. It's the key to the clock shop."

"Everley," she says. "I couldn't."

"You can. Open your ammunition shop and start building on your creations. The giants have a gun that fires multiple rounds. I know you can create something even better. You don't have to worry about the queen anymore. She's going to leave you and Claret alone."

Laverick accepts the key, her eyes big as the owl's. "What about you?"

"I'm the Time Bearer," I say, my tone falsely light. "I'll be all right."

"No matter what happens tomorrow, I'm proud of you, Evie. You chased Killian across the worlds and never backed down. Most people would have given up."

"Maybe I should have."

"No," Laverick says thoughtfully. "There will always be monsters. We can't let them go unchallenged, or why get up in the morning and face the worlds?" I lean into her side and wrap my arms around her waist. Laverick shares her shawl with me and tips her head against mine. "Do we have to go back inside? It smells."

I choke on a laugh. "We can stay out here as long as you'd like."

"Forever it is, then."

Chapter Twenty-Five

Loud thudding comes from outside. I wake and push to my feet. Jamison is already at the window, his pistol drawn. Everyone else sits up, each of us waiting for the roar of a giant or a huge fist to slam its way through the door.

Jamison lowers his gun. "Everley, we have guests."

We both step outside. Countless blue lights float together in the predawn dimness like dangling azure stars. It takes a moment for my eyes to adjust to their glow and recognize they are pixies. Hundreds and hundreds of pixies.

Radella flies over and perches on Jamison's shoulder. She wears a helmet and breastplate made from waxy leaves. Her troops are also dressed for combat.

Marching out of the night behind them is a vast army—elves, spriggans, trolls, and gnomes walking on foot and driving wagons full of supplies. Some of them ride horses, while others sit astride bareback upon centicores. All the soldiers wear light chain mail over black clothes and bear bows and arrows and blades. Commander Asmer rides the queen's stallion at the front of them. Behind her is the elven guard, as well as a motley group of field hands and servants from the royal chateau. A member of the elven guard wrangles the leashed barghest as the bloodhound sniffs around and whines to be released.

My friends amble outside of the hut to view the commotion. Quinn's gaze darts this way and that, taking in the assortment of fantastical creatures that moments ago only existed to her in storybooks.

Asmer dismounts her horse and shakes our hands in greeting. "We're a troop of five hundred. These are all the soldiers I could gather in this short a time."

"They'll fight against their king?" I ask.

"They were loyal to Imelda. She served our people for a long time. Many loved her." Commander Asmer's eyes have run dry of tears, her countenance hard. She gestures, and an elf brings forth a familiar white mare. "Our stable hands said you two got along well before, so I brought you Berceuse."

I pet the mare's diamond mark on her nose. This isn't necessarily a sign that what Father Time showed me of the battlefield will come to pass, but it doesn't instill confidence.

"Hello, Berceuse," I say. "I thought I told you I didn't ever want to see you again." The mare's brown eyes slide to me. "Let's make the most of this, shall we?"

The elves pass out helmets and chain mail to our party members. Alick pulls Quinn aside to speak to her about her assistant-medic duties. She complains about not participating in the heat of the battle, but Alick holds strong and convinces her that's the safest place for her and her cat, Prince, since she refuses to leave her feline behind. Asmer shows them to the medic's wagon.

Vevina persuades a handsome elf to turn over the reins of his centicore so she may ride the wild beast. I warn her they're dangerous, and Vevina says that's why she chose the animal.

The Fox and Cat scout out a seat in a wagon full of black powder, ammunition, and firearms. Laverick finds herself a six-shot revolver, and in seconds, she has puzzled out how to load and fire it. She pushes another revolver on Claret to carry and teaches her next.

Jamison slips a chain-mail vest over his shirt and selects a horse. "The Black Forest is a three-hour walk," he says. "With an army this size, it could take twice that long."

Transporting everyone to the forest by portal isn't practical. We could never all manage to enter a portal before it shut, and we are so numerous in size, including our wagons and horses, that to go through one small party at a time would separate us. We're better off traveling on foot as a group. We have the time.

I vault into the saddle, my sword hanging at my side. "Then let's march out."

Our army tramples out of the woods and past Elderwood Manor. In the dusky morning light, the full damage from the giant's attack is visible. Jamison and I ride slower as we pass the smashed windows and wrecked front door. From his expression, I can tell he's already planning the repairs. A stony lump forms in my throat. This day will end in triumph or defeat, and for me, neither ending includes coming home.

Eventually, the manor drops out of sight. I ride on, my joints wooden and my movements mechanical. I force my gaze ahead and trek west toward a daybreak horizon.

Be a machine. Be indifferent, like time.

I stop myself. As much as this hurts, I will not spend my final moments with Jamison hardening myself for what's to come. Love may hurt, but it hurts a lot less than caring for nothing at all.

"Evie?" Jamison asks.

My gaze snaps to his. His concerned gaze searches my face. He must have been watching my shifting moods. The love I see there, the patience, nearly cracks my heart open. I never wanted to keep secrets from him again, but if he knew what I'd done—what I intend to do— he would stop me. I know, because if the roles were reversed, I would do anything to stop him too.

I press my lips into some semblance of a smile, some arrangement of reassurance, to confirm that everything will be all right. Let him hang on to that picture of the two of us in the clock shop. Let him grasp it with both hands, with a full heart. I need him to do that; I need him to believe, or I don't know if I can do this. I don't know if I can see this through if he doesn't think I can.

My half-hearted smile is not enough. He's still watching me, his worries rising. I sense they will soon take over, and then we will both be more afraid than hopeful. I whisper three little words, the biggest words I have ever said. They come out soundless, but they sing. His eyes soften and shine, and his lips pull up into a grin that has always come easier to him. He says those little, big words back to me, loud and clear, so there's no doubt I will feel them.

"And I love you."

Now my smile is quick and genuine and bright. Because he loves me. He has loved me when I was broken. When I was lost. He has loved me when I was wrong. When I was done. And he loves me still. His love will help me see this through.

Commander Asmer lowers our pace as we roll into a village. The huts and cottages have sustained even more damage than the manor, the structures smashed apart and abandoned.

"Don't look too closely," Jamison warns.

Bloodied debris is strewn across the road and yards. Most of us keep our eyes straight ahead until the devastation is behind us, on alert for the giants that caused it. Outside the village, we travel past wheat fields trodden down with huge footprints. The former location of the skystalk is desolate.

I separate from the caravan and ride out into the field, stopping at a huge hole—all that's left of the skystalk. Commander Asmer and Jamison ride up behind me.

"Where did it go?" I ask.

"The giants must have chopped it down," says the commander. "Skystalks shrivel when they are cut off from creation power and shrink back to the ground."

"This is for the best," Jamison says. "It's gone instead of falling over and flattening our countryside."

I shift in my saddle, still unsettled. The skystalk grew from Madrona's creation power, and her power connects the worlds, the very absence of which has made her sick. Did the giants topple the skystalk? Or was it brought down by Madrona's sickness?

"This will make it harder for Osric to lead the giants here from the Silver-Clouded Plain," Jamison remarks.

Osric and the giants could leave through an exit portal, but without the Creator reopening all the portals for entry, the giants could never go back home. Their help may not be coming.

The three of us ride back to our troops. We plod on into the late morning, clouds steadily gathering until they weaken the sun with their dreariness. Our arrival at the remains of the Black Forest casts another sort of gloom over our ranks. The swiftest path is straight through. I ride to the front and lead the way through the wreckage.

A solemn quiet grips us as we navigate around the fallen trees. The casualty of life harrows me. Markham has uprooted so many lives one would think I would be numb to it by now. But this forest had withstood the test of time, surviving and thriving over centuries. In minutes, all of that was leveled.

Near to the noonday hour, we emerge onto the field where the Black Forest used to be. A mist has settled over the clearing, obscuring what lies across from us, but I can hear our foes' footfalls and clanging weapons.

Asmer orders our troops to spread out. Once we are in line, I glance left and right down our ranks. Laverick and Claret have chosen positions near the ammunitions wagon, while Vevina rides closer to us. The medic's wagon is at the far back. Quinn stands on the driver's bench to see over the heads of the army in front of her, cuddling her cat, Prince, in her arms.

I take in the formidability of our troops. We are so few in number. Too few.

"You told the general noon?" Jamison asks.

Radella perches on his shoulder, her color changed from her usual azure to a grayish purple, the shade she wears when she's angry. Or afraid.

"The council knows." I force myself to maintain a firm grip on my calmness, praying silently that my optimism doesn't end in defeat. "They will come."

Commander Asmer finishes organizing the troops and rides back to me to hand me a helmet. I slide it down over my head, the metal light in weight yet thick. The barghest whines and strains against its chain, then howls at the mist. It has scented our target.

Markham is here.

A carnyx horn blows far off in front of us. The eerie battle cry whirls my stomach into an eddy of dread. After the noise dies away, stomping sends quakes across the land, the vibrations growing stronger and closer. Through the slots in my helmet, I see the outline of the opposing army take shape, towering ghouls materializing in the gloom. I grip the reins to steady my horse, my clock heart ticking wildly. The marching escalates to thunderheads colliding in my ears, then halts.

In the beat of silence, the whole of the world seems to cower from the army of giants, and in that frozen cringe, my heart stops for what feels like an eternity before thrusting onward.

Their soldiers are massive and thick as megaliths. Every one of them is adorned in heavy armor in a style of olden days—helmets with plumes, shields engraved with intricate skyscapes, and thick silver chain mail. They carry an array of sharpened arms—long swords, battle-axes, and maces. Since seeing them yesterday, they have painted their faces in blood.

"Holy Mother of All," Vevina breathes.

Commander Asmer wrangles her agitated horse. "Steady."

The giants ram the long end of their battle-axes into the ground again and again, their pounding thunderous. The barghest whimpers and hides beside his handler.

Harlow and Markham ride to the front of their army and continue into the center of the field. Asmer and I ride out to meet them. Neither elf wears their glamour, their features sharp.

Commander Asmer hesitates when she sees Harlow's elven features. "Killian, your woman is an elf?"

"Half elf," Markham replies. "Her father smuggled for me before I left home. He found me here in Wyeth, met Harlow's mother, and fell in love. We took a glamour charm from a sorceress in exchange for smuggling her potions when Harlow was little so she could stay in the human world with her mother."

The commander scrunches her nose. I was told elves don't mate with humans, not that they couldn't.

Markham's gaze rakes down me, taking in my helmet and chain mail and sword. He finishes his assessment and laughs. "You've come to battle well prepared, Evie. Surrender now and your friends will live. I'll even let you keep your helmet."

"I'll cut the smirk off your face for what you did to Imelda," Asmer snarls.

"I think I will amend my offer," Markham answers smoothly. "Everyone except Commander Asmer may surrender. She will go to her grave."

Harlow snickers, her posture relaxed in the saddle.

"We're not surrendering," I say.

His voice coarsens to a cautionary tone. "This is your last opportunity, Everley. Surrender, or your people will die, and you will lose this war."

His conviction cuffs me like a well-timed blow. Am I leading my friends to their deaths? Would it be better if they were taken captive and compelled to serve a wicked king? I sit in the muck of that thought, rolling around in it until I can no longer withstand the stench. I cannot agree to limiting anyone's dreams, nor restricting their freedoms. Human hearts are strong. Human hearts are free. And no one will take that from us.

I lean forward in my saddle, resting on the horn, and curl my lip. "Go sit on a pike, you blaggard bastard."

Markham's wolfish eyes flash a vow of violence. Commander Asmer and I turn away and ride back to the front line. My poise collapses at the sight of our little waiting army.

A carnyx blows, this time from our side of the field. I squint into the felled forest, and out walks a battalion of giants, at least a hundred strong. In the lead, Captain Redmond flies the banner of the Silver-Clouded Plain, the symbol of their green world surrounded by clouds. Osric walks beside him, armed with two big revolvers, one on each hip.

I gallop over to them and leap off my horse, dropping right onto Osric. He catches me with an "oomph."

"You came," I say.

"Did you really doubt me?"

"I thought you were angry with me about before. What I said about you and Killian—"

"I'm not upset with you, Evie. Our argument helped me realize the Land of Promise is my home, and I'm not going to let anyone or anything chase me away from it anymore."

I watch his face as I ask, "Did Asmer tell you about Dalyor?"

"Yes, and I wasn't surprised. I was reticent to talk to you about Dalyor because I could tell he was hiding something. He was a loyalist to the prince. I'm glad I found out before . . . before our connection grew."

Neely grabs me away from Osric and strangles me in his hug. It isn't until he puts me down that I see he's wearing a green vest Mistral knitted him under his breastplate.

"The curse has been lifted," he says. "We came through the same tunnels the warriors traversed all those centuries ago. The Silver-Clouded Plain is free."

I press a hand over my clock heart and send a silent thanks to Father Time. Maybe time isn't indifferent to us. Maybe time cares so much about us that he has to be careful how often he intercedes.

Neely's sisters flank him. Both wear full body armor, Corentine with the carnyx and Mistral wearing fingerless knitted gloves.

"Where did all these giants come from?" I ask.

"Why, they're our cousins," answers Mistral. "They've come to represent our kind."

Corentine glares across the field at our enemies. "Those things have no right to call themselves giants. They aren't creatures of Madrona. They're kreachers."

The warriors across the field are nothing like the giants I have gotten to know. They've been corrupted, kreachers of night, not of light.

Redmond steps forward in battle gear, his formal wardrobe of velvet and silk replaced by utilitarian wool, but he is not without polish. A silk kerchief is stuffed in his pocket, and his mustache is perfectly groomed.

He extends his hand, a peace offering. I slide mine into his and we shake.

"Returning home showed me something I was blind to before," he explains. "Aye, this world of yours is beautiful, but it cannot compare to ours. The Silver-Clouded Plain is where we giants belong."

"Let's show them how true that is." Corentine raises her arm and directs their battalion to spread out.

Our new recruits filter into our ranks. Osric goes to stand with the archers, and Corentine and Mistral find their way to the ammunitions wagons. Neely hangs back with Alick and Quinn, and they agree to bring him on as a second assistant.

I mount up and ride back to Jamison at the front lines. Radella has regained her color, the addition of the new troops bolstering her confidence.

Across the field, the warrior giants—the kreachers—blow their carnyxes in unison.

I raise my sword. "For Avelyn!"

Our army bellows and hollers. In the next breath, all is silent. Then the kreachers release gut-shaking roars and charge.

"Bowmen ready!" calls the commander.

The kreachers' strides eat up the land, barreling across the divide. Asmer waits to signal until they are closer. The bowmen's arrows fly. Several kreachers are pelted in the arms and legs, their heads and torsos protected, while more rush on unscathed.

Commander Asmer instructs the bowmen to release another volley. They shoot up and out, peppering their marks. The kreachers do not slow, the arrows mere beestings.

I hunch in my saddle, sword raised, and lead the charge.

Jamison and Vevina ride hard beside me. Radella flies ahead of us with her troops; and they meet the kreachers first, sprinkling their dust to disappear holes in the ground. The first row of kreachers leaps around the holes, while those behind them fall in. The pixies dive down and vanish their weapons in showers of shimmering light. I ride into the kreachers' line and slash at the back of their legs, searching the field for Markham.

A kreacher picks up a fallen tree and tosses it into a group of bowmen, knocking them down. Laverick and Claret fire their revolvers repeatedly into him, emptying their chambers. The kreacher sinks to his knees and falls face forward to the ground.

The Fox and the Cat have taken down our first foe.

The trolls attack with their poles, aiming for the kreachers' weak spots—their throats and behind their knees. Gnomes scale up their backs and drive daggers into their eyes. A willowy spriggan grows roots from the ground that grip a kreacher's feet and topple him.

Redmond bellows and charges. A kreacher whams him with his mace, and he's thrown. Mistral and Corentine open fire. The kreacher bends down and roars at them. Corentine turns the end of the carnyx around and shoves it down his throat. The kreacher picks her up and tosses her.

Mistral stabs what looks like knitting needles into his foot. The kreacher bares his teeth and raises his fists to smash her. Cannon fire sounds. The kreacher pauses. A cannonball shoots across the field and plows into him.

Secretary Winters has arrived on foot with hundreds of troops, and they brought firepower. Laverick raises her revolver into the air and whoops. She and Claret run to join a cannon crew.

Jamison fights across the way from me, dodging blows from a kreacher's battle-axe. I still don't see Markham, so I whistle.

The elven guard unleashes the barghest, and the big canine takes off into the fray.

"Everley," Jamison yells, "go!"

We lock gazes, stealing a moment we don't have to spare, and then I ride hard after the bloodhound.

Nothor sweeps his spear at me. I duck down in the saddle, but not low enough. He knocks me to the ground, and Berceuse gallops away.

My helmet comes off in the fall, and I drop my sword. Nothor stabs at me with the end of his spear. I roll to dodge him, but he grabs me in his meaty hand. His fingers crush around me, squeezing my breath away.

He lifts me toward his face, his mouth opening to shove me inside with his stained teeth and foul breath. Another cannon fires, and Nothor is slammed in the middle by a cannonball. He drops me, and I fall to the ground near my sword.

I scoop up my blade and sprint after the barghest, my clock heart ticking in time with my footfalls. The bloodhound stops to sniff at a fallen tree. I slow my approach, on alert for Markham. Harlow steps out from behind the tree, wearing Markham's jacket, and shoots at the barghest. The bloodhound skitters away, unhurt, and she levels the revolver at me.

"Hello, Everley. What a puppet you are, doing whatever we need of you."

"Where's Markham?"

"Right behind you." He presses a gun between my shoulder blades. I glance over my shoulder and see the infinity sandglass in his other hand. He must have used it to trick the barghest.

Harlow strides over to disarm me. I slam my elbow into her side and pull her in front of my body, raising my blade to her throat, and rotate us toward him.

"Pull back your troops," I say.

"I don't control them. You know that." Markham wears a look of disappointment. "You were there when they woke. You saw that I merely set them loose to finish what they started. Before we can rebuild, we must tear down what exists."

He takes a step forward, his gun raised.

I hold the blade tighter to Harlow. "I will kill her," I vow. "For Jamison and my friends and my world, I will do it."

"Killian," Harlow says, utterly calm. She has absolute trust in him.

He leaves his gun on us. Any shot at me would hit her.

"Killian?" Harlow repeats. A question. No, a plea.

He puts on a mask of false penitence. "I'm sorry, my dearest. You have been more loyal than I ever imagined, but I cannot give up the worlds for you or anyone."

Harlow gulps against my blade. "My love—"

He fires, and she recoils against me on a breathy moan. She stays on her feet a moment in defiance of the pain and then goes limp, falling through my arms and sinking to the ground.

I try to grab hold of her, but her weight drops all at once. Harlow lands twisted, like her joints are floppy and broken. I gape down at her as she bleeds and struggles to breathe, and I swear, when she exhales her last breath and the light goes out of her eyes, I hear the stars sigh.

Everything in me turns wobbly—knees, belly, elbows.

Markham checks the chamber of his revolver and snaps it shut. "Don't look at me like that, Evie. The second she joined me, she chose this fate."

"She loved you."

"Don't be dense. She was *half human*. Did you really think I could love something that belonged kneeling at my feet?"

"No one should kneel to you."

"Maybe not the Time Bearer." He points his revolver at me and shakes it like a finger. "You have something else inside you, something that attracted a star and garnered the sympathy of a god. Even I know not to dismiss your usefulness. Look at what we've achieved. You and I reunited the triad. Our brothers and sisters will fight, and they will lose. Then I will guide them to peace and order like my father would have done. There's only one thing left to do."

He fires at me. I feel something shatter in my arm—explode, rip, tear—then I'm shoved to the ground by the propulsion.

Markham stands over me, taking aim again. "I would never have gotten to this point without you. It was fate that you didn't die all those years ago. Fate that I let you live so many times." He lowers the pistol to my head. "But everyone has a day that they should die, and, my dear, today is yours."

I grab my sword, and with the last of my strength, I drag the blade across the ground under us. Markham yells as we drop into the portal.

We land on our backs in the Everwoods. Markham hits the ground hard and releases his pistol in favor of protecting the infinity sandglass. The firearm drops into the brush, out of sight. I grip my bleeding arm with one hand, my sword in the other.

Markham rises and stomps down on my injured arm. He waits until I stop screaming to speak. "You are so predictable. The last act that I needed you to perform—bringing me to the Everwoods—is why I let you live time and again. I've savored this time together, but your usefulness has come to an end."

He wrenches my sword from my grasp and plunges it through my belly. The blade goes in and out the other side again, smooth, relentless steel. My pain paralyzes me, pinning me to the ground. The sprites near us zip away and hide.

Markham leaves the sword impaled in my middle and gazes up at the trees. "This sacred place has been cut off from the worlds for far too long."

My lungs fill with heaviness, my throat wet. I cannot die. I cannot die *here*. My whole existence will be erased.

"Every creation began with destruction," Markham goes on, igniting the fire striker in his hand that's used for lighting smoking pipes. "Time erodes everything. Our worlds were formed from the ash of other worlds, and thus, the cycle of life must continue."

He touches the lit fire striker to a branch. The leaves ignite, and the sprites that were hiding there fly away as the fire spreads up the bough and jumps to another. Markham stands back and watches the elderwood burn.

Screaming fills the woods, not from one of the creatures. From the tree on fire.

"How do you usurp a god?" Markham muses, picking up the infinity sandglass. "Their power exists even without them. The worlds are still hung in the universe. Madrona may tie the worlds together, but it is the Creator that binds them, and the Creator will not let the worlds fall.

But this place, this bridge between them, can be rebuilt. The Everwoods will be in my image."

He smashes the sandglass into the ground, picks up a handful of the sand, and holds up a kernel. Not sand. The vessel was filled with tiny seeds.

"How curious that something so small could grow into something so mighty." The prince squints and compares the little seed to a full-grown elderwood tree before him. More of them have caught fire around us. "Once these trees are gone, I will plant a new conclave of elderwoods that will grow in my name to hold up the sky and tie the worlds together. I will live with them forever and see a new Avelyn take shape."

My sword glows, its inner light pulsing.

A hand grabs the hilt. While Markham admires his destruction, Father Time presses a finger over my lips to quiet me and yanks the blade from my middle. A withheld scream burns in my throat, pushing against my lungs. My stomach bleeds so much I'm not sure where all the blood came from. Surely, my veins must be near to dry.

I cannot win. I cannot fix everyone, save everyone, change every awful thing the prince has done. The ruin he has caused has rippled out too far.

Father Time lays the sword into my palm. "Get up, Everley," he whispers.

"I can't."

"You can and you will."

Father Time vanishes, and a pulse of vigor pushes out from my clock heart. The momentary boost emboldens me to rise. My wounds pound in agony. I only know of one way to take away the pain, and it means causing myself more.

I pull myself up onto my knees. I'm bleeding so badly I cannot look down at myself. The end is nigh, but it will be an end of my choosing. I'll be damned if I let Markham have the satisfaction of killing me.

My legs quake as I try to stand. Mother Madrona said my family was with me. I call upon them for strength. *Be with me. Help me stop Markham once and for all.*

A hardness runs down my spine, strong like a rod of steel. My hurt arm loses some of its sting, and the sword wound in my belly drifts to a faraway ache.

I pull myself upright and plant my feet. The firelight above brightens the forest to midday, the screaming of burning trees torturous. Dragging my sword at my side, I trudge toward Markham. With each step, daisies sprout at my feet, growing up and laying the path before me.

"Markham."

He swings around in surprise.

I raise my sword. "You're no god."

He throws a handful of the seeds in my face. I blink them clear, and he strikes me. I fall to the ground on my stomach, my wounds throbbing daggers. Markham grabs a fistful of my hair and wrenches my head back.

"We're done here. Now be a good lass and die."

I place my hand over his on the back of my head and reach for his spirit. His hand starts to let go of me, so I push my spirit out of my body and drag his along with mine.

Our bodies lie on the ground beneath us. From above, my gunshot and stab wounds appear critical. Markham glances around in alarm. The Everwoods have taken on a new form. We could be inside a frozen sun. Everything that was green is now white. In the core of the trees, their heartwood pulses like real hearts of flesh and blood, soft red lights, sparks of verve. A glow radiates off everything, and the fire Markham started burns blue. The color matches the heart of a flame, the purest blue imaginable, serene, treacherous.

He tries to dive back into his body. My blade slashes through his arm and sends him sideways.

"You were right about one thing," I say, following him. "My temper was going to get me into trouble."

Blue sparks rain down around us. He leaps for his body again. I lunge, stabbing him through the leg. He sinks to the ground one knee at a time.

"Look who's kneeling now."

Markham tries to get up. I slice at his other leg, and he falls to the ground, writhing.

Around us, the fire spreads down the trees toward our bodies. I cannot see a tree that hasn't caught fire. All the sprites have gone, and Father Time is nowhere in sight.

"Evie, please," Markham says, gripping his legs. He cannot get up. He does not bleed, not while in spirit form. The wounds are there, but his body will not manifest them until he returns to it.

"You have the gall to beg me?" I ask.

"Everything I've done will be undone. All the work, all the sacrifices. It will be as though none of this ever happened."

The prince starts to crawl for his body. I raise my sword, and a picture of Jamison comes to my mind, the two of us standing in a gazebo beside a pond. Letting go of it, of him, aches worse than my wounds, but I have my family with me to lift me up. Calling upon them one last time, I lift my sword over my head with both arms.

"This is for my father."

I drive the blade down, straight through Markham's chest. He goes still, eyes bulging. The blue light of the fire around us flashes to searing white. As the light melts away, I find myself back on the ground in my body, in so much agony I can scarcely breathe.

Markham lies beside me, my sword lodged in his rib cage. I muster the willpower to roll over to him, my face in line with his. He wheezes, his mouth open, but nary a sound comes out.

"I don't hate you any longer, Killian Markham. You don't get to have that from me anymore."

He shuts his eyes. Between each breath, he says a word. "I. Should. Have. Killed. You. When. You. Were. A. Lass."

I roll onto my back, clutching my wounded side, and stare up into the inferno. He coughs, and then his coughs turn into choking. I don't care for death, but his is one I want to be sure of. I roll onto my side and watch the prince of elves, the king of lies, succumb to the end of his days.

A clap of thunder ricochets across the sky. Embers rain down on me, smoke skulking all around. Markham's soul peels off his body and floats up through the halo of fiery treetops and into the heavens. A shadow waits in the blackest spot, toothy jaws grinning.

"Good night, sweet prince," hisses the cythrawl.

Markham screams.

One death of his was enough to witness. I close my eyes and let his screams become swallowed up by the crackling flames.

I rest my sword on my chest. The fire above is mesmerizing, a wash of reds and yellows and oranges, a terrifying last sunset. My mind begins to meander away from me, seeking the end to this exhaustion and pain.

My vision slowly fades to emptiness. Right before everything goes blank, I see my family's faces above me, and my father smiling.

I wake up in a bright, immaculate white room, lying on a fragrant bed of daisies. Music plays all around me, its origin uncertain. I recognize it as the everafter song, but in a more buoyant key, sung by a woman I cannot see.

Father Time stands beside me wearing his top hat and suit. "Do you know where you are?"

"No." All I remember before waking up was fighting on the battlefield. "Where's my sword? I have to get back to the battle."

Father Time eases me to lie back down. "The battle is no more, Everley. You have reset the fracture in the timeline. The Evermore has returned to its predestined state. You bore the weight of the worlds upon you and made Avelyn whole."

I deflate into the daisies, my ache so deep I cannot move. "Everything is gone. I have nothing to go back to."

He smiles widely, an odd sight on his austere face. "Dear girl, you have everything to go back to. What you have done will always exist at the back of your mind and the bottom of your heart."

"But I won't remember Jamison."

Father Time plucks a daisy from the bed and lays it on my chest. "You would be surprised what the heart can hold on to."

The pure white light around us strengthens, and the woman's singing grows louder. A star shines over my head, dazzling and strong; her prongs look as though they were broken and someone sewed them back together.

"Centurion," I whisper. "Please don't send me away yet. I don't want to forget her or them."

Father Time begins to fade into the brightness. "They're all waiting for you. Go to them."

The intense radiance burns through my mind, removing everything except the delicateness of the daisy petals against my skin and the contented sigh of a star.

In Another Time

A bell rings as the door to the shop swings open. I set the map I was studying beside my half-eaten pastry and look up as a young man enters. He walks straight, his shoulders lifted and his gait steady. I watch as he peruses the clocks, stopping at one decorated with pixies.

His eyes, a glorious morning-sky blue, dart to mine.

"May I help you?" I ask.

He points at the clock. "Is this one for sale?"

"I sure hope so, since it's on the shelf." I notice pastry flakes have fallen on my chest and quickly brush them away. Isleen is going to strangle me if I stain her dress, and then Mother will tell me that's what I get for taking it without asking.

The young man walks over to me at the clerk's desk. He's dressed impeccably, his blond hair brushed back and face shaven. I stare longer than I probably should.

"I'm looking for a timepiece for my sister's birthday. She'll be thirteen next week." He spots a map on the desk. "Is that from one of Brogan Donovan's expeditions? The king's greatest explorer?"

"It is."

"His adventures are why I almost joined the navy, but my father needs me at home running the estates."

I smile wide. "Brogan Donovan is my father."

"That's grand," he says, delighted. "Have you any interest in exploring?"

"I've thought about it, but my father is gone for months at a time, and I enjoy being at home. This is my uncle's shop, and I'm his apprentice. Someday, presuming I learn to carve well enough, this will be mine."

He smiles wider, his gaze lingering on my face, and extends his hand. "I'm Lord Jamison Callahan."

My mother would disapprove of me touching a gentleman stranger—even a lord—but what trouble could I get into when my uncle is in the workshop behind us? I place my fingers in his, and he lifts my hand to his lips.

Something jangles at the back of my mind and the bottom of my heart. A recollection dawns on me. I have seen this man before, at night, when I'm falling asleep. His face has come to me, among many others, but his I have seen the most. "I'm Everley Donovan," I say, my words slow. "Have we met before?"

"I think I would remember meeting you," he replies softly, his stare intense.

"Let me show you my favorite timepiece." I walk him over to the daisy mantelpiece clock. "My family has almost an identical clock like this in our home."

Lord Callahan looks at me slantwise. "Forgive me, but I think I was wrong. Maybe we have met before. My father is an admirer of your uncle's work." His gaze does not let up on me. "Pardon my forwardness, but would you like to go for a walk? There's a bakery down the street that sells soda bread. I told my mother I would bring some home to celebrate the growing season."

"Thank you, but my uncle Holden needs me here." I would go with him right away, regardless of the scolding my mother would give me, but I have to prove to my father and uncle how badly I want this job. I take out a wreath I made from twigs and daisies and set it on my head.

"My family is meeting later in the quad for the prayer circle. Maybe I'll see you there?"

"Sorry, but no. My family celebrates with a picnic, a tradition my mother started." He appears genuinely put out that he will not see me again later.

We stand together in silence, neither one of us making an effort to part ways. My uncle hammers away in the workshop behind me while he sings an old ditty about the Creator. The whole city is in good spirits on the celebration day for the growing season.

"I'll take this one," Lord Callahan says of the daisy clock. He counts out a stack of notes as payment and places them in my hand. "May I have it delivered?"

"Would tomorrow be all right?"

"Would you bring it? My sister would be delighted to meet Brogan Donovan's daughter."

"I usually go on the deliveries with my uncle."

"Maybe afterward we can go for that walk?" he asks, his eyes bright.

"I'd like that."

"Grand." Lord Callahan shoves his hands in his pockets and strides to the door. "It's been a pleasure to meet you, Miss Donovan."

"A pleasure to meet you as well."

He tips his head at me and slips out.

I run to my desk and open my journal. Flipping to a fresh page, I start a new entry before this feeling of lightness passes.

Today I met the gentleman with morning-sky eyes. We both felt like we knew each other, though neither of us could remember from where. I didn't tell him I've seen him before in my imagination. It's strange to even write that, but as I sit here and listen to the ticktocking clocks, I feel certain our meeting was not happenstance.

I pause, my ink quill poised over the paper. Isleen bought me this writing journal for my eighteenth birthday last month. I write about my life, but more so, stories about giants and elves and pixies, and merrows and sea hags, and princes and ladies of the night. Tavis says my stories are wonderful. Even Carlin likes me to read them to him. My siblings think the stories are fanciful, but when I'm writing them, nothing has ever felt more real.

"Everley," Uncle Holden says, stepping out of the workshop, "your father will be here in a minute. Are you done?"

"I'm finishing something, and then I'll be right there." I shut my journal and Uncle Holden reads the title.

"'The Evermore Chronicles,'" he muses. "What's it about?"

"Nothing of interest."

"I'm interested in everything you create, especially why you put a tree rune of protection on the front."

"To keep my brothers out, of course." I chew on my inner cheek. "The tale has to do with fanciful creatures and far-off worlds. All the things I wish were true but aren't."

"And who is the hero of this tale?"

"A girl."

"What's special about her?"

"She's not a normal girl. She has a clock for a heart."

"Does she now?" Uncle Holden smiles, amused by my imagination, and probably flattered that I included some of his own craftsmanship in my story. He picks up the journal. "Does this girl have any companions?"

"She knows a pair of best friends who love each other, one who looks like a fox and the other a cat; a kind surgeon; a gambling woman who stashes cards down her corset; an ornery girl with a pearl brooch; and a vain, charming man who adores apples. Oh, and one more, a young lord with clear blue eyes who plays the violin. Those are the ones I see—I mean, write about the most."

Uncle Holden hands me back my writing journal. "Does this story have a villain?"

"No." I sigh. "None of my ideas have felt right yet, but I'm working on it."

My father calls my name from the house connected to the back of the clock shop. I stuff my journal into my bag beside the figurines I whittled today—a pixie, a sea hag, and a sleeping giant.

"Are you coming, Uncle Holden?"

"I'll lock up and meet you there."

I kiss him on the cheek and run out the back door.

Father sits atop his horse. "Ready to meet up with the family, Evie?"

"Ready, Papa." He pulls me up to ride behind him, and I sit side-saddle in my skirt. I wrap my arms around his waist, closer to him and his smell of leather. As we set off, I say, as neutrally as I can, "I met a gentleman. We're going for a walk tomorrow."

"Oh?"

I can tell Father doesn't want to be interested, but my mention of a man is unusual. Despite his and Mother's best efforts, I have avoided all their attempts to meet gentlemen callers. "His name is Jamison Callahan. He thinks you're a great explorer."

"I like him already," he says with a chuckle.

I rest my cheek against my father's back and hum his favorite sea chantey. Father whistles along with me as we ride down the streets beneath strands of apples strung over our heads. A daisy slips from my festive crown and drops between us. I catch the sweet-smelling flower before it falls to the ground and hold it over my beating heart.

ACKNOWLEDGMENTS

No writer finishes a series without a big band of supporters. Warmest thanks to these colleagues and loved ones:

Marlene Stringer, for coaching me and cheering me on through thick and thin. I respect and admire you very much. Keep hustling. Jason Kirk, for your steadfast guidance and calming spirit. You're a rock in this up-and-down business. Thanks for believing in me time and time again. I hold your praise in the highest regard. Clarence Haynes, for always knowing how to mold my work into a better vision. Your thoughtful direction and intuitive suggestions never fail to broaden my mind. I'm so grateful to have taken this journey with you. Brittany Jackson, Colleen Lindsay, Kristin King, and Katie Kurtzman, for working so hard on my behalf. My copyeditor for the whole series, Michelle H., and my proofreader, Katherine. Thanks for your sharp eyes. Lauren Ezzo, for bringing Everley's voice to life with verve, care, and immeasurable talent.

John, Joseph, Julian, Danielle, and Ryan. Another series down. Boom! Let's go on an adventure. I'll bring the sunscreen. Hugs to my mom and dad, for never failing to check in with me and help out where needed. You're not just my parents; you're my buddies. Kathryn Purdie, for answering my texts no matter the hour and for talking me off many ledges. Kate Coursey, Veeda Bybee, Sara B. Larson, Annette Lyon, Teralyn Mitchell, Breeana Shields, Caitlin Sangster, and Kate

Watson. You ladies keep me on track and remind me often that friendships matter most in this industry.

Krysti Meyer, Sharon Rios, Brad and Britney at AudioShelf, and Cassie Mae, for being the bestest book bloggers on the planet. And the supremely talented Kirk DouPonce at DogEared Design for my amazing covers.

Finally, my Father in Heaven, who loves all his children equally. Thank you for your continued strength and peace that you give my family and me. You've proven this to be true: "God is never late and rarely early. He is exactly right on time."

ABOUT THE AUTHOR

Photo © 2015 Erin Summerill

Emily R. King is a writer of fantasy and the author of The Hundredth Queen Series and *Before the Broken Star* and *Into the Hourglass*, the first two books in The Evermore Chronicles trilogy. Born in Canada and raised in the United States, she is a shark advocate, a consumer of gummy bears, and an islander at heart, but her greatest interests are her four children. Emily lives in northern Utah with her family and their cantankerous cat. Visit her at www.emilyrking.com.